To The Thomas Family

To The
Thomas
Family

Book One

On the Wild Side:

In the Heat of Arizona

Scott H. Peterson

ON THE WILD SIDE: IN THE HEAT OF ARIZONA

Cover Design by Sara Fisher

Book Formatting and Interior Layout by Carlos Torrejon

To all those that helped me make this book a reality. My editors... Starla Butler and Jennifer Peters. My cover artwork... Sara Fisher. My chapter heading artwork... Alex Vinciguerra. My friends, school teachers (Mr. Martensen, Mr. Grandi, Ms. Smith, Ms. Murray, Ms. Caviness, Mr. McDowell, and Ms. Thorvardson) and my wonderful family. And most importantly to my parents... Jeff & Penny Peterson who helped me every step of the way.

I love you all.

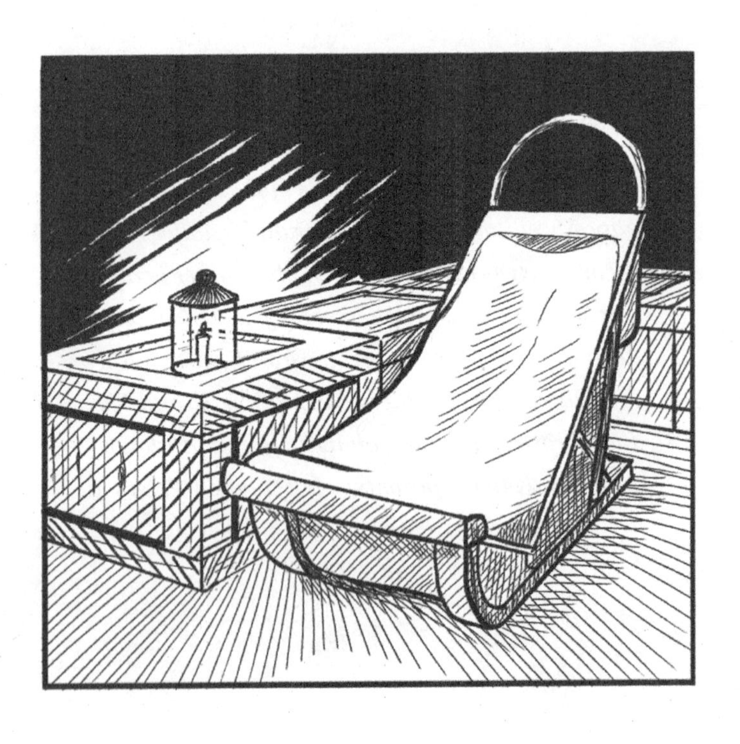

CHAPTER 1

In the Winter's Cold

Thick winter snow covered the town of Fairbanks, Alaska. Rex opened his almond-brown eyes and blinked. The snow outside his tent was beginning to sparkle in the early morning light. Rex lifted his long, gray nose and sniffed the cold morning air. He could hear the master moving around in the house that stood near the tents. It was nearly time to start the day's run.

Rex heard a quiet snore next to him. He nudged Lilly's warm, white fur. Lilly yawned wide and stretched, then stood on her four feet.

"How are you doing?" she asked through another yawn.

"Fine," Rex answered, "Sleepy, but awake."

Rex treasured Lilly's friendship. Her cheery and helpful nature made the slim Samoyed a pleasant companion.

The master stepped out of the house and whistled to his

dogs.

"Breakfast!" yipped Duke, scrambling to the front of the tent where the dogs slept. Duke was kind of a wild card; a Greenland dog with copper-brown fur, he could be a little crazy and at times quite annoying. His thoughtless tendency of barging into the other dogs' conversations left them exasperated with him more often than not.

The master pulled open the tent flap and began scooping meat into the bowls lined up near the flap. Duke charged for the food and bumped right into Alpha. Alpha growled. Duke immediately stepped back, whimpering.

"Let's go," said Lilly to Rex, hurrying to their master. The master finished serving the meat and gave each of his dogs an affectionate pat and some kind words before he stepped out of the tent to ready the sled.

The moment the flap closed, Alpha rounded on Duke.

"What was that for?" Alpha asked angrily.

"I was just having fun. Jeez," muttered Duke grudgingly.

With his share of the meat finished, Alpha stepped out of the tent—away from Duke—to find Beta. The slim, black-and-white Siberian husky was lying down on the snow, enjoying the quiet sounds of the early morning around them.

"Hey, how are you doing?" Alpha said sincerely to Beta.

"I'm fine, just a bit sleepy," she replied, blinking her light blue eyes in the sunlight.

"Are you ok with hauling all of this cargo?" he asked her, concern coloring his voice.

"I'm ready!" she barked excitedly.

He smiled at her happiness. Beta was the only dog who was herself around Alpha. She was a very happy dog and made Alpha very happy as well. What did not make him happy was how some of the dogs made fun of him for this.

Their master called all nine of his dogs to the sled. He harnessed them in specific order. Alpha was in front, then Duke, Beta, Lilly, Rex, and four other dogs. They would haul this cargo load from their home in Fairbanks along the Anchorage run to the south.

"Are you all ready?" asked Alpha, being the leader.

"Yes!" the team answered enthusiastically.

Having finished loading the cargo onto the sled, the master walked towards Alpha and gave him an encouraging pat on the head.

"You'll do great."

That bit of confidence from his master added to Alpha's excitement. He was ready to begin this trek!

The master got on the sled and shouted, "Onward, mush!"

The dogs ran. Their master cracked his whip. The dogs ran faster. Alpha pulled as hard as he could. Beta and Duke strained at their harnesses, and Lilly and Rex's feet barely touched the snow. The master cracked his whip again, and the dogs soared across the snow toward Anchorage.

All day the team ran through forests, down valleys, and around mountains. When the sun began to touch the horizon, the master called the dogs to halt. They made their camp near Denali. It wasn't long before their master was asleep, and so were several of the dogs. Rex was starting to drift off next to Lilly. She was happy and felt safe being near him. Alpha and Beta were stretched out on the snow near some pine trees chatting. Duke was being his usual, annoying self.

Duke was a bit of klutz . . . socially, mentally, and physically. Other dogs often left him alone because conversations with Duke included the most random and odd things you would ever hear in your life. If dogs went to school, he would be the class clown. However, he wasn't a loner; he was friends with Rex and the others and they were fine with him. They tried to be nice because he was sensitive and could get sad easily. But he was also resilient and liked to have fun, and with nine friends, it could get crazy. Duke did act serious sometimes, though those times were few and far between.

Duke ran over to two dogs who were talking.

"What are you two talking about?" he interrupted nosily.

One of the dogs rolled his eyes and snapped, "Do you have to be this annoying?"

Duke bounded away from the two dogs, ignorant of their irritation.

"That crazy mutt," said the other dog.

A short time later, all of the dogs were asleep under a sky dotted with stars and a tiny sliver of a moon. In the morning, the sun sent its first rays into the sky, shining on the snow like a white mirror. The master woke and got ready, took out meat for the dogs and himself, and whistled. The dogs woke up and began to stir. Alpha was sleeping near Beta. Both yawned, stretched, and walked over to their breakfast. Likewise, Rex woke next to Lilly and stretched.

"How did you sleep?" Rex asked heartily.

"I slept great because of you," she said sincerely.

That made Rex smile. They ate with the other dogs, then got in line for the master to harness them to the sled.

The dogs went on running as they had the day before.

Though the snow was very cold on their paws, sled dogs are meant to brave the cold. The dogs usually loved traveling over Alaska because it meant time with each other and their master, and the work was fun. This run was not turning out like one of those usual times. As they ran, the air became chillier than normal. Despite their thick fur coats, the dogs and the master began shivering. Rex and his friends started to feel nervous. They kept running, but they were very cold. Rex glanced up at the sky. The sun that had risen so brightly a few hours earlier was now nearly invisible behind dark gray clouds.

Tiny flurries began to fall out of the sky. Soon they grew heavy and thick. The wind gave a low, moaning whistle. The master looked up at the dark clouds.

"It's going to be a mighty fine blizzard tonight," he called out to his dogs. As if in response, the wind howled and wailed like a screaming banshee.

"It's getting kinda cold," braved Lilly, who really felt like her tail was freezing off.

"Ditto on that," answered Rex through teeth clenched tight with cold. The dogs struggled to run against the fierce wind. The snow fell more thickly, and then a freezing burst of wind hit the dogs and their master.

"It's freezing!" yipped Beta, who was running as fast she could.

"You'll be fine. I know you can do it," Alpha said confidently.

Lilly glanced at Rex. "How are you doing?"

"It's kinda cold, but I'm doing just fine," Rex lied.

They ran through a depression where the snow rose like walls on either side of them. It was becoming hard for the master and the dogs to even see, but they continued cautiously through it. Then Mother Nature threw all of her wrath upon them.

THUD! A tall, thick pine tree fell in the middle of the path before them. The master pulled on the lines as hard he could, but the sled continued to slide forward. The dogs stopped and Alpha was thrown away from the tree and flew into the snow. Beta barked with concern as their master leapt off his sled and fought through the snow to where Alpha had crashed. The master pulled Alpha out. Alpha licked his master and the master patted him on the head. The master checked on the other dogs; they were all fine. He checked the cargo; it was still intact. Beta, scared to death, ran to Alpha.

"Are you ok?! Are you hurt?! Are you—"

Alpha interrupted kindly. "I'm fine, I'm fine."

Beta smiled with relief.

The master turned to his sled dogs.

"This blizzard is too dangerous. We'll camp here and try to continue in the morning."

The master got back on his sled, turned the dogs around, and searched through the heavily falling snow for a place to camp. A few miles away they found a cave big enough to fit him, his sled, and all of the sled dogs. He carefully maneuvered his sled and team into the cave.

Finally, with the sled and team in the cave, he could unstrap the dogs. Alpha collapsed on the floor in exhaustion.

Beta went to him. "You did great," she declared proudly. Alpha smiled and scooted over so Beta could lay near him. She plopped down right next to him.

Duke, Lilly, and Rex chatted while their master cooked

dinner for himself and the dogs.

"Do you think we'll be ok?" Lilly asked. Out of the cave they could see only blowing white snow.

"We'll be fine. Our master said so," Rex replied. Lilly was happy and grateful for Rex's reassuring presence.

The master finished cooking the meat and whistled to his dogs. The dogs liked meat, and they weren't picky because they knew it was easier to cook. Stomach rumbling, Rex ran, followed closely by Lilly and Duke. Alpha, Beta, and the rest came too.

After they had eaten, the dogs settled down for sleep. Alpha was snug on the cold ground far away from the entrance of the cave with Beta nestled close to him. Duke was near the master's sled, and Rex and Lilly were asleep near the entrance of the cave. Lilly cuddled close to Rex. The blizzard was still raging and it was freezing, but she felt good next to him.

When Rex awoke around midnight, their master and the other dogs were asleep, but Lilly wasn't next to him. He opened one of his eyes and saw her outside, a good distance from the cave's mouth. She was standing in the middle of the blizzard like a statue.

He ran out to her and yelled, "Lilly!"

She didn't answer. He yelled to her again even louder, "LILLY!!!!"

He made it to her side. She looked petrified. He was relieved she was all right, but her fear made him anxious. "Are you ok?" he asked, concerned.

"Be quiet," she whispered.

"Be quiet for wh—" he began to ask.

"Be quiet!" she said more loudly. He followed her gaze and saw bright glowing eyes—five or six pairs near the tree line. Lilly and Rex pricked up their ears as a low growling sound began.

"Timber wolves," Lilly whispered in terror. A howl rang out. The growling got louder. A timber wolf emerged from the trees.

He was large with dark gray fur and deep scars and scratches across his face. His bright yellow eyes petrified both Rex and Lilly as their eyes locked.

"Well, well, well, what do we have here?" the timber wolf sneered.

"We're just going now," Rex said nervously.

"No, stay. You two look tasty," the timber wolf said, licking his chops with a pink tongue.

"We can find you something better," Lilly offered anxiously.

"I already have," the timber wolf said, creeping forward.

Rex shouted, "Run!"

Lilly and Rex dashed toward the cave. The big timber wolf was faster. He darted in front of the cave's entrance and growled at them. Lilly ran in the opposite direction, back toward the woods, and the timber wolf shot straight for her.

"Lilly!" Rex charged the timber wolf. The wolf was close to Lilly.

"Lilly, watch out!" Rex repeated. Lilly was sprinting as fast as she could. Rex slammed into the timber wolf, who twisted and sank his teeth into Rex's right shoulder. Rex cried out in pain. The timber wolf pinned him on the snow, a deep red spreading onto the snow around his shoulder.

"REX!" Lilly cried in horror. She turned back, snarling, and charged the timber wolf.

"Get off him!"

She lunged forward, tackling the timber wolf. The wolf turned his attention from Rex to Lilly. She snapped at him before he tackled her. He pinned her down and growled, then Lilly surged upward and threw the timber wolf off her. He flew a few feet away and slammed into a tree buried in the snow. He crawled out, limping and bruised. Lilly snarled at the timber wolf.

"Retreat," he called to the other wolves, then he ran back into the woods, the other timber wolves following him.

Red-hot anger pulsed through Lilly. "Yeah, you'd better run!" she threatened, before rushing to Rex.

"Are you ok?" she asked, worried.

He stood up and limped for three seconds before collapsing. The cold snow had slowed his bleeding, but his fur was stained with a red splotch. She was relieved he wasn't still bleeding, but he was falling asleep.

"You have to stand up, please," she urged.

"I'll try," he said, fatigued.

He stood up with Lilly against his side. She tried to hold him, but the blizzard was still raging, making it hard. Finally, she saw the cave entrance.

Alpha, Beta, Duke, their master, and the four other dogs were all still asleep. Rex managed to stumble into the cave before he and Lilly both collapsed in exhaustion. She let Rex lay on her so he wouldn't freeze to death.

When morning came a few hours later, the blizzard had died down. The dark clouds had rolled way and the sun's golden rays shone on the snow once again. The master woke up and got everything ready, then whistled for his dogs. They all stirred except Rex and Lilly, who were beaten with exhaustion.

Alpha and Beta got to their feet, as did Duke and the other dogs. They all looked at Rex and Lilly with confusion. Alpha and Beta walked up to them.

Beta chuckled a little bit, but asked in concern, "Are you two ok?"

"Yeah, what happened to the two you?" Alpha asked with a snicker.

Rex and Lilly woke up slowly. Lilly lifted her weary head and turned to look at Rex.

"So, it wasn't a dream," she murmured. Dried red splotches marked the wound on Rex's shoulder.

"What wasn't a dream? And is that blood on your shoulder, Rex?" asked Beta, confused.

"Wolves." Lilly told Alpha and Beta what had happened during the night.

The dogs listened in shock. "Wow!" they said. They called the other dogs over, and they were just as amazed to hear the story, but the trail couldn't wait. They ate breakfast and got harnessed up, ready to go... especially Alpha.

"Onward, mush!" The master cracked his whip and the dogs started to run.

Rex was lagging behind, which caused the other dogs to go slower. The master noticed and called his dogs to a halt.

He went to Rex and for the first time noticed the blood splotches and stains on his right shoulder's fur. He felt it and pressed on it as gently as he could. Rex whimpered in pain.

"Oh Rex, what happened to you?" the master asked Rex

sympathetically. "It must have been those blasted timber wolves," he said angrily.

He unharnessed Rex and carried him to the sled. After rearranging the cargo, he put the injured dog in the cargo bed.

"Okay, since Rex is too injured to run, I'm going to give him a break for the rest of the day and we'll head back to Fairbanks and I'll let my supervisor know what happened," the master told the rest of the dogs.

He rearranged their positions then got back on the sled and called out, "Onward, mush," and the dogs began to run. The master turned the sled around, called out to his dogs again, and they began the run back to Fairbanks.

In four hours, they were just leaving the northern border of Denali National Park and Preserve. The park's forest was dense and they stopped next to the Nenana River's rocky banks.

The master watched with a smile as all of the dogs ate lunch together, having a grand time.

"So Rex, how are you feeling?" Duke asked.

"I'm fine, just fine, but you should thank Lilly," Rex said, looking at Lilly.

Lilly started to chuckle a little bit and one of the other dogs said with a snicker, "You're so lucky, Rex, that Lilly was with you or you would have been dead meat."

"Ha ha, so funny," said Rex sarcastically.

Then Alpha asked the gang, "Hey, who wants to have some fun?"

"We will!" two of the dogs said.

"Ditto," said the other two dogs.

"A little fun never hurt anyone," said Duke.

"Yeah," Beta chimed in.

"So, what about you, Rex?" Alpha asked. "You up to it or will you be sitting on the sidelines?"

Rex shook his head glumly.

Alpha turned to Lilly, "Lilly, you?"

"I'll sit this one out with Rex," Lilly said, declining his kind invitation.

"Aw, it would've been fun with you two," one of the dogs said trying to persuade Rex and Lilly.

"Leave them alone, if they don't want to join us, they don't have to," Alpha said, trying to defend both Rex and Lilly while not hurting the other dog's feelings.

"Remember, Lilly and Rex dealt with a timber wolf and Rex was a casualty," Alpha reminded the dogs. "Let them have a break, they deserve it," he said calmly.

"Thanks," Lilly said to Alpha.

"Don't mention it," he replied.

"But we'll watch you guys," Lilly said, "won't we, Rex?"

"Yeah," Rex replied.

Alpha began sprinting to the river, followed by the rest of the dogs. As soon as his paws left the sturdy bank he began slipping and sliding on the frozen river that had been blanketed in ice by the cold winter's grasp. He began to tumble and fell flat on his belly.

The master heard Alpha's tumble and looked over to the frozen river and laughed, "That rascal! At least he's having fun."

Beta jogged over to the river and asked, "Alpha, you okay?"

He stood up and slid his way over to her.

"Yeah, I'm alright." He climbed back up onto the bank. "Come on, Beta, have some fun!" he said as he bumped her onto the slippery ice where she slid uncontrollably.

"Alpha! You sly husky," she shrieked.

Alpha began to get carefully back onto the ice, but as soon as he got on Beta slammed into him, making him topple over.

"Oops! I'm so sorry, Alpha, I didn't see you there," Beta said wryly.

"Even?" Alpha asked.

"Even," Beta replied before losing her balance as the four other dogs slid through. Lilly and Rex sat chatting on the frozen river bank.

"So, how's your shoulder?" Lilly asked.

"Better than when it was bleeding," he smiled. "It's fine just a bit sore. How are you doing? That must have been quite a fight you put up with that timber wolf."

"It was frightening, to say the least, but I tackled him, showing my dominance, and I came out on top," she stated frankly.

"Thank you, by the way," he told her with gratitude.

"You're welcome," she replied with a warm grin.

Rex looked around the forest. "Where's Duke?".

"Dunno," Lilly shrugged, right before they saw Duke barreling through the trees towards the frozen river. He made contact with the ice and slid with great speed toward the clump of dogs. Duke slid closer and closer before striking them like an out-of-control bowling ball, sending dogs every which way.

"DUKE!" the clump of dog all growled in annoyance.

"That's our Duke," Rex said with a chuckle.

Rex and Lilly burst out laughing while Alpha chased after Duke and Beta across the ice.

The master then called all the dogs back to the sled.

"I'll race you," said Lilly.

"You're on!" replied Rex.

Rex and Lilly ran to their master. The other dogs all shook themselves free of ice and snow before following them.

Lilly reached the master first.

"And Lilly comes in first!"

A moment later Rex arrived, panting from the exertion.

"And Rex comes in second!" Lilly cheered.

"I guess you won?" he panted.

"Sure," she said with a wink. Rex laughed.

The master fed his dogs dinner and the gang chatted until it started to get dark. Their master checked the perimeter for timber wolves and found none. Soon he, Alpha, Beta, Duke, and the other four dogs were asleep.

Lilly and Rex lay talking as the dusk grew darker.

"Ah, this is better, isn't it?" Lilly said, relaxed.

"Yeah," Rex said calmly. "Could I ask you something?"

"Sure, what do you want to ask me?"

"How were you feeling last night when the timber wolf attacked me?"

"It was terrifying when he bit you and you started bleeding. But I mostly felt angry. That's why I tackled him," Rex smiled at her and she smiled back.

"At least you didn't get hurt," Rex said. Soon they both fell asleep.

After a good night's sleep, the sun rose bright and clear.

The master got up and got everything ready for the day, then sat down to eat breakfast with his dogs.

"It's kinda nice right now," one of the dogs said, relaxed.

"You can say that again," Rex said.

"Do I have to?" the dog asked, surprised.

"Nah, it's just an expression," Rex said, relaxed.

The master called his nine dogs, strapped eight up, and put Rex back in the cargo bed. The master then called, "Onward, mush!"

They ran off across the icy snow. As they were running across the white snow, Rex noticed a white blur weaving in and out of the trees.

He peered at it, confused. He pushed it out of his mind, feeling like it must have been some type of snow flurry. But as the eight dogs continued to run, Rex again saw the same quick, white blur weaving between the trees. Now this caught his attention and was making him nervous.

After a few miles of running, the master called his dogs to a halt.

Rex climbed off the sled and hobbled over to Lilly, who stood next to Alpha.

"Hey, how was the ride? Was it refreshing?" Lilly asked him.

"It was . . ." Rex began to say in an unnerved way, but he paused. ". . . good."

Lilly noticed his nervous abruptness and asked. "You okay? You look . . . nervous."

The master whistled to his dogs, and Rex went back to the cargo sled. The master called out "Onward, mush," and the eight dogs began to run.

A few hours later the master saw Anderson, a small town in the middle of Alaska, a day's ride southwest of Fairbanks. When they got into Anderson, the master let Rex walk next to the sled and called out for the dogs to go a little slower.

Rex began to look around at the forest and saw the white blur looking at him, then run away into the deep forest.

Lilly noticed Rex's uneasiness.

"Are you ok?"

Feeling a bit jittery, Rex answered honestly.

"I keep seeing a fast-running white blur by the forest's edge."

Lilly didn't think he was crazy. Rex was the most honest dog she knew, but she was scared for him. *Could someone be following him, maybe tracking him?*

They got unloaded and the master talked to some people he knew and told them what happened.

"Yeah, we have the same problem you have," one agreed. "Most of our cargo has been backed up three days coming from Seward."

"It was too dangerous to fly in by air," another added. "They almost crashed a plane in the river."

"Do you know of a hotel or inn where I could sleep?" he asked his friends.

They helped him find one, then the master went and had dinner with his friends while his dogs ate some meat he had bought from the local butcher shop. They were all eating together near the restaurant when Rex heard rustling in the alley and got up to investigate. He looked and saw the white blur again. It ran up a board and onto a trash can, then quickly jumped over a fence.

Rex ran after it.

When Lilly realized Rex was missing, she was worried. She knew Rex might have been followed and have gotten into trouble. She hurriedly followed his scent, but paused when she noticed something interesting-- another scent. Lilly followed and discovered nervously that the two scents led back into the forest.

Rex ran, but with his injured shoulder, the white blur was too fast for him, and after a moment he didn't see it anymore. He looked around, perplexed. Suddenly the white blur lunged out of the snow and tackled him. Rex opened his eyes and saw a white fox on his chest, staring at him with its brown and light blue eyes.

"Who are you and vy vere you running vit zat human?" the white fox demanded in a Russian accent.

Rex didn't understand.

"He's my master," Rex said. "I have to follow his orders."

The white fox got off of him with a confused expression. "So, you're not vild."

"Right!" he said then he introduced himself. "I'm Rex. I'm an Alaskan malamute. I live in Fairbanks with my friends. We had some complications on our sled run, so that's why we're here."

The fox introduced herself. "My name is Khitrey, and. . . ."

Rex interrupted. "Wait, wait, wait. . . . Your name is Khitrey?" he asked, chuckling a little bit.

Khitrey's temper rose. "It's Russian for 'ze sly and cunning one'!" She began to circle him. "You're odd."

Just then Lilly ran up, having followed their scents and paw prints. When she saw Rex being circled by an arctic fox she yelled, "Rex, are you ok?"

"Yeah, I'm fine, why?"

She stared at him and yelled, "YOU'RE BEING CIRCLED BY AN ARCTIC FOX!"

Khitrey turned and growled at Lilly. Lilly growled back at her before they both charged. Before they could hit each other, Rex darted into the middle. Lilly and Khitrey both saw Rex and tried to stop but slid instead, both hitting Rex.

They were both a little embarrassed and calmed down. Rex introduced them.

"Lilly, this is Khitrey, and Khitrey, this is Lilly."

"Nice to meet you," Lilly said to Khitrey.

"Same vit you," Khitrey said politely.

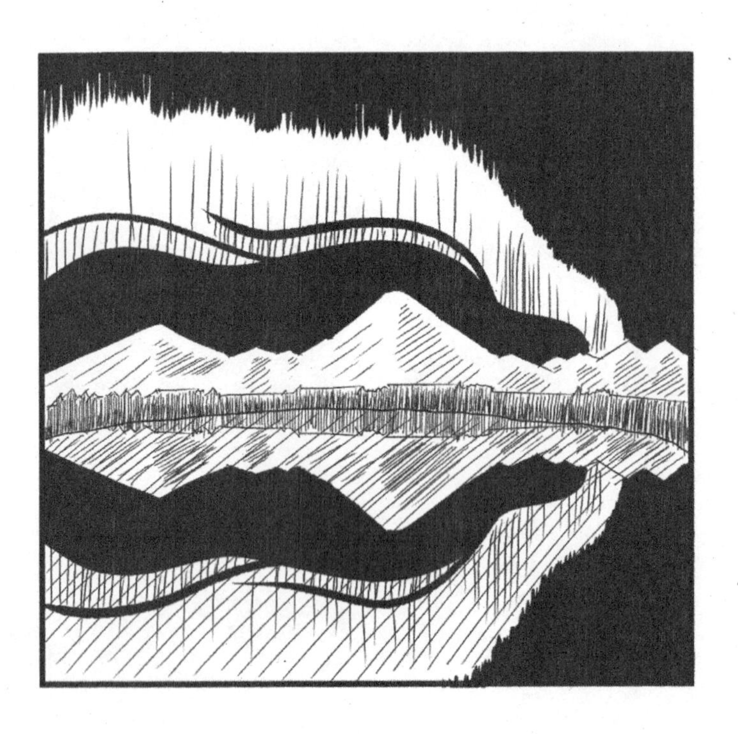

CHAPTER 2

AMBUSHED

"So, your name is Khitrey; what a unique name," Lilly said, intrigued.

"It's Russian for 'ze cunning one'!" Khitrey declared boldly.

"Well, you were very cunning with Rex, so I think the name fits," she laughed.

Khitrey chuckled. Suddenly they all heard a boisterous howl. They heard growling and all looked towards the sounds. Bright amber eyes glowed in the distance, but they couldn't see anything else in the dense trees. The growling got louder, then a bulky white wolf came charging toward them.

"Oh no!" Khitrey cried. She ran in front of where the wolf was charging.

"Are you crazy!?" Lilly said.

"Stop, Dukhoveny!" said Khitrey.

"Dukhoveny?" Rex and Lilly asked together.

The big white wolf ran to Khitrey and spoke angrily in Russian. Khitrey responded defensively in the same language.

"Uh, can you two talk in English?" Rex asked, confused.

"Yeah. Sorry, he doesn't trust anyone but me," Khitrey said.

Dukhoveny apologized. "I'm sorry I charged in here and got angry. I'm just trying to protect her."

"So, do you live together?" Lilly asked Dukhoveny.

"Yes, ve do."

"How did you two meet?" Rex asked, intrigued.

Dukhoveny told the story. "Ven I vas very young, I lived in a pack. My mother and father gave me ze name of Dukhoveny, vich is Russian for 'ze spirited one.' Ven I was grown, I got in a horrible fight zat almost killed my opponent-- niet, niet, my friend—because of my spirited nature. I vas banished from my pack, but my parents pleaded to the alpha to let me back in. He said, 'Niet. He is a danger to our pack. He could have killed zat volf.' My father told him, 'He vasn't too spirited,' but ze alpha dismissed zem. So I left, pack-less. Zen a few monts later I found zis town and my luck started to change. One day I vas valking around in ze forest and I saw her lying on the ground." He looked at Khitrey, then continued. "I ran to her and I asked, 'Are you ok?' She didn't respond, but she stood up shakily, looking famished. So, I ran and stole some meat from the local butcher in ze town, zen I brought it to her and told her to eat it slowly. As ve got to know each other ve became friends, but zen ve became family."

"Khitrey, why were you in the middle of the forest starving to death?" Lilly asked.

Khitrey answered, "I used to live in a tiny group vit my

family. Zen some people in fancy clothing came and tried to take us avay, but I escaped. I ran and ran, but food was scarce in ze forest, so I vas starving. Zen Dukhoveny found me and took me in. Now we are like family."

As they talked, Khitrey had an idea. "Vat if you sleep vit us at our place tonight?"

"Our master would not be happy if he found us gone." Lilly and Rex both said.

Then Khitrey reassured them, "You don't have to vorry. Ve're vell-known ziev—"

"Enough!" Dukhoveny interrupted. Khitrey stopped. Rex and Lilly were confused. Rex thought, *Ziev? That's not a word. What was she going to say? And why did Dukhoveny interrupt her? It's like he didn't want us to know something.*

"Sure," they said together, but while Lilly's voice was kind, Rex's was suspicious. They went to Khitrey and Dukhoveny's place.

When the gang realized that Rex and Lilly were missing, the dogs barked to their master, who realized they were missing, too. The master was nervous for them. He went all over Anderson talking to people.

"Have you seen two dogs? One is an Alaskan malamute and the other is a Samoyed."

But he only heard, "No," or "No, I haven't, sorry."

As he walked back to his hotel with his dogs and a friend, the master remembered the day that changed his life.

When the master was five, he heard of the sled dog Balto and his serum run to Nome, Alaska in 1925. He knew then he wanted to have a sled and to be the best, just like Balto's master.

When the master was six, his parents got him a sled for his birthday, and didn't leave it without a sled dog. His father let the tiny Alaskan malamute go. The dog ran to the six-year-old master.

"I love that puppy!" he said. "Now I should give you a name, Spot?"

The puppy shook his tiny head.

"Fido?"

The little puppy looked bored.

"Max? Keith?"

The tiny dog yawned.

Finally, he said, "Oh, I've got one. What about Rex?"

The tiny little Rex jumped on his little master and licked his face. The six-year-old master laughed and asked his parents if he could ride his sled with Rex.

"Yes!"

The young master and tiny Rex ran outside. He leashed Rex and the master stood on his new sled.

"Onward, mush!" the master said.

Then little Rex started running. They went all over Fairbanks. The master had so much fun. The streets and sidewalks were covered in snow, so no cars were on them, but there were people in and around the town.

He and Rex were pals. They did everything together and were never apart. When something went wrong for one, the other would try to cheer him up. (Mostly Rex cheered up the master, but on occasion, the master cheered up Rex.)

As he grew older, the master found out about sled racing and knew he would need more than one dog to race. He bought

Lilly, and Lilly and Rex became best friends. They had fun being together as the master trained them. Then the master got Alpha, and a while later he got Beta.

The day Beta was given to him was the saddest and happiest day of his life.

The girl he liked was moving to a far-away city in Germany because her father got a job there, and she didn't want her Beta to get stolen or hurt. She thought the master was trustworthy, so she gave Beta to him. Now when he sees Beta, she reminds him of the girl.

Alpha would always nip at his master, and sometimes it hurt pretty bad. Then he introduced Beta to Alpha, and Alpha calmed down. The two dogs became best friends.

The master found Duke when he was older. He saw Duke being pulled and dragged by the leash by some people in strange formal clothing with some kind of crest on the breast pocket. The formal people were near a toy shop, and the master eavesdropped on their conversation. He heard that they had stolen Duke from a city in Greenland and were going to send Duke to Arizona, to a person they called the "Boss."

The master went to the people in fancy clothing. "What are you doing to that dog?" he asked. "That's no way to treat him."

"Beat it kid," one of them said harshly. When they were both distracted the young master ran, unclipped the leash, and said to Duke "Run!" He ran with Duke, and the strange men tried to catch him, but he got to his house and told his parents what happened.

His parents threatened to press charges against the strange men for trying to hurt him and for stealing the dog. The men gave up and left, but they threatened the master.

"We'll be back for that dog one day," they warned. "You won't keep him forever."

But Duke was his now.

The master got two more dogs, then finally started racing. He won every race and was known as the sled dog champion of Fairbanks. He made his mark. Now when he raced, he often had very little competition because no one dared to race against him. The other contenders were inspired by the master and his dogs, but they feared them too. The townspeople said he was faster than an avalanche.

Eventually he got nine more dogs and competed in the Iditarod trail race, and he and his dogs took second place overall. After the race, a man dressed in a nice suit came up to him.

"You're phenomenal, son. Would you like to do this as a job?"

"Yes, sir!"

A few months later he got fourteen dogs and his dogs were officially his life.

The master walked back to his hotel with his buddy and his dogs. The two men entered the lobby of the hotel and sat down to eat dinner while the dogs ate theirs outside.

"We've checked the whole town for Rex and Lilly and we still haven't found them. I'm worried for them, Jack," the master told his friend.

"Don't worry. They'll turn up sometime, sooner than later," Jack reassured the master.

"But what if I don't find them?" the master asked his friend with concern.

"You have plenty of dogs. Two gone missing won't be that

bad," Jack told him.

"Jack, they were the first two dogs I got when I was young and I don't want to lose them!"

"I've met Rex and Lilly. They're the smartest dogs you got. Something might have happened to them, but they wouldn't've run away, because they love you and you love them," Jack replied.

The master pondered the situation and then suddenly thought, "What if they're not in the town, but in the forest? They love to explore." The master sprung up from where he was sitting. "Yeah, that has to be where they are. I'll go look for them," he said to himself, putting on his heavy coat and heading for the door to go round up his dogs.

"Jack, I'm going to go look for them. If you need me—" the master began to say before Jack rushed over and grabbed his shoulder.

"Whoa there, you're getting ahead of yourself," Jack told the master directly. "I don't think it's a good idea going out in the wilderness at night. You could run into those pesky white thieves or, even worse, you could be attacked by a pack of wolves or a bear. Didn't you say Rex got a wound from a timber wolf recently? I know you're worried about them, and I'm worried about them as well, but I'm more worried about you. I don't want you to get hurt and, as I said, they're smart dogs and they'll be fine," Jack stated.

He then grabbed his own coat, putting it on as he walked to the door. "Get some sleep. You'll feel refreshed in the morning and then we can try to find them." Jack turned to the master "Please promise me you won't do something you'll regret," he asked the master.

"I promise," the master dutifully replied.

"Have a good night, my friend," Jack said before heading out the door.

Then the master went to his room with his dogs, and before he went to bed, he said a silent prayer that Rex and Lilly would be safe.

Rex and Lilly were at Khitrey and Dukhoveny's place, a hidden cave where no one could find them. They stayed in the cave with Dukhoveny while they waited for Khitrey to get dinner.

Khitrey walked in with a tiny rabbit and mouse hanging from her mouth. She opened her mouth and the mouse and the rabbit fell out, cowering in fear. Khitrey said, "Bon appétit."

Dukhoveny looked at her. "Zat's not Russian. Ven did you learn zat?"

She said lightly, "I heard a townsperson say it."

"Vat! A townsperson? I told you to stay avay from zem and ze town!"

She stayed quiet for a little bit, then they both went to eat the small animals. Rex pushed them away so the rabbit and mouse could run away. As they ran out of the cave, Rex heard in the distance two tiny thank-yous.

Dukhoveny glared at Rex, then stalked toward him, saying fiercely, "Vat vas zat?" He growled at Rex.

Rex was a little scared, but he growled back at him.

Lilly and Khitrey both got up and said before either could lunge, "Stop, you two!"

Rex and Dukhoveny both stopped and looked regretful.

Lilly had an idea. "What if we have berries?"

"Zat's a great idea! I know ver some are," said Khitrey.

She went out of the cave, running and blending in with the snow around her. She found a bunch of golden berries with a hint of redness, and there were enough for all of them. She grabbed a big leaf from a bush in her mouth, picked the golden berries, and put them on the leaf. When she had a lot of berries, she grabbed the leaf's stem and the tip of the leaf and carried the berries back to the cave.

As she ran, there were two things on her mind that she wouldn't dare tell Dukhoveny. One was that she liked the humans that lived in Anderson, and the other was that she wanted to help the humans and see the world instead of spending all day hiding in a cave. She had thought about it for a long time, but she didn't want to do it alone. She wanted Dukhoveny to explore the world together with her.

When she came into the cave, she set the leaf down and the golden berries were revealed like gold to a miner. Rex licked his lips.

"Dig in," Khitrey said. Khitrey and Dukhoveny waited until Rex and Lilly had each taken their first bite before they started eating.

"Mmm, these are good," Lilly said. "What are they?"

"Yeah, they're delicious," Rex agreed.

"Zey're cloudberries," Khitrey told them.

"Cloudberries?" Rex and Lilly both said, intrigued.

"Zey're berries zat grow in arctic regions like here, northern Canada, and other places like zat."

A few minutes later the cloudberries were gone.

"Oh, those were amazing," Lilly said with a full stomach.

They all went to sleep. A while later Rex opened his eyes and saw Lilly fast asleep right next to him and heard Dukhoveny snoring really loud, but he didn't see Khitrey near him. He got up slowly, so Lilly wouldn't wake up, then checked the whole cave, but he didn't see her. He heard rustling outside. He left the cave and found Khitrey staring at the sky.

"Are you ok?" Rex asked her, concerned.

She didn't say anything, so he lay down next to her.

Finally, she said in wonder, "My father and mother vould tell me zose lights in ze sky vere called ze dancing lights. I've alvays loved zose lights."

He looked up and saw the northern lights bright and full of color, dancing in the sky that glittered with stars. "Oh, you mean aurora borealis," Rex said.

"Aurora borealis?" Khitrey said, intrigued.

"Or the northern lights," he clarified. "My master told me and my friends that. He learned it from his parents when he was a boy."

"Vell, zey're very pretty," she yawned. "Ve should get some sleep."

They stayed laying there on the snow and didn't go back in the cave. They slept under the lights dancing across the sky.

In the morning Dukhoveny and Lilly woke up and didn't see Rex or Khitrey, but they went out of the cave and saw Rex and Khitrey both asleep on the snow.

"Vake up!" Dukhoveny said loudly.

Rex and Khitrey woke up and both looked tired.

"What are you two doing out here?" Lilly asked.

Rex jumped to his feet. "We need to go Lilly, right now!"

Lilly and Rex started to run, but then Khitrey said, "Ve're coming vith you."

Dukhoveny put his paw down. "No, ve're not."

"Please! I vant to go to Fairbanks. Maybe ve can live there," she pleaded.

He thought about it and looked at her face and knew she had wanted to go someplace else for quite some time now. If it made her that happy, he could be fine with it. "Ok, fine. Let's run."

"Ok, but don't get spotted, and when we run, follow the sled." Rex said.

After running from the forest, they all found a hole in the fence. Rex and Lilly went through it into a long alley, and Khitrey and Dukhoveny went around the town to meet the sled.

Rex and Lilly ran out of the alley into the streets. When they saw the other seven dogs and their master on his sled, they both yelled, "Stop!" but the team was too far ahead to hear them. Rex and Lilly sprinted after the sled.

The master was heartbroken because Rex and Lilly were gone, but he had to get back to Fairbanks. As he drove his team through the town, Rex and Lilly almost caught up, but the master cracked his whip and the two dogs fell behind again. They followed the master's sled into the forest. Rex glanced behind him and saw the white blur he knew was Khitrey, but then he saw a bigger white blur that he realized must be Dukhoveny.

The sled went faster. Rex and Lilly were still running, with Khitrey and Dukhoveny right behind them, but they ran for miles before the Master finally stopped.

As the master was unstrapping the dogs, he saw Lilly and Rex running up to him. They jumped on their master and licked him. He was so happy, and he felt such a sense of relief as he checked on the cargo.

The other dogs stared at Lilly and Rex. Finally, Duke said, "Where were you? It was like you vanished."

"We'll tell after the master goes to bed," Lilly said.

"We also have something to show you," Rex winked.

"What do you mean you have something to show us?" Alpha asked warily.

Neither dog replied. Without saying anything, Rex and Lilly stepped away from their teammates to find their white-furred friends. Khitrey and Dukhoveny were behind a huge rock hidden by trees.

Lilly said, "You two stay here, then when our master goes to sleep, we'll introduce you both to the other dogs."

"You just need to lay low for a while," Rex added.

They both nodded and lay down on the rock. Lilly and Rex went back, and the master gave them dinner. The dogs all ate the meat, but Lilly and Rex tore their meat in half. The rest of the seven were perplexed. Then Lilly and Rex left some meat for themselves and grabbed the rest in their mouths and secretly brought it to Dukhoveny and Khitrey. Rex gave his half to Dukhoveny, and Lilly gave her half to Khitrey. They both thanked them quietly and dug in.

As Rex and Lilly were walking back, all seven of the dogs were looking straight at them. Rex and Lilly lay down, and one of the four other dogs said, "You two are acting pretty secretive."

"Yeah," the rest agreed.

"Yeah, you're going 'show' us something? Now you're acting weird," Alpha said.

Lilly and Rex started to get nervous. They stalled for three hours until the master was finally asleep.

"Master is asleep," one of the four other dogs said.

"Now show and tell us," Alpha demanded.

"All right," Lilly said. "You promise you won't do anything, or freak out, or bark for the master?"

"Yeah."

"Sure."

Rex grinned and called, "Come out, guys!"

The other dogs stared as a white fox and a white wolf came walking out of the trees. They were all nervous.

"Everyone, meet Dukhoveny and Khitrey," Lilly said.

Dukhoveny walked over to Duke. Duke was nervous, and when Dukhoveny came in front of him, Duke covered his eyes with his paws.

"Nice to meet you," Dukhoveny said politely.

Duke lifted his paws off of his eyes and stood up. He looked at Dukhoveny, then said, "You too."

Khitrey had started walking towards Beta. Beta was scared, but Alpha was in front of her to protect her. Khitrey got to Alpha and said politely, "Kind sir, you're in front of ze dog I vant to talk to."

He stepped to the side so that the polite fox could talk to Beta.

"Hello, my name is Khitrey. Vat is yours?"

"My name is Beta. What an amazing name you have!"

"Beta, huh? The Greek letter for the letter B. My name is

Russian for 'ze cunning one'!" Khitrey said. "And who is zis handsome dog?" She looked at Alpha.

"His name is Alpha."

"Alpha, huh? Another Greek letter. You two make a great pair . . . A and B," she chuckled.

They all talked for an hour or so, then fell asleep. Just before dawn, Rex and Lilly woke up Khitrey and Dukhoveny so that the master wouldn't panic when he found a wild fox and wolf sleeping with his dogs. They walked with them back to the huge rock, and Dukhoveny and Khitrey hid behind it again.

"Wait here," Rex told them. "When the sled starts to go, follow it, but don't get seen by our master."

Rex and Lilly left and lay back down to rest. The master woke up and saw Rex and Lilly were awake. He smiled and got breakfast ready. He whistled to the dogs and all of them woke up one by one. The dogs ate their breakfast, and Lilly and Rex again went to the white-furred friends behind the huge rock and shared half with them.

The master was confused, but the other dogs knew what was happening.

When they all finished breakfast, the master got the dogs strapped in. He got on his sled, then cried, "Onward, mush!" The dogs sprang against their harnesses, and the sled started sliding across the snow.

"Hey, where're Dukhoveny and Khitrey?" Alpha asked Rex, who was behind him.

"Look behind the sled." Rex said.

Alpha looked behind him and saw a big white blur and a fast-running blur. He turned back ahead and kept running.

They ran for miles. They were near Lost Slough when they came into a thick forest still covered in snow. They passed the river and in a few miles were close to Nenana, a third of the way through their journey. The master saw an airplane taking off and knew they were close.

They went through Nenana, but the master didn't stop. Khitrey and Dukhoveny were tired, but they still pressed on. A few miles past Nenana the master came to a dangerous spot on the trail. The trail was on a weak rock ledge. On one side a snowy slope rose up above them. On the other side a twenty-foot steep slope dropped into a raging river. The master slowed down and proceeded with extra caution, as did the dogs.

Lilly was on the side of the drop. She put her paw on a loose piece of the ledge, and it cracked and fell. She lurched sideways and bumped into Rex, and he saw how terrified she was. The dogs were dead silent.

Then Rex saw some snow powder from the slope above them. Rex looked up and saw Dukhoveny and Khitrey creeping along at the top of the slope.

Oh no! He thought. *They might start an avalanche!*

Then a big chunk of the trail broke off the ledge ahead of the team and fell and rolled down the slope into the river. The dogs went around the hole in the trail and the sled passed over it without a problem. Then the master glanced up and saw that an avalanche had indeed started. He looked behind the sled and saw the rock ledge starting to crack with pieces falling into the river.

He cracked his whip and shouted, "Onward! Mush, dogs! Onward!"

The dogs ran as fast as they could, but the avalanche was faster. The thundering snow swallowed them up, and the entire rock ledge crumbled beneath them. The sled careened down the slope towards the river. The master tried to steer, but it was impossible. Half of the cargo fell off the sled. Rex grabbed a box of penicillin in his mouth and threw it to his master, and his master caught it, but the rest of the boxes rolled into the raging river. Then the master got hit in the chest by a medium sized boulder and rolled down the slope and plunged into the raging river.

"Master!" Rex cried. Then he forced himself to focus and said to the others, "We have to pull this cargo and get out of this."

They were working to pull the sled when Khitrey and Dukhoveny literally dropped in on it. They struggled and finally got the sled onto a solid path. They ran a ways until they were safe.

One of the four other dog said, "Hey, it's you two."

"What do we do?" Duke asked Rex.

Rex sighed, "We take the cargo to Fairbanks. We'll do it for the master."

Before they left they decided to search for some berries as best they could for lunch, even though they couldn't get unstrapped without the master. Then the dogs and their Russian friends heard rustling in bushes. All eleven of them growled, but then the master emerged, soaking wet. All of his dogs tackled him and licked him in bliss, and the white-furred friends used the commotion to hide.

"Oh, is it great to see you all!" the master said joyfully, looking at his dogs. He re-tied the cargo, then climbed onto his sled. They started to run, with Dukhoveny and Khitrey following them.

Unbeknownst to them, another party was following them, just out of sight.

At long last, the master and his team arrived in Fairbanks. The master first led his dogs home, where he unharnessed them and unloaded the cargo. When everything and everyone was settled, the master loaded the cargo in his car and drove to see his supervisor.

Back in their home tent with all their fellow sled dogs, Rex and his friends introduced their new white-furred friends to the other ten dogs. As the other dogs were getting acquainted with Dukhoveny and Khitrey, the gang of nine went back out of the tent.

The first thing they saw was two men in suits pointing guns at them. The dogs tensed. One of the strange men shot at Rex, but he missed and hit a pole that supported the tent for the dogs. The dogs saw it was a tranquillizer dart.

"I swear I've seen these people before," Duke muttered, tensed to dodge, "but I can't put my paw on it." Then a dart thunked into Duke's side and he collapsed.

The four other dogs ran into the tent, terrified. Then Beta got shot by a dart.

"No, Beta!" Alpha cried, lunging toward her, but a dart stopped him before he could get to her.

Lilly got shot and fell.

"Lilly!" Rex screamed. He snarled and charged toward the men, but he got shot by a dart and stumbled. He got sleepy and dizzy, then fell.

Hearing the commotion outside the tent, Dukhoveny and Khitrey stepped out to see what was going on. Seeing Rex lying still, they tried to wake him, but he was out cold. Then Dukhoveny and Khitrey saw the men in suits aiming their guns at them. The two darted back to the forest.

The two men in suits lifted the limp dogs into five separate kennels in their vehicle and then climbed in the front and took off. One drove while the other called their Boss.

"Yeah, Boss, we got them," he said in a grunting tone. "We missed four of the dogs and two other animals, yeah, but we got five."

They pulled to a stop at a small airport on the outskirts of town and loaded the dogs into a medium-sized private aircraft. Rex managed to open one of his eyes. He could only see the inside of the plane and his friends before he blacked out. As he faded, he heard the sound of the airplane starting up.

CHAPTER 3
ARRIVAL IN ARIZONA

Rex woke up when he felt the jolt of the plane landing on the runway. Some goons came and checked on the kennels.

When the goons were talking to the pilots up in the cockpit, Rex whispered to make sure the humans didn't hear him, "Hey guys, wake up!" The other dogs all slowly opened their eyes.

"Where are we?' Lilly asked in a slurred voice.

"Dunno," said Rex, "But one thing is for certain—I don't trust these guys."

Rex started looking at the latch and realized it wasn't that hard to slide it open. He opened his kennel with his nose, then quickly unlocked Lilly, Alpha, Beta, and finally Duke's kennels. They were out.

They heard one of the goons chuckling loudly as he walked to the back door of the plane. "Hey, let's get these dogs to the

Boss."

He opened the cargo door and the gang sprang at him, trampling the goon and running down the steps of the plane. The second goon ran after the dogs. The goon that got trampled clambered to his feet and ran after them, too. The dogs ran out of a fenced gate and down the road past a sign that said Marana Regional Airport.

The goons got in a car that had been waiting for them and peeled out after the dogs. It didn't take the car long to catch up with the dogs. The goons drove along behind the dogs who were cutting across a field, trying to figure out a way to stop the dogs and recapture them.

They passed some cotton farms, then ran along a road in the shape of a slender S that passed a huge desert hill. They ran past a huge factory with tall smoke stacks billowing gray smoke out into the blue sky, then over a bridge with cars passing by.

Rex led the dogs under a busy freeway and jumped over a chain link fence. Lilly and the others followed. The goons drove right through the fence, and Rex wasn't sure what to do. Then he heard a loud train's horn and saw a big diesel engine and cargo cars starting to pass by.

He had an idea. It was a long shot, but it might be their only chance to get away.

He saw a cargo car with both the front and back door open. He said, "Onto the train! One . . . two . . . three!" He jumped into the car and clawed at the wooden floor so he wouldn't fall. Running alongside the moving train, Lilly copied Rex's actions. She jumped and Rex grabbed her collar with his mouth and helped pull her in. Alpha jumped next and they both caught him, then they helped Beta and Duke jump on as well.

The dogs collapsed on the floor of the car to rest. Rex stood in the middle of the train door, watching as the goons in their car crashed into a concrete barrier. They shook their fists at Rex. He lifted his paw in the classical "good riddance" gesture, mocking the goons as the train rolled down the tracks.

The other four dogs had moved to look out the door facing the other way. Rex joined them and stared at the beautiful but strange landscape.

He had never seen anything like it. It had tall green spiny plants with many arms and strange trees, some with dark brown bark and some with green. Dead bushes were rooted to rocky, sandy ground as far as the eye could see, and off in the distance he saw one very short but long mountain with patches of buildings on it. Another, taller mountain was covered in snow at the top with large clouds above it. Even more buildings stood at its base.

"This is not Alaska," Rex said in shock. He looked at the tall mountain and had an idea. "Let's go to that mountain. We can hide from those guys there." He pointed to the mountain with his gray nose, and all of them agreed on the plan.

They settled in to wait. It was an empty cattle car, so there was some hay and straw to lay on. Alpha, Beta, and Duke lay down together.

Lilly looked out across the landscape, then looked over at Rex, tears welling up in her eyes.

"Where are we, Rex? Because this isn't Fairbanks or even Alaska."

He looked at her and said warmly, "We'll figure this out together."

She nodded and settled in close to him, feeling much better. They continued to watch the scenery go by. They went under an overpass, then saw a big outlet mall with houses and shops nearby. As they continued to head towards the city, Rex looked over his shoulder and saw a big rocky peak off in the distance that looked kind of like a sombrero hat, with a larger mountain next to it resembling a face staring straight up at the sky. It disappeared behind a huge dirt-and-concrete overpass.

That was about when Duke saw a tall, lit sign. The letter "I" was burned out and the rest of the sign said "HOP." So Duke did just that: he hopped off the train, falling on the gravel beside it. He stood and licked his fresh, new bruises.

A moment later the other four dogs tumbled onto the gravel a little ways down the tracks, each of them moaning from their own new bruises.

"Why in the world did you jump? We didn't need to jump," Rex said to Duke.

"The sign said to HOP." Duke shrugged.

The other dogs shook their heads, and they all set off running for the mountain. They ran for a while in the city, trying not to get hit by cars, and staring around them at this strange, new place. After a while the road went out into the desert. Rex again saw those spiny, tall, green plants with many arms. He reached out and touched one with his paw.

"Ow! That hurt!" There were spines now embedded in his paw. The others watched in interest as Rex grabbed the spines with his teeth, pulling them out one by one.

"What are those things?" Lilly asked.

The last spine out, Rex just shrugged and started running, turning to the side and sprinting when he heard something like a raging river. He saw a whole group of strange, scraggly wolves standing together, staring at the river.

Rex walked up to one of them. "What kind of wolf are you?"

The strange wolf gave him a distracted glance; her attention was on the river. "What? No, I'm a coyote. Can you reach him?"

He was confused until he realized her last question was to one of her pack mates. He looked more closely at the river. It seemed to be very high and very fast. Then it hit him. Flash flood! And there, clinging to a very loose branch of a submerged tree, was a little coyote pup.

The rest of the gang caught up then. "Rex, are those wolves?" Alpha asked.

"They're not wolves, they're coyotes," Rex responded, but his attention was still on the struggling pup. The branch was bending and breaking.

He suddenly leaped into the raging water, making his way to the stranded pup.

"Rex!" Lilly screamed.

He reached the coyote pup and was able to grab it by the fur on the back of its neck, then kicked and swam to the side and managed to put the little pup on a small ledge before struggling to climb and squirm himself up and out of the arroyo. He coughed up water and shook to get dry.

The mom of the young coyote cuddled her pup close and said to Rex, "Thank you for saving my pup. If you ever need anything, we'll repay the favor." The coyote pup barked in agreement and Rex chuckled as the coyotes began to run into the desert.

"How would I be able to find you?" he called to her.

"Just howl!" she called back. The coyotes then disappeared into the distance.

After running for so long, Rex and his friends eagerly drank from the river, being careful not to fall in, then continued their journey towards the tall mountain. Near the base of the mountain, they saw a truck parked at a nearby school. Several people stood near the truck, talking together. The bed of the truck was piled with what looked like camping gear.

"Let's hitch a ride," Duke whispered to the other dogs. "My paws are killing me."

With that, they all jumped in and hunkered down low in the truck bed. They soon felt the truck start up and head up the mountain road. The dogs rested thankfully as the truck carried them up the mountain. When the truck got near the top of the mountain, it came to a stop, stuck behind road construction.

"Looks like this is our stop," Rex whispered.

The dogs jumped out of the truck and ran for a bit. They passed by a camp before coming to a gate that read "Camp Lawton."

"Looks good to me," Beta said. "The men chasing us might not be able to come in here."

They ran in and stopped near some long logs that were cover by a dusting of snow.

"Snow!" Duke said excitedly, and he started rolling around

in it.

Rex and Alpha stood and talked. "If we're going to find out where we are, we need to find a view of the city," Rex said to Alpha.

"Solid plan. Let's take a look around."

They gathered the others and went and looked around the camp. When they saw some people, they dodged into the forest, weaving through the trees as best they could.

"I think we're safe here," Rex said.

"Good, because I'm exhausted," Lilly admitted.

"Me too," the rest agreed.

They all collapsed into a heap in the middle of the forest in the late afternoon. Snow fell softly as they slept and covered them in a light blanket of white. Around midnight the cold, icy wind made Rex shiver, but he cuddled in with his friends and was cozy enough. When morning came, they went all over the mountain and found berries to eat for breakfast.

They spent all morning exploring different parts the mountain. They had fun but didn't find any great views of the city. Even so, they loved how amazing the forest was. This strange, faraway mountain felt like winter in Alaska, but definitely milder. Down in the valley, though, it hadn't felt like winter at all. They continued to have fun exploring this new place, even Alpha.

Far from the mountain, the goons were driving on the south side of the city on their way to visit the Boss.

People called the Boss many names. "El Siervo del Diablo" and "El Loco" were what people called him behind his back, but if people spoke those names around him, they would get killed. His real name was José Tonto, but his goons just called him "Boss."

As the goons neared the Boss's estate, the slender goon with the whiny tone said to the rotund goon with the grunting voice, "We need to get those dogs back or the Boss is going to kill us."

They were on a literal deadline. As they entered the mansion grounds they went through a golden gate, then got to the Boss's zoo complex.

The Boss's exotic zoo was his sole obsession. He had piranhas, giraffes, kangaroos, and all kinds of animals you would see in a zoo, but rarer, and he didn't display any of them to the public. He even had an operation in the works to steal a dinosaur fossil from a famous fossil lab.

When the Boss was a boy growing up in Tucson, he loved animals. He was kind of a nerd and knew everything about them, like how fast a cheetah could run and how much an elephant weighed. He was a good student, but he was bullied by other kids. He found refuge in his dream of having the best zoo in the world someday. As a young man, he opened a small neighborhood zoo and it was the biggest in the city. But then the city opened their Reid Park Zoo, forcing his zoo out of business. His dream was crushed, and his heart turned to stone.

As he got older, the Boss began to steal every animal he could get his hands on, still trying to make his dream come true of creating the best zoo in the world. He became known as the "animal maniac." Then he hired some goons who would go all over the world and steal animals, and he became the "animal Boss" of the city. He even told his goons to try to put other zoos out of business, especially the local Reid Park Zoo. He wanted to destroy that one.

He earned his nicknames and was a feared man. He tried to get some coyotes and other native wildlife that lived around the city, but the local police and the animal control wouldn't allow it. However, he still loved his animals. Sometimes he treated his animals better than his goons. He called his zoo the best zoo in all of the world, and he called the Reid Park Zoo "El peor zoológico del mundo."

The goons went into the Boss's offices. The Boss was a chubby Hispanic man dressed in all white, from his white fedora and white jacket to his white pants and white shoes.

"You let the dogs get away," he said while twiddling a large knife. He abruptly threw the knife, which missed the goons and hit a wall. "Find them or I'll slice both of your throats wide open."

They ran out of the Boss's mansion. "We don't know where the dogs are," the larger goon said to his companion.

"Then we'd better start driving and looking for them."

That afternoon, the gang settled down to rest a few miles from the camp. As they relaxed together, Rex felt uncomfortable.

"Are you ok?" Lilly asked.

"I feel like we're being watched."

Who or what is watching us? She looked around nervously, worried for all of them.

They continued to rest, but all of them felt a little scared. Even Alpha was nervous, and each of them stayed on guard. It was getting late.

Off in the distance, another group watched their prey.

"When are we going to attack?" a small voice asked quietly.

"When their guard is down," a wise and sophisticated voice answered.

A few hours from midnight, Rex, Alpha, and Duke each lay near the base of some trees, with Lilly and Beta in the middle. The two of them slept and were snug and cozy. Around midnight Rex was looking up at the night sky. There were no clouds, just tons of stars and a silver waxing gibbous moon.

Lilly woke, walked over to Rex, and lay down next to him, looking up at the sky with him.

"Isn't this beautiful?" she said.

"Yeah," he replied while still looking at the sky. They relaxed together for a while before they both fell asleep. In the morning they woke up and ate some berries and nuts, then explored more near the camp. They were still trying to find a view of the city, but even though they had no luck, they were having fun. After an hour or so, Lilly and Rex explored south of the camp and Alpha and Beta explored north of the camp. Duke explored both east and west from the camp.

Each group was being stalked by two hidden pairs of eyes.

Lilly and Rex were on a steep downhill.

"Race you," Lilly said with a smirk.

"You're on," Rex said readily.

They took off sprinting down the hill, but as they were running Lilly tripped on a root sticking out of the ground.

She tumbled down the hill, then stopped with a thump.

Rex stopped and ran to her.

"Lilly are you ok?" He looked her over. She was bruised, bleeding a little, and covered in dirt.

"Yeah, I'm fine," she said. "Just a little bit bruised." She stood and shook the dirt out of her fur, but when she tried to walk, she limped and then collapsed.

Rex helped her up the hill. "Let's go back to the camp. I think we've had enough exploring for today."

North of the camp, Alpha and Beta were exploring, but they felt like they were being watched. Beta stayed close to Alpha.

While Duke explored, he looked for bugs and tried to have conversations with the wildlife. He met some squirrels and a cottontail rabbit and even saw a mountain lion, but they mostly ignored him. He was having so much fun anyway.

In the distance, a pair was watching Duke.

"Great; this one is alone," said a rough voice.

"Let's tell the alpha," the other responded. They set off running.

Lilly and Rex rested at the camp, and Lilly was starting to feel a lot better. As they were chatting, Rex saw a fast, red blur dart through the forest before disappearing behind the trees.

"I think we have company," Rex said in a low voice.

"What did you see?" Lilly murmured back.

"Do you remember back in Alaska when I told you I saw a

white blur? And it turned out to be Khitrey?"

"Yeah," she said slowly.

"I just saw a bigger red blur."

She tensed. They waited on edge for the others to come back. Alpha and Beta met up with Duke, then they all ran back to the camp. Rex and Lilly told them what happened, and they spent the afternoon on heightened alert.

In the distance, glowing, blue eyes watched them. The gang thought they heard something a little ways from the camp, so they went all together to investigate, but they didn't see or hear anything.

Rex felt a presence nearby. All of the mountain animals fled into the trees, burrows, and all of their hiding places. The forest was dead silent as they walked.

Alpha snapped his jaws in frustration. "Enough! Let's find whatever this is and be done with it."

The others nodded in agreement, and they started running again. They ran and ran, trying to flush out whatever was stalking them. They made it to the highest peak of the forest, but still had no luck. They had looked everywhere.

Suddenly Rex saw the red blur running in the direction of the camp. He stopped and looked where it had gone, then froze.

"They're here, watching us," he whispered.

The five circled together, petrified with fear. They heard some rustling, then a big, boisterous howl, followed by other howls. They were surrounded by wolves.

CHAPTER 4

On the Mountaintops, Where the Wolves Howl

A whole pack of wolves emerged from the forest, growling.

A wolf with amber eyes stepped forward and said in a dignified but sarcastic tone, "Well, well, well, what do we have here?"

"Where have I heard that before?" Lilly mumbled to Rex sarcastically.

"Who are you?" Rex asked the lead wolf suspiciously.

"I am the alpha of this pack," the alpha wolf replied with lofty pride. "Now, may I ask, who are you?" The alpha wolf's tone was condescending and conceited.

"We're a group of explorers who climbed up this mountain," Rex replied.

"Our mountain, I may add," the alpha wolf interrupted rudely.

"*Your* mountain? Sure. . . ." Rex said under his breath.

"But who are you, really?" the alpha wolf asked, "because a group of domestics up here is quite unheard of.".

"As he said, we're just a group of explorers," Lilly butted in firmly.

"But you domestics aren't allowed on my land. When boundaries are crossed, your fate is decided by the alpha of the pack," the wolf sneered to the gang. "And it so happens that I'm the alpha of this pack," he replied with a wicked grin. "So, you had better get off this mountain or you'll suffer the consequences of your ignorance," the alpha wolf said threateningly. "Now wolves, let's teach these domestic intruders a lesson," the alpha barked to the other wolves and they all started to close in on the gang.

"RUN!" Rex cried and darted off, leading them through a gap in the pack.

"Get them!" the alpha wolf demanded to his pack.

The dogs ran toward the camp, the wolves close on their heels.

"Spread out," Rex commanded, and his friends obeyed.

When they reached the camp, the camp workers saw the wolves coming and fled for the buildings. Lilly, Beta, Duke, and Alpha followed them inside just as the workers slammed the door closed, collapsing to the floor exhausted.

"We're safe," Beta panted.

Lilly looked around, then whimpered, "Where's Rex?"

Rex ran at an angle away from the camp, hoping to lead the wolves away from his friends—but there were no wolves. He paused, listening carefully. He heard rustling and took off running again. Suddenly, something slammed into his side, throwing him to the ground.

A wolf with red fur stood over him.

"Déjà vu," he mumbled.

The wolf pressed her nose to his, very hard.

"Who are you? And why are you here?" Her voice was cold.

He replied quickly, "My name is Rex, and I'm just trying to figure out where I am."

She got off of him and they looked at each other. She had a beautiful maroon-red coat, a color Rex had never seen. Her body was slim and she had exquisite blue eyes. As she stared at him, her stance relaxed, no longer threatening.

"Follow me." She turned and ran.

Rex hesitated for a moment, then followed her.

They ran through another camp, then came to a steep hill and continued down. He didn't see her for a moment, but he then saw her red fur. She was on a big rock. He walked over to her, then stopped when he saw the city below.

He gazed at its vastness for a minute, then asked, "What's your name?"

"My name is Rosy."

"Are you a lone wolf?" he asked, intrigued.

She shook her head but stayed silent for a couple of seconds. Then she spoke. "No, I live with a pack of Mexican gray wolves."

So that's who they were. Rex said to himself. "But you're a red wolf. Why do you live with them?"

Her eyes narrowed and her shoulders tensed. "How did you know I was a red wolf?"

"You're a wolf and your fur is red," he pointed out. "How did you end up in a pack of gray wolves? Have you always lived here?"

Her shoulders relaxed slightly, but she looked away. "I . . . I don't really want to talk about it."

He nodded respectfully, then looked at the city lights. "What city is that?" he asked.

"That's Tucson."

"Tucson? Where's that?"

"Arizona."

Rex froze. "Arizona? We're in Tucson, Arizona!" he said frantically. "We're so far from home! What mountain are we on?"

"We're on Mount Lemmon."

Rex was confused. "Lemon, as in the fruit?"

"No, Lemmon," she said to him.

"Oh, so the mountain is named after a fruit. That's kind of odd. Wait—are there lemon trees on this mountain?"

"L-e-m-m-o-n. Lemmon. It was named after a botanist named Sara Plummer Lemmon."

"Oh, now I get it." Rex said. It was starting to get late.

"Now that I've answered most of your questions, I need to ask you one for myself." Rosy looked questioningly at Rex, and he nodded.

"I have been watching you and your friends for some time. I saw when you and your friends came upon my pack and our . . . leader." She spoke of her alpha more like she was talking about a disgusting slug than her pack's leader.

"When you were running away together from the wolves of my pack, you split off from your friends, who were going to the human camp for safety. My question is, why?" Rosy asked him in utter confusion. "Why would you put yourself in harm's way? You knew there was a possibility that you could have gotten attacked by the wolves and been badly injured or even killed. So, why would you do that?"

Rex began to think. "Because they are my friends and I would do anything for them," he replied honestly. "Even if it is dangerous or risky, I know they would do the same for me. I wanted to protect them even if it meant I would possibly get injured or even killed." Rex spoke with all of his heart, bringing a curious look to Rosy's face.

"It's getting dark," Rosy said. "We can sleep here tonight. I promise the wolves don't know this place, so we're safe."

He nodded. He was sure Lilly and the others were safe back at the camp. She lay down where she was; he lay down a few feet away, respecting her space, where he could see the city lights.

The rest of the dogs were sleeping in the buildings back at camp. The camp workers let them sleep inside until the wolves were gone, but the camp workers were nervous. Lilly was holding on to the hope that Rex was ok. She knew he was very strong and smart.

At the same time back at the big rock, Rex's mind was so full of thoughts that he couldn't sleep. He looked out at Tucson, remembering back when the mother coyote said, "Just howl." There was one problem. He didn't quite know how to howl.

Rosy saw that Rex was awake. It was a little before midnight. She walked over and sat down right next to him.

"Oh, sorry, I guess I woke you up," he said.

"Are you ok?"

He didn't answer at first, then he spoke. "I'm just thinking about a lot of things."

"You don't have to keep it in. I won't tell a soul." Then she smiled, and that made him smile. He saw her red fur gleam from the full moon.

"So how did you meet the gray wolves?" He repeated his question from before.

She was quiet for a long moment.

"It's a long story." She paused. "Are you sure you want to hear it?"

He nodded. She looked out across the city.

I was born in the Alligator River National Wildlife Refuge back in North Carolina, with my brothers and sisters. My mom and dad were so happy. When they saw that I had bright maroon-red fur, brighter than any other red wolf in our pack, they named me Rosy. They would call me "our precious rose."

My siblings all had yellow or green eyes, like our parents. When my parents saw that my eyes were blue, they thought they would change when I got older, but they never did. I was special.

Rosy paused for a long moment, remembering.

Then one day, our pack was attacked. Not by an animal. Some people in strange clothing came. They took my family, and the other red wolves in my pack fled. They took us to an airport and put us on a small airplane. After a short flight, they put us on a flatbed truck, saying something about another airport. It was a bumpy ride and my cage fell off. It rolled down a very steep hill, and I hit my head hard on the side of the cage. Finally, the cage stopped, and I could hear my family howling before I went unconscious.

When I woke up, I was with people in uniforms. I think they're called "Park Rangers." We were in Mississippi, and they sent me to be looked at by some scientists in Yazoo City. The scientists were all very kind, but one scientist in particular was special. Albert was very smart and very brave. The other scientists thought he was crazy to let me out of my cage, but he did. I walked out, and was I ever nervous, but I saw him and wanted to give him a chance. I approached him cautiously, then he slowly eased his hand closer and patted me on the head. I licked his hand, and the other scientists were astonished. We hung out and played and kept each other company, but I was his only real friend.

One day, I saw that Albert was looking at one of his fellow scientists, named Marie. I knew he liked her. When she was getting ready to leave for the day, I tried to encourage him to go after her, but he seemed depressed. I ran out of the lab after her and saw that her car was driving away. Albert ran out of the lab just as I started running for the car. He chased after me, and I kept running for her car. He yelled at me to stop, but I didn't, because if you love someone you must do something. I howled and she stopped. She looked out of the window and saw nothing, then she rolled down her window. I popped up in the window and she was startled. My friend Albert walked up to me and told me to come, and we both walked slowly back towards the lab. I was sad. I knew she had felt something, and she called out for Albert to stop. As she got out of her car and walked up to him, he tried to speak, but he was so nervous that he couldn't get words out of his mouth. I looked at him, then at her.

He looked at me, then took a deep breath and said to her, "Will you go out on a date with me?"

She happily said, "Yes!"

He was so happy. They went on their first date and I was happy for them. They worked and studied me and we all became so close and had so much fun together. They got married and both got promoted and were transferring to a new facility in Phoenix, Arizona.

They decided to bring me to their new home in Phoenix, and they thought it would be better to drive than to fly. So we drove, and I saw lots of things. We went through Bowie. It was a quaint little city in Texas, and we stayed and looked around. We stayed on the down-low because people were so confused when they saw me. Once a police officer saw us and asked, "Is that a wolf?"

"Yes," Albert said, "but I promise she won't hurt anyone." He told the officer about what happened, then the officer bid us adieu. We drove a long way, all the way to New Mexico, sometimes stopping in little towns and keeping me hidden in hotels.

Finally, we hit Albuquerque, New Mexico. Albert and Marie wanted to see some sights. We first went to the Albuquerque BioPark Botanical Garden. It had a huge glass pyramid on the top of it, and as we went in, one of the employees told them that they couldn't bring me in. My friends asked for the manager and the manager came and told them that that I was a wild animal and couldn't come into the park, but that they could go in if they left me in the car. Marie told her that I wouldn't hurt a fly and that I acted more like a dog. Well! I had heard and seen dogs back at the wildlife refuge in North Carolina, and I was miffed.

The manager was still hesitant, but she put her hand out in front of my mouth. I licked her hand, and she was impressed. She said, "Enjoy!" and let us all go inside.

We saw all types of plants. I sniffed a goldenrod and sneezed loudly, and everyone looked at me and laughed. I saw some roses and stood in front of them, and my friends laughed because my fur matched the flowers, and they called me Rose. We went on a small train that took us around the garden and went into a big hollow log. People around us thought I was amazing. They knew I was a red wolf, but I acted more like a dog (which I got used to being called), even though I still had wolf in me. They came and patted me and the people said, "That wolf is amazing and very friendly."

After the garden, we drove to the New Mexico Museum of Natural History and Science. It had a large dome on the top. My friends were excited because they were both scientists. As we walked inside, one of the museum's employees came up to us and said, "Excuse me, is that a red wolf?" He looked at us and got excited. He said, "Wait, you're the two from Yazoo City. And this must be Rose. I'm a big fan of your work." He squealed with excitement. He seemed like a nerd.

"We're just passing through here on our way to Phoenix," Marie said.

"Oh, well it is a pleasure to meet you! Welcome to the New Mexico Museum of Natural History and Science." He started walking toward the exhibits, then stopped and turned, asking, "Are you three coming?"

"We're confused," Albert said. "We didn't pay to get a personal tour."

The tour guide said politely, "It's on the house."

"Thank you!" my friends both said.

"No problem. Now, let's get started. This museum was founded in 1986 and is near the old town of Albuquerque. Here we have Stan, our Tyrannosaurus rex."

Stan was posed in attack mode. He was gigantic, and his bones were amazing. He looked like he was roaring with his mouth wide open, and we could see all of his sharp teeth.

"Stan is one of the largest predatory dinosaurs of all time."

My friends were impressed.

"He lived about 66 million years ago, hunting in the jungles and savannas of Western North America, near the end of the age of the dinosaurs. Stan was a powerful, agile, bipedal killing machine. Nearly 40 feet long and 12 feet high at the hip, Stan weighed as much as six tons.

"Stan hunted with his acute sense of smell, 3D vision, and he had great speed from his huge and muscular hind legs. He probably used his thin arms like meat hooks to stab his prey. Stan had about 60 huge, blade-like teeth set in a powerful skull that he used to tear his victims apart. T. rex fossils are rare, but several have been found in New Mexico. However, no complete skeleton has ever been discovered."

"Well, you know your history and science," Marie said.

"Yeah, this job is amazing!" replied the enthusiastic guide. "I have loved dinosaurs ever since I was a kid. I wanted to be a paleontologist, but it's a hard job to get, so when I heard the museum was hiring tour guides, I took the job. I fell in love with the dinosaur exhibit, and Stan is my favorite dinosaur.

"Now, back to Stan. The T. rex in this exhibit is a replica of a nearly complete skeleton that was found near Buffalo, South Dakota, in 1987. Stan is named after his discoverer, amateur paleontologist Stan Sacrison."

He showed us the museum's other exhibits and the planetarium. At the end we bid him farewell, and he thanked us for coming. We got in our car and drove on to Arizona. Finally, we got to Phoenix and went to Albert and Marie's new work facility. Their boss greeted them and introduced himself, and my friends introduced themselves, then introduced me.

Their boss said, "So, this must be the famous Rose I've been hearing all about." He patted me on the head, and I licked his hand. He told them to come into work tomorrow morning and to be sure to bring me.

We went to the apartment Albert and Marie had rented, then we checked out Phoenix a little bit. It was a wonderful city. It's known as "Arizona's Urban Heart." We went to Heritage Square, where we saw a lot of old houses from the Victorian Era. As we were walking, I saw two shady men in fancy clothing following us. I saw the same crest on their clothing from when my family was taken back in North Carolina, but they were different people. I realized they must have been friends with the people that took me and my family.

Oh no! I have to be careful. They might try to take me again, *I thought. My friends and I were walking near an old two-story house. I saw the two men following me and I started to walk faster. I ran around the house, hoping my friends would realize something was wrong, but they thought I was just having fun looking at the old house. They didn't know I was running away from the two men.*

Oh, this is bad, very bad, *I thought nervously. I stopped to go back to the safety of my friends, but suddenly one of the men grabbed me by my fur and threw me into a kennel the other man held ready. I howled to my friends. They heard my distress and started looking for me, but one of the men opened the kennel door and put a muzzle on me. He closed the kennel door and they took me to a car. One of the shady men opened the back door of the car and threw the kennel in. I saw my friends frantically looking around trying to find me. I tried to howl, but I couldn't with the muzzle, and I scratched at it. One of the men said in a raspy tone, "It's no use. Even if you got it off, they'll never hear you. You're the Boss's now."*

They started the car, and Raspy Voice made a phone call to someone he just called "the Boss."

"Wait, wait, wait!" Rex interrupted her story. "Did you just say they called him 'the Boss'? And that they had a crest on their fancy clothing?"

"Yes. . . ."

"My friends and I were stolen by men just like that! I heard them call their Boss, and they had a crest on their clothing!"

"What?" Rosy looked at him with eager eyes. "You were taken by them, too? Where did they take you? Did you see any red wolves? Did you see my family?"

Rex shook his head. "I'm sorry, Rosy. We escaped before they got there, like you."

Rosy sighed. "I suppose it was too much to hope, after all this time." She was quiet for a moment.

"What happened next? In your story?"

"Oh right, my story. Where was I? Do you remember where I was in the story?"

"I think you were telling me about the men who captured you and their Boss, right?"

"You're correct, my good sir. I was testing you."

"Right," Rex said sarcastically.

Rosy smirked, "Right."

So, the men drove out of Heritage Square with me in the back. After a few miles I saw a big airport, and a huge airplane was taking off. They turned down a road, and I saw a large river. I was scared because I didn't know where they were taking me, and I wanted to be back with Albert and Marie. Then the man with the raspy tone called his Boss, turning on the phone's speaker.

"Hey Boss, it's us."

"Ah, the Phoenix crew. You have something?"

"Yeah, we got something. We got a red wolf."

I growled.

"There was her that growled, she's in the back."

"A red wolf? Aren't you there for gray wolves?"

"Yeah, we're going to Pinetop for some gray wolves, but we came across this beauty while we were in Phoenix. She has very bright red fur. You'll love it."

"Bright red fur? Hmm. I had some men pick up some red wolves in North Carolina a while back. There was supposed to be a bright red wolf in that group, but they lost it. Of course, as a punishment— "

"Okay, okay, I don't want to hear what happened to them."

"Good work. Get the gray wolves, and don't lose that red one." The Boss hung up before the goon could respond.

I was intrigued, but they just kept driving and driving. When they stopped for gas, Raspy Voice told the other goon to take the muzzle off so I didn't overheat. I tried to bite him, but he was quick. They got back in the car and I growled at them.

"Be quiet, you flea-bitten mutt."

After a long drive, we got to Pinetop, Arizona, up on the Mogollon Rim. They went and checked into a hotel and put me in their room on a table by the door, and they forgot to close the door fully.

One of the goons said to the other, "When should we go and get those gray wolves?"

"When the park rangers are done with their day, you idiot," the other goon said.

As they kept talking, I saw that the kennel had a latch. I carefully slid the latch of the cage open with my nose. One of the goons looked at me and saw that I was laying down, then went back to his conversation. When they were both facing the opposite direction, I slowly pushed the kennel door open and stealthily dropped on the carpet. Their heads turned and they both saw me. I sprinted for the door and squeezed through, and the goons came after me. I ran down the road, and the goons got in their car and followed me.

I saw a thick forest beside the road, and I ran into it. The goons stopped their car and followed me on foot. I ran deeper into the forest and hid behind a large tree to catch my breath. Ten minutes later I heard a sarcastic, "Come here, red wolf, we're not going to hurt you.".

I took off running again.

"Get it!" one of them shouted. I glanced back to see how close they were, tripped on a tree root, and tumbled down a steep hill. I hit a big rock and bruised my whole body pretty bad. I tried to stand up, but I was too weak and collapsed. One of the goons appeared at the top of the hill and sneered, "Come to papa."

The other goon emerged to one side. As they advanced on

me, we heard a big, boisterous howl. The goons both stopped and looked around. A big, dark gray wolf jumped in front of me and growled at the two goons. The goons circled around, trying to outsmart the gray wolf, but he growled and snapped every time they got close to me. Then he howled for backup.

The goons were nervous. I heard others howling off in the distance, and the gray wolf smirked. We all heard numerous howls, and the goons were becoming petrified. A group of about ten gray wolves emerged from the trees, growling at the goons. The biggest one lunged at the goons, and they both turned and fled to their car and drove away. The gray wolves ran into the woods, and the big, dark gray wolf said, "Follow me."

He started to run, but he stopped when he realized I wasn't behind him. "Are you coming?" he asked, concerned. I stood up and tried to walk but collapsed again.

The big gray wolf said nicely, "You'll be ok. We don't have to be in a rush."

I managed to get to my feet and slowly walked, and he walked with me.

"What's your name?" I asked.

"My name is Hunter."

"Hey, that my brother's name," I said with a smile, but it faltered when I thought of my captured family.

"Is that so? Now, what is your name?"

"My name is Rosy."

"What a lovely name," he said sincerely. I chuckled a little bit and blushed. We walked and chatted for a while, then we entered a decent-sized valley with a lot of gray wolves milling around. Hunter and I went down into the valley and he took me to their alpha. He was the oldest Mexican gray wolf in the pack.

The alpha said in an old, wise, tone, "Hello, young lady. I'm Clements. I'm the alpha of this pack. Who might you be?"

"Hi, I'm Rosy. I'm a red wolf from North Carolina. I was stolen by some very shady people."

"Yeah, I believe they were going to take her to this place down south of Tucson. They were going to take some of us, too," Hunter said, concerned.

"What? Who's taking us?" Clements said frantically.

"They're people who steal animals and do who knows what with them." Hunter told the alpha.

Clements called the wolves' council together and told them what was happening. As the council began to discuss the issue, Hunter said to me, "Let's let them talk it out. You can come to my place and hopefully sleep there with my family, and I can introduce them all to you."

We walked to Hunter's place, and I was kind of nervous. He saw and said with a smile, "Don't worry, they'll like you. I promise." He seemed like a trustworthy wolf. "We're close to my place. Just follow me." His place was secluded. There were huge rocks that had fallen down from the mountain. I saw four gray wolves. One fit-looking wolf with vanilla-white fur walked up to me and said in a warm tone, "Hello, young lady. Who might you be?"

"I'm Rosy. I'm a red wolf from North Carolina."

"North Carolina? How did you end up here with us in Arizona?"

"I was stolen from a wildlife refuge where I lived, but I escaped and two scientists found me and brought me to Phoenix. But then I got stolen again by two other people, who brought me to Pinetop. I escaped, but got hurt pretty bad. They were going to

get me, but Hunter protected me and brought me here."

"I'm Shira. I'm Hunter's mother. It's a pleasure to meet you. What an amazing travel story! This is my husband."

Another bigger, dark gray wolf came up to me and introduce himself in a deep, welcoming tone.

"My name is Robert, but you can call me Rob. It's nice to meet you. I'm so happy that our boy saved you." He was a big wolf.

So Hunter gets his size from his dad, I thought.

Then two pretty wolves walked up to me. Hunter said, "Rosy, these are my two younger sisters, Star and Mary."

Star, a vanilla-white gray wolf like her mom, said bashfully, "Hi, I'm Star. It's nice to meet you." She darted away and hid behind her parents.

"She's a little bit shy around others, but she'll get use to you." Hunter said.

Mary, dark gray like her dad, said, "Hi! I'm Mary. Your name is amazing and unique."

"Thank you."

Then Hunter spoke. "Mom, Dad, can Rosy stay here for a while?"

Rob said, "As long as she's comfortable with it." He turned to me, "Would you like to stay with us?"

"Yes." I trusted them.

"Then she can stay, and you need to watch out for her," Shira said.

So, Hunter showed me their valley. It was kind of like the wildlife refuge, just smaller.

"How is your body doing?" he asked after a while.

"It's actually feeling a lot better," I said honestly. To prove it,

I ran and jumped on some big rocks nearby. He laughed, and I sprang on additional rocks even faster. His laughter died down a little. I saw another larger rock and jumped on it. I looked back to Hunter, but he had stopped laughing and was dead silent. I jumped off the large rock and landed gracefully on the ground, and he ran over to me.

"You almost gave me a heart attack!"

I shrugged my shoulders and gave him a smirk. I met a lot of new friends and acquaintances until it was getting late and the pack was going to sleep. Hunter and I got back to his place. I slept a few feet away from him out of respect. I looked up at the sky. It was a new moon and I could see the Milky Way with millions or even billons of stars. It was beautiful. As I was looking at the majestic sky with its countless number of gleaming stars, a bright red shooting star streaked across the sky, then it was gone. It was hard to see the wonderful night sky when I was in North Carolina because my family and I slept under the trees.

Rosy looked at Rex. "Stargazing that night reminded me of when I was a young wolf. I would sneak away to the Alligator River inlet. Near its coast, you could see the bright silver moon with billions of stars around it."

On the night prior to the strange men coming to steal red wolves and breaking up our family, I went to the coast with some friends of mine. We were just goofing around on the beach, but the beauty of the sky entranced us with wonder and awe. The river inlet mirrored the sky, like a vast ocean filled with glowing fishes swimming. The blackish-blue waters had a thin silver crescent-shaped boat sailing slowly across it.

Then, as we were gazing at the beauty of the sky, a bright blue shooting star streaked across the ocean-like sky.

"A shooting star!" one of my friends cried out. "Give it your deepest wish."

So I did. As the blue shooting star disappeared beyond the horizon, I thought in my head, I wish I could have a more adventurous life.

I think often of how my wish has come true. I both thank and curse that shooting star for what it has done to my life.

Rosy resettled her position and continued her previous tale.

When I woke up in morning, I looked for Hunter, but he wasn't in the spot where he slept. I walked to where his mom lay and asked her quietly, "Where's Hunter?"

Shira said sleepily, "Hunter is usually an early bird . . . or early wolf . . . but he doesn't usually get up at this hour. He must have a good reason for it."

"I'm going to go look for him."

"Ok, be careful and be safe."

"I will," I said to her as I started around the rocks.

I saw some gray wolves who were awake and went over to greet them, and they greeted me back.

"Have you seen Hunter?"

I mostly heard "No," or "No I haven't, sorry," but then I heard someone say, "I know where he is."

A healthy, light gray wolf came running toward me with a grin on her face.

"Where is he?"

"I saw him near the river," she said.

"Thank you. I don't think I know your name."

"My name is Aquamarine, but the wolves in the pack call me Aqua."

"What a unique name. How did you get it?"

"When I was a wolf pup, I loved to go to the river. Every time the older wolves led me away from the river, I would always go back. Because of my desire to be near the water and because of the color of my eyes, my parents named me Aquamarine." Her eyes were an aquamarine color similar to an actual aquamarine gem. "Forgive me, I never got your name?"

"Oh, my name is Rosy. My parents named me for my maroon-red fur."

"That makes sense. Now, I'll take you to the river and help you find Hunter."

We searched all around the river for him. We finally found him sitting on some big rocks in front of a steep rock face covered in grape vines with wild grapes everywhere. He was tugging determinedly on the vines. As he tugged, one of the vines snapped and he fell backwards into the river with a big splash. I was concerned at first, but he emerged out of the water and swam to the other side. He was soaking wet.

"Hunter, what are you doing?" I yelled to him.

"I'm getting some breakfast for you. I see Aqua is with you. Hi Aqua!"

Aquamarine smiled at him. He picked up the vines in his mouth, then swam across the river to where we stood. He climbed out of the river, shook himself vigorously, then said, "Dig in!" He had gotten a lot of grapes for all of us and we enjoyed our breakfast.

Several days after that wild grape experience, Hunter, Aqua, myself, and some of their friends were resting in a grove of trees on a hot afternoon. The trees shaded us from the blistering sun above. We were all chatting pleasantly, when two gray wolves from the wolves' council approached us.

"Rosy, Clements needs to talk to you."

My mind swirled nervously. Did I do something wrong? Why does Clements need me?

"Why?" I asked.

"Clements and the council need to talk with you," the lighter gray wolf, a male, simply replied.

"Come on, let's get a move on." the darker gray wolf said to me as she began to walk away, with the lighter wolf right on her tail.

I turned to Hunter and Aqua. "Why do Clements and the council need me? Did I do something wrong?" I asked, panic coloring my voice.

"Rosy, Rosy! You're not in trouble. They probably just want to talk to you," Hunter said, trying to calm me down.

"Yeah, Hunter's right. It's not like you killed a wolf or something," Aqua joked, chuckling.

"Rosy, Clements and the council probably just need to talk to you for the benefit of himself, the wolves' council, and all of the wolves of the pack." Hunter's reassuring words calmed me down a bit.

The light gray wolf turned back to me and called, "Rosy, we must go now. Clements told us 'time was of the essence.'"

"Ok. Let's go."

Hunter and Aqua walked with me. I was grateful for their presence.

As we walked, the dark gray wolf walked next to me with the light gray wolf close to her other side.

"What are your names?" I asked.

"I'm Willow," the dark gray female answered, "and he's Rowan."

"Hi," Rowan said to me with a smile.

"You two seem to be very close friends."

Willow smiled. "Yeah, we're very close. We have been friends since we were young."

"Wow, that's pretty amazing."

"We're mates also," Rowan added.

"You are?"

They looked at each other, smiling, and said, "Yes," as they both sighed happily.

"You and those men who almost took you seem to be the talk of the pack," Willow said.

"Me?" I looked at her, surprised. "Really?"

She nodded.

"She's right, you are quite the news around this valley." Hunter replied.

"You're the first wolf to come to this pack who wasn't born into it," Aqua added.

"Let me explain," Hunter began. "Rosy, you coming to this pack is like a single seed blown in by the eastern winds to a field of gray and white flowers. And from that seed blooms a red rose. No pun intended," he told me. "But that doesn't mean you're a newcomer."

"But Hunter, she is a newcomer," Aqua reminded him.

"Yes, you're right, she is a newcomer," he agreed. "But that doesn't mean she's not a wolf." He looked at me and gave me a

kind smile. "As my father has always told us, 'a wolf is a wolf, no matter what type it is.'"

We all nodded in agreement.

"The stories of you almost getting kidnapped near the outskirts of the forest, and even wolves in our pack nearly being stolen by those men, have spread around quickly and caused quite a panic within the pack," he said.

"This has been a persisting problem for the wolves' council to solve," Rowan stated.

"I heard you came all the way from North Carolina to here. That must've been quite the journey," Willow said to me with a grin.

"It was."

We kept walking until we got all the way to a spot high up in the valley, near the meeting place of the wolves' council.

Willow and Rowan told Hunter and Aqua that they had to wait here near the entrance because of secrecy. They both complied and sat down to wait for my return.

"This way." Rowan gestured to the entrance.

I looked back to Hunter and Aqua, who both looked at me with friendly smiles.

"You're going to be fine," Hunter told me.

I entered the meeting place of the wolves' council with Willow and Rowan. We entered an open area on the edge of a cliff that was known to the wolves and other wildlife of the valley as Poplar Point. The whole area overlooked the valley, and towering cottonwood trees shaded the group of about twenty wolves. The wolves were sitting down talking with one another, their opinions and ideas weaving and intertwining like a well-crafted spiderweb.

"Hello," I called out, but my words were drowned out by the council's discussions. Willow and Rowan both cleared their throats to get the wolves' council's attention.

"Alpha, members of the wolves' council: I would like you all to meet Rosy of North Carolina." Rowan spoke to the group of now-attentive wolves.

The council looked at me with eager eyes. "Thank you, Rowan and Willow, for bringing Rosy. You may sit with us," Clements said gratefully.

They both nodded respectfully and sat down. "Rosy, it's great to see you again," Clements told me in a kind voice that made me less nervous. "You may sit with us."

I noticed a vacant spot right next to Willow, so I went and sat down next to her. I looked at Willow and she smiled at me kindly.

"Rosy, we need you to answer a few questions to the best of your knowledge about these men who tried to take you," Clements told me.

"Yes, Ms. Red, we need to know about these thieving men!" a large black wolf said in a tone of self-importance. He sat on Clements's left.

"Um, that's not my name. My name is—" I began to say.

"Ms. Red, we must find out who these men are and why they are trying to steal wolves from our pack." The black wolf interrupted in a demanding manner. "Our problem is more important than your name. We'll get to that subject later."

At this, Clements gave the large black wolf a stern look that clearly deflated the large black wolf's pride.

"Do you know who these men are?" asked a wolf with yellow eyes.

"No, I don't know who these men are. They just came to my pack and took me and my family."

"Do you know who they work for?" Willow turned and asked me.

"The only thing I overheard was them talking quite a bit about a person they referred to as the 'Boss'," I replied.

"Did you notice anything strange or unusual about these men?"

"Well, for starters, they dress formally in a fancy kind of way," I recalled. "They also had a sort of gold-colored crest on their clothing." That was etched into my brain and was something I would never forget.

"What was on the crest?" asked a wolf with dark brown eyes.

"Well . . . it showed two caged animals. The one in the right was a large bear grabbing the bars of its cage, and on the left was a mountain lion lying down."

I heard murmurs and whispers among the council. I continued, "There was a plant on the right side of the bear's cage that grew in North Carolina. It was called devil's tongue, or eastern prickly pear. A type of cactus-like plant with large spines and branched pads with its fruit on top. The crest also showed another tall, tree-like plant, but it wasn't a tree. It had large green arms with spines. Above the cages was a rifle and spear crossed over making the shape of a diamond with a curved hat," I continued. "At the bottom of the crest was a sentence in Spanish."

"But why are they coming for our pack?" a small wolf inquired.

"Why they're trying to steal wolves from this pack, I don't know," I told them. "But I believe these men came to my

pack because we're protected red wolves. We are on a list of endangered animals because our habitats are being altered, and frankly, we are worth a lot of money for trappers, sellers, and buyers in illegal markets"

Rowan asked me. "What does that have to do with our pack?"

I thought for a moment and then asked, "How is your pack doing in numbers?" This question silenced Clements and every member of the wolves' council.

"Rosy," Clements began solemnly, "Our pack of Mexican gray wolves, as well as other packs of Mexican gray wolves, have been threatened by livestock owners trying to protect their livestock. Because of that, o-other p-packs as well as o-our p-pack w-w-were. . . ." His voice began to shake and tremble in sorrow as tears fell from his gray eyes.

"Killed," the large black wolf who sat next to Clements said angrily, his face as cold as stone.

Every wolf of the council bowed their heads sorrowfully and respectfully for their fallen members. Even the large black wolf bowed his head with a sorrowful look on his face.

I bowed my head in respect along with them.

The sun had lowered to the horizon as we'd been speaking, and as it slowly sunk behind the mountains, a warm red color slowly descended down the towering cottonwoods until red hues filled the whole valley. This redness enveloped the tall red cottonwoods that were silent as if joining our moment of respectful silence.

"Thank you for that, it's much appreciated." Clements' kind voice brought a warm aura to the council.

"The disrespectful humans come killing our wolves and

others, hunting us down, ensnaring us with abominable traps and even resorting to lethal poisons," the large black wolf snapped, breaking the peaceful moment. His face contorted angrily. "Savages!" he said with utter disgust, like the farmers were some sort of cruel beasts.

"I've got it!" I yelled out loud.

Every wolf looked at me expectantly.

"Ok, I think I may know the reason these men stole me and my family, and why they're trying to steal wolves from your pack," I began. "Both of our species are declining and are considered by humans to be 'endangered.' This happened to both me and my family in North Carolina and I saw it again in Phoenix."

"That sounds plausible, but how does that tie in with us?" a brown-eyed wolf asked.

"Clements, you said the Mexican gray wolf population has seen a decline, right?" Clements nodded. "Well, if red wolves and Mexican gray wolves are both considered endangered, this could be why this 'Boss' is having them steal me and my family along with trying to steal wolves from your pack," I explained to the council.

"Thank you, Rosy, for your insight on our pressing matter," said Clements. "We all appreciate it. You can go now."

I got up and was about to leave when Clements called out, "Rosy, wait."

I turned around.

"I want to talk to you after the council to discuss a few more things."

I nodded and he smiled. Back outside the council area, I found Hunter and Aqua resting on the ground.

"How'd it go?" Aqua asked me.

"It was fine, actually. They just asked me a few questions about the men who tried to kidnap me."

"See, there was nothing to be scared of," Hunter replied, and I chuckled as he and Aqua got up and started to walk away.

Realizing I hadn't moved, Hunter and Aqua stopped and turned. "You coming?" Hunter asked.

"Actually, I need to wait here. Clements said he needed to talk to me some more after the council's discussion," I told them with sheepish chuckles.

"Okay," they both sighed, and we all settled down until the council was done with their discussions an hour later.

As wolves began to leave, Rowan and Willow came over to us. "We're done with our discussions, so you can go back in and talk to Clements now. He's just talking with his head counselor," Rowan explained.

"Okay, thanks."

"Thanks for your help today. The council really appreciated it," Rowan told me with gratitude.

"Yeah, it means a lot to us," Willow chimed in.

"Have a good night!" Rowan called out as he and Willow walked away.

"Yeah, sleep well," Willow exclaimed.

"See you later," Hunter and Aqua called out to them.

"Safe travels," I added as I turned and headed for the entrance. I looked back and saw both Hunter and Aqua giving me kind smiles.

"Clements is a reasonable wolf, don't worry." Hunter reassured me.

I walked back into Poplar Point. Clements was talking to the large black wolf who had sat next to him during the meeting.

"Clements, we need to leave immediately before the men who tried to take that red wolf come back and take us."

"Relax. Hunter and Rosy said there were only two men and that Hunter and ten of our wolves scared them away," Clements said reasonably. "And we have more wolves than just two humans."

"You don't know for sure how many men there are," the large black wolf quickly interjected. "This 'Boss' could have hundreds of men who could steal our whole pack away in no time."

"How so?"

"The red wolf—" the large black wolf began to say before being cut off.

"Her name is Rosy! Just say her name! Is it that hard to put four letters together?" Clements exclaimed in frustration. "Calling her 'the red wolf' and 'Ms. Red' is an insult to her, especially when the pack and I are trying to welcome her with our hospitality, and you can't even say her name."

The large black wolf looked frazzled by Clements's outburst.

"Ok, Clements, I'll follow your wishes, but there is no need for such anger." The large black wolf scoffed. "But Rosy said there were men who stole her and her family in North Carolina, as well as men in Phoenix. We could get further away from those men by invading the land of Olive's pack."

"No, we cannot do that." Clements said firmly. "Greatness is not achieved by brute force. Olive and I have kept the peace between our packs. We've respected each other's territories and it has been a wonderful relationship."

"Yes, I agree with your notion; but instead of fleeing to some place near the valley, what if we. . . ." he paused and then the large black wolf leered his gaze at me slightly but his head was

pointed at Clements.

"What if we what?" Clements asked.

The large black wolf moved close and whispered something into Clements's ear.

"I don't know. . . ." he said hesitantly. "What if it doesn't work? It could turn into an utter disaster."

"It's the only thing we can do for the safety of the pack," the large black wolf said firmly.

Clements sighed and nodded. "You're right. If it is for the welfare of the pack, then it's the right thing to do."

I cleared my throat. Clements and the large black wolf turned and looked at me.

"Rosy, your presence never ceases to bring joy to this valley," Clements said to me kindly.

His kind words put a smile on my face and I walked up to them.

Clements had a warming smile on his pleasant face. Next to him was the large black wolf who stood tall and proud. His eyes gleamed like two pieces of hardened tree sap encompassed in darkness.

"How has your day gone, Rosy?" Clements asked.

"It's gone pretty good, except for the hot weather. I was with Hunter and Aqua and some of their friends cooling down in a grove of trees."

"Yeah, it's quite a hot day. I'm glad you and your friends found a way to cool off."

I looked at the large, black wolf. He still stood with proud arrogance.

"Oh, Rosy, this is my head councilor." The large, black wolf was silent and looked down at me over his scrunched nose and

squinted eyes that hid their amber color.

"Hi, I'm Rosy. It's nice to meet you," I said politely.

He stepped back with a look of disdain.

"A pleasure."

"What's your name?" I asked. He remained silent. "You have a name, don't you?" I asked him, chuckling a bit.

Clements nudged him. "Come on, tell her your name."

"Oh, my name is De-Vil," he said with his chest puffed out.

"Your name is De-Vil?"

"Yes, De-Vil is my name and have we not just gone through this?" he said in frustration.

"But. . . ."

"But, what Rosy?" he questioned as his voice deepened, marking his frustration.

"But doesn't De-Vil sound an awfully lot like devil? You know, an evil spirit from the fiery regions below."

He gave me a look that said I had just insulted his family and even his ancestors.

"It is a family name," he said stiffly, obviously affronted. "It means 'of the brave.' It was my great-great-grandfathers name." He growled, making me step back.

"Calm down, De-Vil." Clements said calmly, stepping between us. "She meant you no harm. I know your name is special to you and your family. My name was the name of my father and I hold it dearly, just as you do,"

"I'm sorry, Rosy," De-Vil apologized half-heartedly.

"Now that we have gotten to know each other and resolved our problems, De-Vil, I need to talk to Rosy alone." Clements looked at De-Vil, who nodded and stepped aside quietly.

"De-Vil, I said alone!"

De-Vil nodded once more and left Poplar Point.

"So, Rosy," began Clements, "the council and I have devised a plan that I think you might have heard me and De-Vil discussing. But before it's finalized and presented to the pack, I would like to know what you think about it."

"You want . . . my opinion?"

He nodded at me with a friendly smile.

"What do I think of it?" I paused to think. What harm could it do?

"But now, looking back, I wish I had never had that thought." Rosy shuddered and continued telling Rex her story.

"Yeah, I think it's a great idea if it will help the entire pack."

"Oh, that is wonderful. Your help in this is greatly appreciated. Thank you."

"No, thank you," I said. "You and the pack have gone above and beyond by welcoming me into this pack like it's my own."

"Well, you are a wolf," he pointed out. "Wolves work together to help other wolves. Are you sure my plan is going to work?" he asked me nervously.

"Yes, Clements, I think it's a good plan. It will help the pack to get away from those men who took me and my family," I told him frankly.

"Oh, marvelous. How absolutely marvelous," he said as tears of joy welled up in his eyes. "Rosy, I can't thank you enough."

I chuckled with him.

"Rosy, you are like a ray of sunshine that has brought light to our valley, breaking through the dark, ominous clouds that

have been looming over us."

"Well, I'm happy to help you and the pack out. Do you want to know why?"

"Why?"

"Because wolves work together to help other wolves." I echoed his words back to him.

He smiled and laughed, both of which warmed my heart.

"I know I've said this already, but thank you, Rosy."

"It's been my pleasure."

"You're free to go now."

I left Poplar Point and found Hunter and Aqua both asleep right where I had left them. "Hey Hunter, Aqua, wake up!" I exclaimed and they slowly opened their eyes.

"Finally! It took you long enough." Aqua said.

"Yeah, just in the nick of time. It's getting quite dark, and we'd better start heading back home." Hunter yawned, stretched and got up.

All of us began to walk at a brisk pace to the bottom of the valley. "So, how did your talk with Clements go?" Hunter asked.

"It went pretty well, actually," I replied. "He was nice and considerate and made me not nervous at all."

"Yeah, he is pretty well-known for his kind-natured leadership." Aqua explained.

"Well, everything was fine until Mr. I-Am-Better-Than-You started talking," I said in an annoyed tone.

"Who?" Hunter and Aqua asked simultaneously.

"His pompous head counselor," I grumbled.

"Oh, you're talking about De-Vil. Yeah, he comes off as . . ." Hunter paused to think of how to word it. ". . . not the friendliest wolf in the pack."

"Or the humblest." I heard Aqua muttered under her breath.

"He is a bit prickly, to say the least," conceded Hunter, "but he is the head counselor and Clements must trust him."

"Yeah, like anyone would trust that puffed-up nagger," Aqua muttered.

We continued to walk and talk.

"I've heard that De-Vil killed a wolf because he was jealous," Aqua told us out of the blue.

"What?!" Hunter and I responded in shock.

"So, you're saying that De-Vil killed a wolf?" Hunter and I said in unison. His voice sounded doubtful; mine was a mixture of shock and fear.

"Yep."

"Aqua, you know that the 'De-Vil killing another wolf' story is just a rumor wolves in the pack tell because of his unpleasant nature," Hunter said.

"How sure are you that he didn't kill a wolf?"

Hunter's muscles tightened in his face. "Aquamarine, think about what you're saying. If De-Vil did kill a wolf, don't you think that it would have been brought to Clements and the council?"

She just shrugged.

"Why in the world would Clements, the alpha of the pack, appoint De-Vil as his most trusted head counselor? He is with him all the time, and if he killed a wolf, wouldn't he be considered a threat?"

"But what if he did kill the wolf?"

"Aquamarine!" Hunter raised his voice. "It's..." he began to say to her as his calm face turned into a grimace. "It's just a stupid rumor! Ok, I have another question for you. If he really did kill a wolf, why haven't any wolves or wildlife found any

evidence of the crime?"

"Because they didn't find the carcass of the dead wolf," she said in an unnerving way.

Hunter seemed creeped out by her statement; I was absolutely terrified.

Aqua went back to her normal, relaxed face and started laughing. "You should have seen your faces," she gasped, laughing hysterically, and then she made a face of alarm and fear, mocking our previously frightened faces. "It was priceless!"

Hunter was not amused by her scaring both of us, and that fact was reflected in his face as well as in his voice. "Aqua, that was mean of you, insulting De-Vil with this stupid rumor."

"He's not here, so I can say anything I please about him."

"Plus, you scared Rosy half to death!"

She tried to speak but he spoke over her.

"Aquamarine, a stupid rumor of De-Vil killing a wolf compounded with his mean nature," Hunter paused, his face growing angry, "does not mean he actually did it!" he shouted angrily. "By the earth below me," he sighed in frustration.

"Whoa, calm down, Hunter. I was just joking."

"Oh, were you?"

They glared at each other, looking like they were going to have an argument.

"Hey, I have an awesome idea. Let's channel these negative feelings and use them in having a friendly competition," I interjected quickly.

"What kind of competition?" Aqua asked.

"How about a race of who can get to the bottom of the valley and to the river the quickest?"

"And whoever is last has to jump into Mud Cave," Aqua

added looking at Hunter with a sneer.

"Yeah, that sounds fun," Hunter replied. "I'm in."

"Okay, if Hunter is racing, then I'll race too," Aqua responded.

We all lined up, shoulder-to-shoulder. I looked over at Hunter.

"You ready to lose?"

"Is that smack-talk I'm hearing?"

"Maybe," I replied with a smirk.

"Ok, I want a fair race. May the best wolf win," Hunter told all of us. "Three . . . two . . . one . . ." he counted down. "Go!" he shouted, and we all took off running.

Aqua was ahead of me from the start; Hunter was behind me as we ran from high up in the beautiful valley. "Eat my dust, Hunter," I shouted while sprinting as fast as I could into the dusky evening.

As we got lower and entered the forest, Hunter was way behind, but Aqua was in my sights. I noticed her bluish-green eyes flash in the starlight as I overtook her, and then it was literally downhill from then on.

I raced down the hill on the forest's underbrush that echoed my crunching paw steps. The feeling was invigorating as I contrasted being trapped in a confined space with those thieving men to how I felt in this moment. I was as free as I ever was. I felt the crisp air rushing past me as I weaved between the towering trees. I started hearing the sound of rushing water as the river was coming into view. I sprinted as fast as my legs could muster as I approached the river bank's finish line. Its water gleamed from the starlight—and I was the winner!

I was waiting for who would come out of the trees next when I caught a glimpse of someone running. It was probably Hunter because of his speed. I of course wouldn't tell that to Aqua's face, but she isn't the fastest runner in the pack. But to my surprise, it was Aqua and she ran right up next to me.

"Good job, Aqua!"

"Thanks," she panted back.

"Where's Hunter?"

"He was behind me but fell behind."

"Do you think he'll be arriving soon?"

"Yeah, he'll be here. He's one heck of a runner," she replied looking into the forest.

About a minute later, Hunter came running up to us. He was huffing and puffing.

"Hunter, you ok?" I asked concerned.

"Yeah, I'm fine. Just a bit winded from all of that running," he said, panting vigorously.

"Well, you can walk now. You deserve it."

"But you're going to have to saunter over to Mud Cave and jump into its muddy mess," Aqua added with a grin.

His happy face went glum.

"Hey, you did great!" I reassured him, which put a smile back on his face. I then leaned in to his ear, "And we can have some 'fun' with Aqua in Mud Cave." The smirk on my face put a smirk on his as well.

We walked all the way to Mud Cave. As we trekked through its entrance and down a narrow tunnel, our steps echoed off the walls.

"Hey, move faster, ya slowpokes," Aqua called out. "Especially you, Hunter. That mud is just waiting for you to jump in."

"We'll get there soon enough, Aqua. There's no need to rush things," he called back.

My chuckles bounced throughout the tunnel as we came into a damp, cavernous room. It was deep, sloping further down and becoming quite large. Everything we did or said sent echoes throughout the cave. I saw a whole mass of mud and watched Aqua walk into its muddy mass. She stuck one of her front paws into the mud, and it made an audible squelching noise.

"Do you hear that, Hunter?" she asked. "Do you hear those wonderful noises? Doesn't that make you want to jump right in?"

Hunter began to move behind her. "Yeah, that would be nice . . ." he paused, "but how about ladies first?" he said as he ran and knocked her into the muddy mass.

"Hunter!" she shrieked. "You are so dead!" she yelled while trying to get up on all fours.

I then pushed Hunter into the mud. "Oh, I see how it is, you crafty wolf," Hunter said to me, his dark gray coat drenched in a mucky brown layer of mud.

Just then he was tackled by a slimy Aqua, pushing him deeper into the mud.

Hunter got up from the depths of the muddy pit with his face all covered in mud. "Oh, is this a mud battle now?"

"Sure, if you want me to smother you into the mud," Aqua replied with a wide grin.

"Come on Rosy, let's have some fun!" Hunter called out to me. "Or are you afraid to get your coat dirty?"

I jumped into the muddy pit, coating my red fur muddy brown. "Does that answer your question?" I smirked.

We had so much fun playing in the mud and flinging it everywhere. I ran as fast I could in the muddy depths while

Hunter and Aqua battled, trying to get each other's head down in the mud. Our splashing and tumbling reverberated throughout the whole cave. As I ran near a side tunnel that led to other caves and caverns below, I caught a whiff of an unpleasant smell rising up. It was a putrid odor that made my nostrils burn.

"Hey, Rosy don't go too deep down that tunnel. It could lead anywhere and you could get lost," Hunter warned.

"Oh, I wasn't going to do that," I began tell him. "There's a horrible smell coming from it."

Hunter and Aqua came over towards me through the mud, both sniffing. "Oh, holy skies!" Hunter uttered with a face of revulsion. "You're right, Rosy, that smell is disgusting!"

"Ugh, it's making my nose burn." Aqua turned away from the unpleasant smell.

"What do you think it is?" I asked Hunter.

"Dunno, but it probably smells worse down there."

"I wonder what could make that bad of a smell?" I muttered. I began to step closer to the foul-smelling tunnel's entrance.

"What in the name of the Clements are you three doing here?!" someone behind us shouted angrily. The loud words reverberated through Mud Cave, making the stalactites above us quiver and shake.

We turned around to find De-Vil. He looked like a furious wasp who had been doused in water.

"You three are in a heap of trouble," he growled angrily.

"We were just having some fun; is that a crime?" Aqua asked him frankly.

"Don't talk back to me, Aquamarine."

"Ok. . . ."

"What was that?" he asked her sharply.

"Nothing," she quickly replied.

"Now, come out of that mud this instant and you better do it quickly, because you're testing my patience."

We walked as fast as we could through the thick mud to the cave's solid ground as De-Vil glared at us. But as soon as we got near him, he would move away from us, treating us like we had some kind of horrible disease.

"Now, I'm going to escort you three imbeciles to your parents and inform them of what you have done."

As we closely followed De-Vil up through the tunnel, he scolded each of us for our stupidity. When we came out of the cave's entrance, he said, "I hope my words have brought change into your thick skulls. Now, let's get going. The sooner we get to your parents, the sooner they can know of the idiotic decision you all have made."

We walked behind De-Vil like lambs to the slaughter. I leaned close to Aqua.

"Aqua, Aqua!" I whispered softly so De-Vil wouldn't hear me.

She hissed back. "What are you doing? You could get us in a lot more trouble!"

"I need you to run and get Hunter's parents and tell them what is happening."

Aqua nodded. As we were walking, she broke off of De-Vil's walk of shame in a sprint.

"Hey!" he shouted as she ran as fast as she could away from all of us to go and find Hunter's parents.

"Aquamarine, come back here! Aquamarine!" he screamed angrily. But she was gone.

"Stupid wolf," he growled.

Hunter and I continued walking behind De-Vil as he headed to find Hunter's parents.

After an hour or so of walking in tense silence, we saw Aqua coming up to us with Robert and Shira as well with two other wolves, Doris and Tiberius.

"What seems to be the problem here?" both Doris and Shira asked.

"These three miscreants have been fooling around in Mud Cave when they're supposed to be sleeping," De-Vil explained harshly.

"Mud Cave?" Tiberius asked in confusion. "De-Vil, isn't Mud Cave a recreational spot?"

"Yes, it is. But—" he started answering.

"Then why are you getting mad at them when they aren't doing anything wrong?"

"Because they could have got lost in the caves or even died."

"We were just having fun and had no intentions of going too deep into the cave. We were just playing in the mud," Hunter answered.

"And why were you getting close to the other tunnel's entrance that could have led you to who-knows-where?" De-Vil countered.

"We were just trying to find where that horrible smell was coming from."

"A horrible smell?" Robert asked.

"Yeah, it was this gut-wrenching odor that smelled like something was rotting down in its depths," I explained.

"It was probably a skunk living there that got startled by your obnoxious behavior," De-Vil quickly responded, suspiciously dismissing my description of the foul odor.

"No, it was stronger and more rancid than a skunk's spray," I told him.

"Are you doubting me?" De-Vil asked sternly.

"Well, we were there for some time before you busted in and started being nasty to us," Aqua replied.

"You fleabag!" De-Vil growled.

Everybody gasped in shock.

"Hey!" Tiberius shouted. "Don't you talk to my daughter like that," he said sternly and then calmed his voice. "They were just having fun, big deal. That gives you no reason to punish them."

"Yeah, why would you snap at them when they were doing nothing wrong in the first place?" Robert asked.

"I told you, those three fleabags were messing around in a place they weren't supposed to be."

"A place they weren't supposed to be?" Robert repeated De-Vil's words in confusion. "De-Vil, they can go in that cave as they please. And you are not the parent of my son, daughter or their friend."

When he called me his daughter, I was shocked. Did he call me his daughter? Did he misspeak? I was confused.

"Did you call her . . . your daughter?" De-Vil asked while sneering at us.

"Yes."

"Robert, Rosy isn't your daughter."

"Is she not?" Robert said. "She most definitely is!" he went on powerfully. "Why do you think she's in my family's care?"

"Because those thieving men who stole her brought her here trying to steal wolves from our pack," De-Vil sneered.

"Then why did my son take her to Clements?"

De-Vil didn't respond.

"It's because she is a wolf and she was being hunted by those men, and Clements, with his good judgment, adopted her into the pack to become a fellow wolf, just like you and me," Robert stated.

"She's not originally from our pack, Robert!" De-Vil growled.

"But is she not a wolf?" he asked. "Is she not a wolf, De-Vil?" he asked once more sternly.

"Ok, yes. She is a wolf." De-Vil admitted. "But she's. . . ." De-Vil was beginning to say.

"A wolf is a wolf, no matter what type it is." Robert told De-Vil firmly.

His words echoed in my head from Hunter telling me the same thing previously when we were walking to Poplar Point.

"Yes, she is a wolf," De-Vil conceded. "But what I was trying to say is, she is not a Mexican gray wolf."

"What is it with you that she is or isn't a wolf?" Robert asked.

"Because your 'daughter' has disrupted our pack's social order."

At this point, everyone was getting annoyed by De-Vil's rude and countering statements and comments. De-Vil was again about to speak his mind but was interrupted by Robert.

"Oh, look at the time. Thank you, De-Vil, for your helpful comments and statements. It's getting late and we wouldn't want to waste your precious time, would we?" he said to De-Vil with a friendly but mocking undertone.

De-Vil was about to speak again, but I interrupted him this time. "Yes, thank you so much, De-Vil. We hope you have a wonderful night," I said with a happy, cheerful voice, and, of course, a sarcastic undertone.

De-Vil stood there, stunned. The rest of us started to walk away, and as we walked, I looked back to see if he was still there. I just saw him there . . . staring at me. Just staring at me. But I blinked and he was gone. It was a little creepy.

"You okay?" someone asked.

I turned around. Hunter and Aqua were smiling at me. I smiled, too.

"Now, you three go wash the mud out of your fur over there in the river, okay?" Robert told us.

The four parents waited as we got into a shallow part of river and cleaned our fur coats. The water around us turned brown from the mud.

"De-Vil is such a jerk," Aqua said, annoyed.

"Aqua, that wasn't a nice thing to say," Hunter replied.

"No, Aqua's right. He didn't have to be so rude and condescending," I told Hunter. He thought for a few seconds and nodded.

"But why was he so protective of that odor-filled tunnel entrance?" I asked.

"Yeah, he sure was," Aqua replied.

"Do you guys want to find out?" I suggested to the both of them.

"We could, but if De-Vil caught us again, he wouldn't be too pleased," Hunter answered. "But whatever was in the tunnel giving off that foul odor was as clear as the mud in Mud Cave itself."

We got out, shook our fur dry and then joined the adults. We all began to walk again. I walked next to Robert.

"Oh hi, Rosy. How are you doing?" he asked me in a kind voice.

"Good," I replied. "That was quite the talk, wasn't it?" I

chuckled.

"Yeah," he sighed. "And I apologize for De-Vil's rude behavior. He can be a stick-in-the-mud sometimes." I chuckled at Robert's pun and he quickly joined in. He then leaned in and said, "This is just between you and me, ok?" he said to me quietly. I nodded. "The thing about me slipping up and calling you my daughter—that wasn't a mistake."

"Really?"

"Well, you have lived with us for a long time, and you feel like a member of my family and our pack," he replied honestly. "And even if De-Vil can't accept you as a fellow wolf in our pack doesn't mean you don't fit in. Clements is a wise wolf with good judgment—something De-Vil will never grasp. Clements adopted you into this pack because of his mercy and hospitality. But most of all, he brought you into this pack because he saw what a great wolf you are," Robert explained in a heartfelt manner. It made me happy to hear such wonderful things.

"What are you two talking about?" Doris asked.

"Oh, just about De-Vil," I told her.

"He gave us quite the yap, didn't he?"

"You said it," Robert sighed.

"Why is he so angry and rude?" I asked.

"It's just who he is. He doesn't like things that interfere with his ideals," Robert replied. "It's either his way or nothing at all," he said with a sigh.

"He just wants what's best for the pack, albeit in his own way," Shira added.

I left Hunter's parents talking to Aqua's parents and walked over to where Hunter and Aqua were chatting.

"That was quite the argument," I said.

"Yeah, it was crazy. But the good thing is that my father got the message across to De-Vil."

"Your dad is a brave wolf to stand-up against De-Vil," Aqua told Hunter.

"Yeah, that's his greatest quality. He can be the kindest wolf in the pack, but if you insult or mess with his loved ones, then you get a whole different side of him—his protective side."

We continued to talk until we got near Aqua's home.

"Doris, Tiberius, I can't thank your daughter enough for running and getting help when she and my children were being berated by De-Vil," Robert said with gratitude.

"We are too, Robert," Doris replied.

"But we also need to thank you for your bravery in standing up against De-Vil," Tiberius acknowledged.

"I hope you all have a nice night," Shira called out.

"We hope you can do as well," Doris replied.

"Bye Aqua, sleep well," Hunter called out.

"Yeah, have a good night," I said.

"'Kay, I'll do that. Good night," Aqua responded before she and her parents disappeared into the woods.

As the rest of us continued on to our home, Hunter and I began to chat.

"So, that was an interesting situation, wasn't it?" I chuckled.

"Yeah," Hunter chuckled as well. "And I'm sorry for De-Vil's rude behavior. He's typically uptight when it comes to what he calls 'rule-breaking' or 'idiotic antics.'"

"It's okay," I replied. "The only good thing was when De-Vil finally got the concept."

We walked on quietly, just listening to and enjoying the sounds of the valley at night. We heard owls hooting in some nearby trees and the river calmly flowing past us.

As we were getting closer to Hunter's place, I was looking around at the beautiful scenery and noticed something up above on the mountain slope. I saw something that I really wish I hadn't."

Rosy paused in her story, her face filling with dread.

"As I was looking up the rising slope, I saw something that made every hair on my body stand on end. High on a tall ridge was a large shadowy creature that stood out with the bright silvery light of the full moon. It was staring at me intensely, with glowing scarlet eyes as red as the blood in my veins."

Rosy's tense body shuddered once more as she remembered this terrifying creature.

"It was . . ." she turned her terrified expression on Rex. "S-s-staring at me," Rosy replied with great fear. "But after I blinked, this terrifying creature had vanished."

Hunter called my name a few times but I just stared at the ridgeline where the scarlet-eyed creature had stood.

"Rosy! Rosy!" Hunter shouted.

I turned to him.

"Are you ok? You seem scared."

"I . . . saw something."

"You want to tell me what you saw?" he asked, but I shook my head because I didn't even want to think about it. He respected my answer and we walked on in silence. I walked so close to Hunter that he noticed my uneasiness, which made him feel a

little uneasy too.

We finally got to Hunter's place. "Mom, Dad," Hunter began anxiously. "Rosy seems very nervous, and it's kind of making me nervous too."

Robert and Shira both turned to me, and Shira asked, "Are you ok, Rosy?"

"Yeah, is everything all right?" Robert asked. "Was it because of De-Vil?"

I shook my head and they were confused.

"She said she saw something," Hunter explained.

"What did she see?" Shira and Robert both asked.

"I have no idea. She didn't want to tell me and I respected her reply. But whatever it was gave her quite a fright." He looked over at me with concern.

"Aww, Rosy, you poor dear," Shira said in a comforting tone.

Hunter's sister Mary had noticed our arrival and sat up from her sleeping place, annoyed.

"There you all are! Star and I have been waiting hours for you guys! Where did you go?"

"Mary, calm down. We've had a rough night," Shira expressed tiredly.

"Yeah, we just want some sleep," Robert yawned.

"What happened? Why did Aqua come here looking for your help?" Star asked curiously.

"It's none of your concern, dear," Shira told her.

"Now, let's all get some well-deserved sleep," Robert called out to everyone.

As we were all settled down for the night, Shira came over to me and said, "If you get scared, my advice is to hum a pleasant tune. It has helped me since I was your age. But if that doesn't work, you can definitely come to us if you get too scared."

"Thanks."

"No problem."

Robert settled down next to Shira, Mary, and Star, who were already fast asleep.

Hunter settled down next to me.

"Hey, how are you doing?"

"Good enough. It's been a long evening."

"I apologize for being probably a little too concerned about whatever you saw."

"No—thank you. I'm glad you and your parents are concerned for my well-being."

"Well, goodnight," I said to him as I was settling down.

"Good night, Rosy," Hunter said with a yawn. "And if anything happens, know that you can come to me or my parents."

"Ok, thanks."

"No problem, my friend," he said with a smile which made me smile also.

I slowly drifted off to sleep. I felt calm at first because the shadowy scarlet-eyed creature on the high ridge wasn't stuck in my brain. I thought maybe I would have a good night's sleep—but oh, how wrong was I.

I woke up at Hunter's place, but he was nowhere to be seen. I looked around. Robert, Shira, Mary, and Star weren't there, either. I stood up and checked the whole area, but none of them were anywhere. I then heard someone whisper my name. In shock, I looked around to see if anyone was there, but I couldn't see anyone. I heard the voice a second time, farther away. I followed the voice and it led me to no one. I was perplexed, but then I knew where I was. I looked up and saw the high ridge, now empty, where the terrifying, shadowy creature had stared down at me with its scarlet eyes. I heard the whisper again. I continued to follow the voice, beckoning me with its ominous whisperings of my name. I soon found myself in front of Mud Cave. As I got closer to the cave, I saw an old wolf cowering at the entrance.

I walked closer. "Are you ok?"

The old wolf was crying profusely and muttering to himself.

"Sir, are you ok?"

The wolf lifted his head.

"Clements?!" I asked in confusion. "Are you okay? Why are you crying?" But as I looked at him, I realized his body and face were covered in scratches and cuts, with blood staining his whitish-gray fur.

"Oh my heavens!" I uttered in complete shock. "Wh-who did this to you?"

He continued muttering wildly. I couldn't understand anything until two words jumped out at me, clear as day: 'staring eyes.'

Staring eyes? I thought to myself.

"Clements, who did this to you?"

"Th-th-the beast," he uttered in terror, his voice trembling. "A d-d-demon or f-fiend of some sort," he stuttered fearfully. "Some wolves told me they saw a b-b-beast guarding something in Mud Cave," he explained, trying not to stutter.

"What was it guarding?" I asked.

"I went in to see this b-b-beast and found it guarding a sub-cavern entrance." He broke down in tears. "And there was . . .

blood. So—much—blood. It was too much to bear all at once," he cried in agony. "But this beast, whoever or whatever it was, had gone too far." His voice changed from sadness to unbridled anger. "I confronted this fiend and told it to leave at once. Leave this valley and never come back!" Clements's words were punctuated with ireful growls. "But the beast didn't listen to me, it just stared at me with i-i-its . . . its threatening, bright-red eyes.

"I repeated my demand that it leave, but with more authority. This time it got super mad and started attacking me. I collapsed, too weak to stand, and the monster snarled at me and made it clear that he was in control. He said I was weak. He gave me an ultimatum: continue as the alpha and die, or submit to his will and live.

"I told him I am the rightful alpha of this pack and he was imposing on our peace." Clements's face contorted with rage. "The monster brutally attacked me again, injuring me greatly. I tried my best to stand, to drag myself from the cave. But before I left, I warned the monster that he would eventually face the consequences of his heinous acts."

"Go while you still can," he warned me in reply.

"This beast is cruel and heartless; he won't spare anyone who goes against him."

I again heard a voice. It wasn't the ominous whisperer I'd heard before; this time it was Hunter and Aqua. Judging by the tones of their voices, it sounded like they were in trouble. I started into the cave.

"No!" Clements pleaded desperately. "Don't Rosy—the beast will kill you!".

"I have to help Hunter and Aqua," I told him. "They may be

in serious trouble." I began to run.

"Rosy, NO!" Clements pleaded from behind me, but I kept running through the long tunnel that led into Mud Cave. As I ran, I could hear Hunter's and Aqua's cries. I yelled, "Don't worry, guys, I'm coming!"

As I got closer and closer, their cries became much louder and more desperate. Finally, I got to the large, open room of the cave. I looked around for Hunter and Aqua but didn't see them. The shadowy beast, however, was there, staring at me with its menacing, scarlet eyes.

"Where are Hunter and Aqua?" I growled my demand.

The beast said nothing.

"I said, where are Hunter and Aquamarine!"

The beast finally spoke in a threatening tone. "Oh, your worthless friends? They came snooping in here where they weren't supposed to be." He scoffed. "So, I took care of them," the beast uttered coldly with a malevolent smile.

I looked past the beast then, and what I saw made my legs feel weak and unsteady. In the depths of the mud were two wolves—Hunter and Aqua. They were maimed and looked as if blood were oozing out of every pore of their mangled bodies. Hunter's brown eyes and Aqua's bluish-green ones were glazed and unblinking.

It was too much to bear. My mind rushed like a raging river. I felt dizzy and my legs gave way, sending my entire body collapsing onto the damp cave floor. My mind swam with all of this emotional trauma.

"Tut, tut, tut," the beast taunted. "Looks like I have another weakling."

"You won't get away with this. You'll face the consequences of

your heinous crimes." I spoke as best as I could.

"I've already killed these weaklings and injured the ancient fleabag. What makes you think you won't end up like them?"

I started to cry. It was all too much. My best friends were dead from this bloodthirsty beast and the alpha of my new pack was seriously injured and was up there lying on the ground like a rock.

"Now that I've killed your worthless friends and weakened your virtuous leader. . . ." the beast uttered unapologetically, "what should I do with you?"

I tried to speak, but that's when I smelled that stomach-churning smell again. I realized it came from the shadowy beast who leered at me with its bloody, scarlet eyes. The odor that the beast gave off smelled like rotting meat. Like something that died a long time ago.

"Oh my, so many bodies I have. What should I do with them?" the beast said both sarcastically and sinisterly. "I know," it said fiendishly, a wicked grin sprouting across his blood-soaked face. The beast lunged at me, staring wildly with his bloody, scarlet eyes into the depths of my soul. "HOW ABOUT LETTING THEM ROT WHERE NO ONE WILL EVER FIND THEM?" the beast uttered in a demonic bellow.

Then I woke up in a jolt and started crying profusely.

"Rosy, Rosy, Rosy!" Hunter called out, shaking me to get my attention.

I cried and cried until I was too tired to cry any more. I lay still for a few minutes, then opened my eyes to find Hunter and his family gathered around me with worried looks.

"Rosy, are you okay?" Hunter asked with concern.

"Yeah, you don't seem all right," Star noted.

"What happened?" Mary asked sleepily.

I mumbled that I had had a nightmare.

"What was that?" Shira asked.

I spoke more clearly. "I had a nightmare."

"A nightmare?" she said and I nodded. "Oh, you poor thing," she said affectionately. "Do you want to tell us your dream?"

I took a deep breath. "Yes. I want to tell you all what I saw in my dream and more details about what scared me yesterday."

"Okay, tell us everything. If it gets too disturbing, you can stop at any time," Robert replied.

"So, it happened after the argument with De-Vil," I began. "As we were walking home, I looked up along the ridge and I saw under the moonlight a silhouette of a large, shadowy figure. It stared wildly at me with glowing, scarlet eyes."

"Does this monster have anything to do with your nightmare?" Robert asked.

I nodded and told them everything about my nightmare, from the ominous whisperings, to Clements and his injuries. It frightened them quite a bit, but when I got to the worst part of my nightmare, I couldn't bring myself to tell it.

"Are you ok, Rosy?" Hunter asked.

Right after he asked, I lunged toward him and nuzzled with him while crying uncontrollably. This caught him and the others off guard. I finally stopped crying and let go of Hunter. I turned to Robert and Shira.

"May I talk to you alone?"

They agreed and told Hunter, Mary and Star to leave us and to try to go back to sleep.

Robert, Shira, and I walked far enough away that Hunter and his sisters couldn't hear us.

"Ok, Rosy. Please continue. We are here for you," Shira told me, comfort and concern in her eyes.

I was shaking nervously. It was difficult to tell them details about the worst part of my nightmare. I mean, how do you tell the parents of your best friend that you saw their own son dead and mutilated, along with our other best friend?

"Ok . . . so, I heard Hunter yelling, and he sounded like he was in trouble, so I went after him," I recalled. "And that's when I saw the monster with . . . w-with. . . ." I choked up, reliving the grimmest part of the nightmare in my mind.

"With what?" they both asked.

I then told them that I had seen their son and his best friend dead and mutilated, lying in pools of their own blood in the mud.

Robert and Shira were shocked.

"I can't go on," I sobbed.

"Oh, Rosy," Shira said sympathetically, which helped calm me down.

"We feel so bad for you and what you saw in your nightmare," Robert said considerately.

Their words of comfort helped lift my spirits.

"But it can't harm you," he reassured me.

"But how do you explain what I saw before I had my nightmare?" I asked quietly.

"What about it?" they both asked, confused.

"I told you I saw the beast up on the high ridge yesterday, and that wasn't in the nightmare."

They looked at each other and then back at me. "Are you sure you saw this monster?" Robert asked.

"Yes, I definitely saw it last night. It was there on that ridge

staring down at me with its scarlet eyes."

"Are you sure it was a monster?" Shira chimed in. "It could have been a trick of the light."

"Or it could've been a weirdly shaped rock," Robert supplied.

"No, it was definitely an animal," I insisted. "A large, monstrous, wolf-like creature, to be exact."

"Maybe it was a wolf on a nighttime stroll?" Shira suggested.

"Maybe. . . ." I said doubtfully. "But if it was a wolf on a stroll, why would it be so big? And why would it stare at me so long with those red eyes? I have met every wolf in this pack, and none of them have scarlet eyes, and none of them are large and monstrous like I saw up on the ridge and in my terrible nightmare."

Shira and Robert didn't have answers for my puzzling questions.

"You were awake very late last night. Perhaps your sleepy mind was playing tricks on you," Shira offered.

"Whatever it was will never get to you or Hunter, because we will protect you all from this beast," Robert said confidently.

"What about Aqua?"

"What about her?" Shira asked.

"Won't she be in trouble if the beast comes for her?"

"She's a strong wolf who can handle herself. She's also got her family to protect her as well." Robert looked at the position of the moon in the night sky. "Now, let's get some sleep."

"And if you have any more nightmares, come and get us," Shira told me lovingly.

I walked back with Robert and Shira to where Star and Mary were again fast asleep. Hunter was lying down, awake, and I walked over to him.

"How are you doing?" he asked me.

"Better."

"That creature must've frightened you pretty bad."

"Can I sleep by you?" I asked him, catching him off guard for a moment.

"Sure, that would be great," he said kindly. "And if you get scared, know that I'm here with you and will protect you from any kind of beast."

So I settled in right next to him and we both began to doze off.

"Hey, Hunter," I whispered.

"Yeah?" he whispered back.

"It's really nice to be here with you."

He smiled at my comment. "It's nice to be here with you, too, Rosy," he replied with a warm smile.

We both fell asleep and I wasn't visited by the scarlet-eyed beast at all the rest of the night.

"Did you find out what the beast was?" Rex asked.

"No, it was and still is a mystery to me."

"Do you still have dreams of the scarlet-eyed beast?"

"No, but sometimes when I close my eyes his image is engraved into my mind," Rosy replied with a shudder.

"Still staring at you with its blood-red eyes?" Rex asked glumly, and she nodded stiffly. Rex continued. "Hunter seems like a very good friend."

"Yeah, he was one of my first real friends, and we spent time together from the crack of dawn until dusk," Rosy chuckled. "We were inseparable and enjoyed each other's company." She smiled fondly.

Rex gently interrupted her story. "Is Hunter here?"

"We're getting close to that." Then a tear fell from her eye, though Rex didn't see it.

She continued her story.

I lived there with them and was part of the pack. It was a normal, fun, and new life. Then one day, everything changed.

The wolves' council arranged an urgent meeting. Clements got up before everyone and said, "My fellow wolves, it has been stated by Rosy, a fellow wolf of our pack, that there are dangerous people who want to take us away. The council and I have devised a plan. Half of the pack will go to Southern Arizona for a while with my head counselor De-Vil, and the other half will stay and hold down the fort here with me." He paused, then spoke again. "Yes, I know it's risky, but we all have to make sacrifices. I know we will be with each other in spirit, even though we will be far away."

The entire pack started talking to each other, upset and concerned. Hunter and I split off from the pack and went for a walk. Hunter was quieter than normal. He stopped, and he didn't look happy. His head was pointed toward the ground.

"Are you ok?" I asked. He didn't speak. I spoke optimistically. "This is going to be fun. Me and you and your family and half of the pack are going to travel to Sothern Arizona, and. . . ."

"I'm not going."

"You're not coming?"

"I have been talking with Clements and I'm going to hold down the fort with him," he said seriously.

"But it isn't safe."

"I'll be fine. I don't want you to be taken, and I told my

parents to watch over you. It's for your own good. You'll be okay, and I know we'll meet back together someday." Then he walked to find Clements, and I started to sob, then. . . .

Rosy had begun crying as she told this part of her story, and Rex interrupted her again.

"Wait, did you like Hunter?"

"Yes!" she wept. She sniffed a little, then regained her composure.

We went to bed that evening, woke up and had breakfast together with Hunter's family, but Hunter and I didn't speak to each other. Hunter's family and I got ready to go with the pack and De-Vil, and then I said farewell to Hunter.

"Goodbye. Be safe," I said. I couldn't stop crying.

He rubbed his muzzle against my cheek and said to me, "I'll always be with you."

I was shocked because his mom and sisters were also saying goodbye to him and their dad. Then we left for Southern Arizona with De-Vil and half of the pack.

She paused. "I didn't like De-Vil from the beginning. From his insatiable ego and rude, nitpicking comments and statements, to the Mud Cave incident. All of those examples didn't put a very good first impression of him in my mind."

As we hiked away from the valley, De-Vil snapped at anyone who strayed off the trail.

After a little while, I was walking with Aqua and Hunter's mom and sisters.

As we were all walking, De-Vil came over to me.

"Hello, Rosy."

"Umm, hi, De-Vil," I muttered.

"I wanted to say I'm sorry for all of that Mud Cave drama. I want to start anew. How about we put that Mud Cave business behind us, why don't we?" he said kindly, which raised my suspicions.

"You have a great rest of your day," De-Vil sang as he sauntered off.

I rejoined Aqua and Shira, who were walking with Star and Mary, and said to them, "Is it me, or does De-Vil seem a little suspicious?"

"Why would you think that?" Shira asked.

I shrugged. "He just came up to me and started acting nice, but it didn't seem right."

"He's probably trying to make amends for what happened in the past," Shira said.

"I guess you're right." We continued to walk for the rest of the day.

The next day, Aqua saw that I was sad and being quiet. "What's wrong, Rosy?"

I didn't say anything. I was thinking about Hunter. She spoke again. "Are you ok?"

I didn't want to speak about it, so I just shook my head and walked ahead speedily. I tried to have hope and faith, but I was sad and depressed. After a lot of walking, the forest disappeared into desert, and the land started getting very rocky.

Aqua walked up to me again, concerned. "Are you ok?"

I couldn't hold it in anymore. "I just miss him," I sobbed.

She was confused. "Who are you talking about?"

"Hunter," I told her, and kept sobbing.

"Did you like him?" she asked me softly.

"Yeah," I whispered. I wiped my tears off of my fur with my paw and calmed down.

"Well, to tell you the truth, I miss him, too."

"You do?"

"Yeah, I miss Hunter just as you do. He's my best friend, and I loved spending time with him every day. Since he's not coming with us, I feel your pain," she told me empathetically. "But one thing my parents told me that keeps me going is to always keep moving forward, living in the present. Accept your past, but don't let it bind you down. They say if I will embrace the future and follow it with enthusiasm, I'll appreciate life and be more content. I have and it has done wonders." She paused. "Just look at me, your relaxed friend," Aqua said with a grin on her face.

"Oh, relaxed—I thought you were just lazy," I joked.

"Well, you're right, I am a bit lazy, but at least I'm not a snail," she replied and we both laughed.

"I just think about our explorations and adventures together; they were fun, weren't they?"

"Yeah, it was fun," she said fondly with a smile. "Before you came to the valley, Hunter and I had the most amazing adventures ever."

"Do you think he'll be alright?"

"Probably. He may feel the same sadness about missing Shira, Mary, and Star, and us, but he's resilient. He'll survive."

We walked a long way. I spent a lot of the time talking with Aqua, and we started becoming really close friends. We even talked while she swam in a small creek. You should see her swim—she's amazing.

But as we were talking, De-Vil came up to us.

"Um, hello De-Vil." We both turned our head towards him.

"What are you two doing?" he asked us in a slow and deep voice.

"We're just talking," I answered.

"About what?" he probed nosily.

"How our day is going," Aqua replied.

De-Vil looked as if he was about to speak, but then paused and looked as if in methodical thought. After a bit, he came out of his thoughts and looked at us with an odd leer. "What are you doing?" he asked Aqua without hesitation.

"Swimming, why?" she replied confused.

"Have you not noticed that we're on a migrational journey, or has the creek's waters clogged your brain?"

Aqua and I exchanged annoyed looks.

"What have we've done to you that you have to be so strict and nasty to us?" she asked him in total seriousness.

"You both are mischief-makers who deliberately do things you're not supposed to be doing," he berated. "You have no sense of the consequences of your deplorable actions that will sink you into trouble." He hissed at us and we just stared at him. "But that makes perfect sense when you spend endless amounts of time with an attention-seeking troublemaker. I guess you learned a thing or two from him?"

We were utterly shocked that he would say a thing like that about Hunter. Aqua got out of the river in the blink of an eye and came to me. "Come on, let's go," she told me firmly, and I agreed.

I began to walk away, but Aqua was rooted to the spot,

staring angrily at De-Vil. "I hope you have a good rest of your day, De-Vil." Then she vigorously shook her wet, gray fur, getting De-Vil as wet as if he had just been drenched by a rainstorm.

"You no-good imp!" he growled, baring his teeth.

Aqua sprinted away and I followed quickly behind her. We ran as fast as we could, with De-Vil charging after us. We came upon and startled a group of unsuspecting wolves on the trail ahead of us.

I was so focused on running that I lost track of where Aqua had gone. I looked back to see if De-Vil was behind me, but I saw no one. I slowed to a walk and looked around for Aqua. I passed a clump of moss-covered boulders surrounded by a small thicket, and just as I was passing, I heard a small "Psst."

It came from the mossy boulders. It could possibly have been the wind, I thought. But again, I heard the same noise coming from the mossy boulders.

I went over to see what was making that noise, and as I got to the boulders and peered over, I saw Aqua hiding.

"Come on! I was trying to get your attention so that you would come over here without De-Vil finding us," she said urgently.

So I climbed over the boulders and crouched down next to Aqua. We were as silent as the stones in front of us. Eventually we heard someone running and then suddenly stop. We heard De-Vil's stern voice roar.

"Aquamarine! Rosy! I know you two are around here! Come out now! You two are in even more trouble!" He was quiet for a moment. Then he let out an exasperated sigh. "I know you're around here somewhere! You can't hide forever, and when I find you two, you'll both be in serious trouble!" He shouted this warning as loudly as possible and then began to walk away,

grumbling as he left.

Aqua and I were quiet until we couldn't hear him anymore. Aqua poked her head over the mossy boulders. "He's gone."

We both slumped over the boulders.

"Why did you shake water all over him?" I groaned.

"Because he deserved it," she told me indignantly. I just stared at her with a look of annoyance.

"Hey!" she snapped. "Don't give me that look. He was rude to both of us, and he insulted Hunter, so he got what was coming to him."

"But did you have to goad him like that?" I asked. "You could have walked away, but you chose to do that and make him chase after us. And by the looks of it, if he finds us, we'll both be in deep trouble."

She was about to say something, but paused and thought for a moment.

"Yeah, you're right."

"Let's go find our families," I told her.

We got up from our hiding spot and shook the underbrush out of our fur.

"Hey, wanna hear my impression of De-Vil?" she asked me and I nodded.

Aqua put on her best mock angry face and spoke in a harsh, sulking voice. "I'm De-Vil. I am an angry, rule-abiding fanatic who doesn't like fun or happy people.". Her face was so exaggeratedly angry, I couldn't help but laugh, and Aqua busted up, too.

We then began to walk together, chatting until the sun went down, and then we found a place to sleep. But I couldn't fall asleep, because I was missing Hunter.

The next morning, Aqua and I walked with Hunter's sisters, Star and Mary.

As we climbed a trail that went up a mountain, Mary said to me, "It's so weird seeing you without Hunter."

"Yeah, you were together 24/7," Star remarked.

I was silent for a moment. I didn't want to tell them my little secret that I liked their brother. Finally, I said while trying keep my voice calm, "Y-yeah."

We walked for a long way. We crossed mountains and valleys, and the farther we got from Pinetop, the more overbearing De-Vil became. Finally, we came to a desert valley with a large mountain in it.

"We'll live on that mountain," De-Vil announced.

We ran around the edge of a small town and got to the base of the mountain. We followed a mountain road until we got up near the top. As we approached the top, we noticed a park ranger walking nearby, he noticed our whole pack of wolves. He called his fellow park rangers and they came and caught a glimpse of our pack of Mexican gray wolves.

They seemed perplexed to see me, a red wolf that looked entirely out of place. One of the park rangers pulled out his phone and took a video of us.

The pack ran away from the humans, but I stayed for a few seconds more before I ran and caught up with the pack.

De-Vil seemed to be acting more suspicious than normal after seeing the humans. The pack kept asking him questions with whats and hows, and he finally snapped.

"ENOUGH!" he roared, glaring around at all of us. "I'm the alpha now."

"But Clements is our alpha," a wolf interjected.

"That old flea bag," De-Vil said rudely, and the whole pack gasped in disbelief.

"You really believe that weakling is a better leader than ME?" he asked rudely, breaking out into hysterical laughter. "That's . . . that's the best joke I've ever heard in my life," he said as he rudely laughed. "Come on, laugh," he replied to our unamused faces. "Really? Not a single laugh?"

He was only met with disapproving glares.

"Oh, I see. You weaklings are too loyal to that weak fleabag." His tone grew stern. "You weaklings need to obey my orders. I am your alpha now!" he yelled. "And if I hear another mention of the weakling you call your alpha, you will be met with grave consequences," he snarled.

"At least he's a better alpha than you," I snapped.

Rage bubbled and boiled in De-Vil's eyes like a simmering hot spring. He glared around at the pack. "Who said that?"

"I did," I said boldly. He looked at me, then suddenly charged and tackled me. He pressed me down on the ground and whispered to me, "Don't you ever do that again, or it'll be your funeral."

He got off me and turned back to the pack. "We have to protect ourselves. If you see humans, try to get rid of them. If that doesn't work, attack them."

The whole pack nodded nervously.

Rosy sighed and seemed to pull herself from her memories. "And here we are."

"I'm so sorry," Rex said sympathetically. It was obvious she didn't want to talk more about it. Remembering his conversation with the coyote mother, he changed the subject.

"Can you teach me how to howl?"

She looked at him, surprised. "Why?"

"I just want to know from an expert."

"Ok. The proper way to do it is to raise your head to the sky, then let out everything you have deep inside and concentrate all of it into one noise." She lifted her head to the sky and howled loudly.

Rex tried to mimic Rosy, but the noise that came from his throat didn't sound like a howl. It sounded more like a sick cow trying to make a convincing howl. She howled again, and Rex lifted his head to the sky and howled for a second, but it died down. Rosy showed him one more time. Rex lifted his head straight to the sky and howled—this time achieving a convincing howl, in Rosy's opinion. He was overjoyed, and the two howled together for a few minutes.

Finally, they stopped. "I should go find my friends," Rex said. "They'll be worried about me."

"Oh, right," Rosy said, looking disappointed.

He felt bad for his new friend. "Do you want join me?"

"Yes!" she answered happily. They ran off to the camp together.

Rex and Rosy came to the camp and saw Lilly, Alpha, Beta, and Duke lying under a tree in the shade. The camp workers were all gone.

"You stay here. I'll call you to come out," Rex said to Rosy. She nodded.

When Lilly saw Rex emerge out of the woods, she ran to him and yelled joyfully, "Rex, you're back! You're a sight for sore eyes."

"Long time, no see," Alpha said as he walked up to them with Beta and Duke. "Where have you been?"

"It's a long story."

"How did you survive those wolves?" Lilly asked him.

"I had someone help me."

"Really? Who?"

"Come on out, Rosy," Rex called.

"Rosy?" the other four echoed. They watched in surprise as a maroon-red wolf came walking out of the trees.

The sled dogs were nervous until Rex said, "Guys, meet Rosy. Rosy, meet my friends."

"Hello! Pleased to meet you," Rosy said to Lilly.

"It's a pleasure," Lilly responded kindly.

She walked to Alpha. "Hello, I'm Rosy. What's your name?"

"I'm Alpha."

Rosy was a little confused. "So, you're the leader? Great! What's your name?"

Now Alpha was confused. "My name *is* Alpha. I'm not the leader; Rex is our leader. I'm more like his second-in-command."

"Oh, I get it," she laughed, turning to Beta. "Hello, what's your name?"

"My name is Beta," Beta responded shyly.

"Aw, your names are 'A' and 'B.' You two make a great couple," Rosy said with a wink.

Beta blushed and Alpha bunched the fur on his neck in embarrassment. "We're not a couple," he said gruffly. "We're only friends."

"Oh, my bad," Rosy said, laughing and looking knowingly from one to the other. She turned to Duke last. "And who might you be?"

"My name is Duke," he replied.

Rex bounded eagerly forward, drawing his friends' attention. "I now know where we are."

They fell silent and looked at him eagerly. "We're on a mountain called Mount Lemmon in Tucson, Arizona."

They were silent for a moment, then Lilly said in shock, "Arizona? *Arizona?!* Isn't that in the lower forty-eight??" Lilly's eyes were wide open in shock. "You know how far away that is from Alaska?"

"You're all from Alaska?" Rosy said in surprise. "You're a very long way from home. Even further away than me."

"The mountain is named after a fruit?" Duke asked, going back a few sentences. "That's weird. Wait, are there lemons on this mountain?"

"Déjà vu," Rex muttered to himself. "No, it's L-e-m-m-o-n, Lemmon. It was named after a famous person."

As the animals rested and talked together that day, Lilly noticed that Rex was spending more time with Rosy, talking about their adventures the night before and about how Rosy had taught him to howl. Lilly felt left out. As the day wore on, she got more depressed and irritated by the minute. She had spent the whole night worrying about Rex, and now he was barely talking to her.

As they lay down to sleep that night, Rex was confused. Lilly always slept near him, but tonight she was off by herself.

The gang and Rosy woke up before the camp workers. As they looked around for breakfast, Rex went to Lilly and asked her, "Why didn't you sleep by me?"

She just shrugged and walked away. Rex went to Alpha. "Do you think Lilly is acting unusual?"

"Not that I noticed," Alpha responded.

"It seems like she's avoiding me."

"She was really worried about you when you were missing. Are you sure?" Alpha said.

"Yes," Rex said. He turned to the rest of the group. "Come on," he called. "I'll show you the city." He looked for Lilly, hoping she'd join him, but she walked next to Duke.

They went to the big rock and Rex showed them Tucson down in the valley. "This is where Rosy and I met and got to know each other yesterday," he said. He looked again at Lilly, but she turned her face away. He tried to hide how much it hurt his feelings while Rosy told the others a shorter version of her story.

"Wow. What an amazing story. Incredible," Lilly said sarcastically.

What's wrong with Lilly? She's never shunned me like this, and she's always nice. That sarcasm was a lot snottier than joking.

As they roamed the mountain that morning, Rex continued to get the silent treatment from Lilly. He talked to Alpha again. "Something is definitely wrong with Lilly. She's never ignored me like this before. And when Rosy told you guys her story, she was rude instead of joking."

"She is acting different than usual," Alpha agreed. "Have you tried talking to her about it?"

"I tried this morning, but she wouldn't talk to me."

"You should try again. Clearing things up might help."

"I'll do that."

Rex went to Lilly. "Can I please talk to you?" She hesitated, then nodded stiffly.

They started walking towards the camp, just the two of them. After a moment, Rex said, "What's wrong, Lilly? You're not acting like yourself."

She glared at him in anger.

"Lilly, let me explain. . . ." Rex began.

"No," Lilly yelled. "Don't give some stupid excuse." she shouted. "'Lilly, let me explain,'" she mocked. "I haven't seen you for a whole night, I-I thought you were hurt or dead, but I guess my welcome wasn't appreciated."

"Lilly, I..."

"I was worried so sick about you that I couldn't even sleep, but you seem to have come back neither dead nor hurt but with Rosy, leaving me to be all alone by myself." She calmed down and was quiet for a minute. "Do you know how it feels to be forgotten?" she asked him seriously, looking straight at him. "It feels like you're invisible, like you don't even exist." Tears ran down her face, unhappiness written in her every feature.

"Lilly, I'm so sorry, I really am. I was caught up in the moment." Rex went over to comfort her. "I was just trying to make Rosy feel like she was a part of the group. She's. . . ." he tried to explain.

"Shut up, Rex!" Lilly yelled, her eyes narrowed.

"Lilly," Rex whispered.

"No! You've been talking too much about Rosy," she said irefully. "Rosy this, Rosy that. I'm sick and tired of that name," Lilly growled. "You prize her more than me. I thought we were friends. . . ." she ranted on.

"Lilly, please listen to me," Rex pleaded as she lashed out harsh words that stung like a whip. "Listen to me!" he said in a loud voice which quieted her. "You are my friend, my best friend. I would never in a million years stop being your friend," Rex spoke truthfully. "Lilly, if we weren't friends . . ." he paused, "I wouldn't be the dog who stands in front of you now. But I have to be friends with Ro. . . ."

Lilly glared at him.

"I have to be with Rosy!" Rex pushed on. "You heard her story; she's practically lost everything, and I'm just trying to give her someone she can count on."

"Oh, I get it." Lilly scowled. "Birds and bees must love the two of you."

"Bird? Bees?" Rex was confused. "Lilly, what are you saying?"

"I don't know—you tell me." Lilly scoffed, then added snottily, "Why don't you ask your new best friend, Rosy? Or should I say, your mate."

Lilly's words gave light to her puzzling comments just as Rex felt his face flush.

"I don't like her like that! I like y. . . ." he bit his tongue and yowled.

"Are you ok? What were you going to say?" Lilly asked.

Rex panicked. "Oh . . . . I was going to say . . . dang it. I forgot when I bit my tongue," he lied.

"Oh, Okay. We should get back."

"Lilly, wait. . . ." But she was already walking away.

When they got back to the big rock, Rex went straight to Alpha and said sternly, "Follow me."

"What for?" Alpha asked.

"Just follow me." Rex needed to talk to another male.

Alpha got up and followed him. They reached the camp, and Alpha sat by the snow-covered logs in the camp, but Rex paced back and forth.

"I found out why Lilly was acting unusual."

"What is it?" Alpha asked eagerly.

Then Rex swallowed, mortified, and forced it out as fast as he could. "Lilly thinks I like Rosy, and she even said that I was Rosy's mate."

"Hold on. Do you like Lilly?" Alpha asked.

"Yeah, a bit," Rex said, rubbing his nose with a paw.

"Well, you're not the only one who's been embarrassed," Alpha said, trying to cheer Rex up.

"Really?" Rex asked, intrigued.

"When you introduced us to Rosy, she called me and Beta a couple," Alpha said in utter embarrassment. "Having similar names doesn't make dogs a couple," he muttered, resting with his blushing cheeks on the cold snow.

Rex offered him a half grin. "So, you like Beta?"

Alpha sighed, then smiled and said honestly, "Yeah, she's nice."

Then Rex said, "We can't speak of this to them or anyone."

"Agreed," Alpha said.

"Agreed," Rex replied back. They stayed and rested on the snow-covered logs.

Back at the big rock, Lilly and Beta were resting together while Rosy and Duke scouted the perimeter for gray wolves. Lilly complained to Beta, "Rex has the nerve to like Rosy."

"Wait, do you like Rex?" Beta asked.

"Yes, I like him," Lilly answered hotly. "We were talking earlier, and he was going to tell me something but he 'forgot,'" Lilly said, her tone thick with irritation.

"Can I tell you something?" Beta asked. "Do you remember when Rex introduced us all to Rosy?"

"Of course," Lilly said sourly.

Beta continued, "After she asked Alpha and I our names, she thought they were cute and called me and Alpha a couple. The worst part is, I blushed like crazy."

Lilly raised her eyebrows. "So, you like Alpha?"

Beta dropped her head to her paws. "Yeah."

"We can't speak of this to them or anyone," Lilly said.

"Agreed," Beta said.

"Agreed."

Later that day the group of six met back up to plan.

"All right," Rex said, "How are we going to get back to Alaska?"

There was a long moment of silence, then Rosy spoke up. "I think I can help get you back to Alaska.".

"Really? You can help us get back? How?" Rex asked.

"I think if we go to the airport on the edge of town, we'll be able to get you on a plane to Alaska. The big airport is closer, but there will be a lot more people, which would make it more difficult to sneak you in," Rosy said.

"Wait, there's another town here?" Rex asked.

"Yeah. There's Tucson, and Marana is further north." Rosy pointed with her maroon nose first to downtown Tucson with its skyscrapers, then towards Marana, which was hidden behind Mount Lemmon's peaks.

"Okay, we'll try that," Rex said. As he looked across Tucson, he saw a glittering object in the southern section of the city. Rex then said, "But first we have to find Rosy's family."

"Wait—you know where my family is? Where are they?" Rosy asked in amazement.

"Well, they were taken by the same people who took us, and those people brought us here. Your family must be around here somewhere. My gut says it's there." Rex pointed his nose at the glittering object south of Tucson.

"You mean it? You'll help me free my family?"

"I mean it."

Rosy smiled at Rex, and he smiled back. Lilly growled and tensed.

The group started down the mountain. They ran out of the camp and down a canyon that led towards the city. It would take the group a long time to get down the mountain and trek across the city, but they were determined. They would go to the glittering object Rex saw, and then they would find and free Rosy's family.

Rex made sure to run next to Lilly, hoping it would help her get back to her normal self, instead of that snotty stuff he had witnessed earlier. He missed her, even though she had been there the whole time. Rude Lilly just wasn't the same.

CHAPTER 5

TROUBLE IN DOWNTOWN

They continued down the canyon. After a few miles, Duke was panting heavily. "Holy smokes! Why is it so hot here?"

"You're in a desert," Rosy replied. "The Sonoran Desert, actually. It's always hot here, but you should have been here when we arrived last August. Now *that* is hot. It gets to like a hundred to a hundred-fifteen degrees in the summer."

Duke groaned. "You mean it gets hotter than this?"

She laughed. "In the winter it only gets down like to the forties."

Duke shrugged. "That's not really cold for us, but I guess it must be cold for here."

They kept running. After a while Lilly drew closer to Rex. "Rex . . . I'm sorry for how I've been acting. I shouldn't have let my anger get the better of me."

Rex was thrilled Lilly was talking to him again. "No, it's my fault. I should have paid more attention to you."

She smiled at him, and he howled in happiness. Lilly was confused, but she saved her breath for running.

As they drew closer to downtown, Rex looked at Rosy. "Where should we go now?"

"We're going to where those tall buildings are," she said, motioning to a cluster of skyscrapers off in the distance.

They crossed roads and ran through neighborhoods. After some time, they came out from a neighborhood and into a shopping center with restaurants and shops.

"Act casual," Rex said quietly to the gang. They started walking through the shopping center. "Just act like a dog," he whispered to Rosy.

"What do I do? I'm not a dog; I'm a wolf."

"You're kind of like a dog, so just do the usual. . . . Bark, wag your tail, and stick out your tongue," he whispered. She followed his instructions, and he smiled. They walked on the sidewalk, and people were confused at seeing a cluster of dogs walking on their own.

A mom with her toddler passed by, and the toddler saw Rosy. "Mommy! Mommy! I saw a big red doggy." The mom followed her toddler's pointing finger and saw a maroon-red wolf. She screamed.

Everyone nearby heard the scream and turned to look. Time to run! The gang fled across the sidewalk and sprinted through the shopping center and down into a dry riverbed. They kept running in the riverbed until they had to stop to rest. When their breathing was back to normal, they climbed up out of the dry riverbed. After navigating a nerve-racking intersection, they finally found a small park with a pathway for bicycles and pedestrians, empty of people for the time being. The park was different from any Rex had seen before. There was no grass, and the dirt was a strange reddish color. Most interesting was the enormous snake head made out of metal. It stood taller than a man and was both amazing and scary and incredibly detailed. The snake had two old, sinister brown eyes, and two old, white beams arched from the top of his mouth to the ground like fangs. Its mouth was wide open with a big forked-tongue design on the ground.

"Whoa!" Duke said excitedly. "Look at that!"

He bounded over and the rest followed. When they got close, they saw an English bulldog lying on the top step of some concrete steps. The bulldog was large, had brown and white fur, and was a little chubby. He lifted his head from the step, looked at the gang with a melancholy expression, then rested his head back on the step. The dogs looked at each other in curiosity. Rex approached the bulldog. The bulldog rolled his eyes up to Rex. "What do you want?" he barked gruffly. Slobber dripped from his drooping mouth. A bit taken aback, Rex hesitated. The bulldog laughed rudely. "What? Cat got your tongue?"

Rosy felt her anger rise at the way this dog was talking to Rex. Suddenly an ominous black haze surrounded her, and her blue eyes turned a vivid purple, like two gems.

"Watch your mouth, you cretin!" she snarled. He froze in fear. Rosy slowly stalked toward the bulldog, the ominous black haze following her like another coat of her own fur. Rex shrank back from its dark, violent vibe. Rosy growled at the bulldog as she drew closer, and he inched away from her in terror. She jumped on the first concrete step and he leaped up and took off running. Rosy wildly chased after him, snarling through bared teeth. The bulldog ran as fast as he could until he hit a white crescent concrete bench. He had nowhere to run. Suddenly Rosy tackled him.

"Don't ever disrespect him again! Got it?" she hissed demonically.

"Y-yeah, I g-got it," he whimpered in panic.

She got off the bulldog. The ominous, black haze vanished from her into thin air, and her evil, purple eyes faded back into their normal blue. She realized what had just happened and stumbled back from the bulldog, tail between her legs.

Sensing the danger had passed, the bulldog jumped up the steps and rounded on Rex. "What was that for? You didn't have to sic your crazy wolf on me for being a little snarky!"

"I didn't sic her!" Rex protested. "She did that on her own." He glanced at Rosy, but she had her back to the group, head down. *I've never heard her talk like that to anyone,* he thought in concern. *And she's upset by what she did. And what was with her eyes, and that black haze? That was the strangest thing I've ever seen.*

The bulldog eyed him suspiciously. "What's a group of winter dogs like you doing in my park, anyway?"

Rex sighed and let his head drop. "We were stolen by some goons in Fairbanks, Alaska. We're trying to get home, but first we're trying to help Rosy"—he gestured to her—"find her family, who were also taken by similar goons. We're hoping they're at some glittering thing we saw from up on the mountain."

The bulldog was startled. "Wait—did you say 'goons' and 'a glittering thing'? And they took her family?"

Rex nodded.

The bulldog's face softened in sympathy. "I'm sorry I was snappy with you. That glittering thing is a large mansion on the south side, and those goons steal animals from all over the globe. They make me furious when they come tromping around my park like everything is theirs. The glittering building is the mansion of 'El Loco.'"

"El Loco?" Lilly interjected. "What's that?"

"Not what," Louis responded. "Who. He's known by many names. 'The animal Boss' is one. His real name Is José Tonto. He's known all over Southern Arizona. His goons are notorious, too. You should steer clear of El Loco and his goons or they'll snatch you six up. I'm not surprised he went for you."

"So that's who the goons follow orders from," Rex said quietly to himself. He looked back at Louis. "Do you know where the mansion is?"

Louis looked at him in disbelief. "Didn't I just tell you to stay away from there?"

"We have to find Rosy's family," Rex said stubbornly.

Louis looked to where Rosy stood by herself, her ears down, and sighed. "I can take you there. I know downtown Tucson and the south side like the back of my paw. It will be late before we can get there, though. Come back tomorrow." He waited for them to leave, but the gang just stood there. "Do you guys have a place to sleep?"

"No," they all muttered quietly. He felt bad for them. "Mi parque es tu parque," he said in decent Spanish. "My park is your park."

"Thanks," Duke said brightly.

"But why do you say this is your park?" Lilly asked.

"Kid, I've been around this park for most of my life, so this is my park. People always see me here and see my name on my collar, and they play with me. I live here, but the good thing is, I have company, so I'm never lonely. Well, sorta."

Lilly felt bad for Louis, sleeping here alone night after night. She walked closer to the concrete steps and said to him, "I'm Lilly. It's nice to meet you."

"The pleasure is all mine," Louis said. "Welcome to my park." A pool of saliva gathered on the drooping part of his mouth before falling and hitting the step.

"Ew!" Lilly said in disgust, pulling back.

"Sorry," he said. "That happens all the time."

Alpha came up next. "Hi, my name is Alpha."

"A strong name. I like it," Louis said with a slobbery grin.

"Hi, I'm Beta," Beta said shyly as she stepped forward.

"What a wonderful name. Welcome," he said, then looked at Alpha and winked. Alpha got flustered.

Duke bounded forward. "Hi, my name is Duke!"

"Welcome."

Then Rosy walked slowly up to Louis. With her head down, she murmured, "I'm sorry for my actions. I don't know why I came after you like that. My name is Rosy. I'm a red wolf. . . . And thank you for helping us."

"We've met before, but that's water under the bridge. Welcome," Louis said. Then he turned to speak to all of them. "So, you're all from Alaska?"

"No," Rex clarified. "We five live in Alaska. Rosy here is from North Carolina and had a rough journey after her family was taken. We met her up on Mount Lemmon."

As the sun began to set, Rex noted, "That's an amazing snake head."

Louis chuckled. "It's not just a head; it's actually a bridge that spans the road."

"Really?" Rex said, intrigued.

"It's known by two names: Diamondback Bridge and Rattlesnake Bridge, or, if you put those two together, Diamondback Rattlesnake Bridge. I'll take you on it if you want."

The gang all jumped up. "Sure!"

Louis jumped down the steps and led them towards the bridge. "This bridge was built back in 2002 and was designed by a local artist. It's not a famous bridge, but people walk and bicycle on it every day."

They all walked into the snake's mouth. Its head was hollow, and the inside had a diamond pattern on its back. As they walked through it, Rex noticed that Louis seemed sad, but he didn't say anything.

The bridge sported some graffiti painted here and there. Beta looked over the edge, saw a big drop with cars passing under the bridge, and whined in fear.

Louis reassured her. "Don't worry, you're not going to fall out."

"This is amazing," Rex said as they walked. They continued to the other side of the bridge and out of the snake, where they saw a large metal tail sticking out of the ground with a rattle on top.

"Well, how was crossing the Rattlesnake Bridge?" Louis asked.

"It was amazing!" Rex said, and the gang all agreed.

Suddenly a loud rattle from the large tail startled them all and Lilly ran to Rex and Beta ran to Alpha.

Rosy and Duke were a little startled, but Louis laughed hysterically and said, "It's supposed to do that." He went to a desert bush and lifted up the leaves with his head, revealing a grate with a speaker. They all walked back across the bridge and out of the snake's mouth to Louis's park.

"It's getting dark," Louis said. He jumped up to his place on the top step where he had been when they arrived and said, "Sleep anywhere you like."

They each looked for a spot to sleep. Rex jumped on the first step and lay down, and Lilly settled in next to him. Rosy jumped over them both and lay down on the second step. Alpha and Beta lay down on the white crescent concrete bench, and Duke lay down under Rex and Lilly on the first step.

"So," Rosy asked Louis as they lay there under the stars, "why do you live here?"

He sighed. "When I was a small puppy, I lived in a big pet store, and I was very happy. Then the day came that I had been waiting for. The other puppies and I heard the front door open. *This is the day, the day I get adopted,* I told myself. *Just be yourself.* A man walked toward the puppies. He was a happy, jolly fellow. He looked at all the other dogs, then he looked at me. I jumped and ran over to the glass window, and he laughed and said to the saleslady, 'I want this one,' pointing at me. He took me home and put a new collar around my neck.

"'Your new name is Louis,' the man said. He played with me a lot, and we quickly became best friends. One day he brought me to this very park. He said, 'This is Iron Horse Park. My parents brought me here all of the time when I was a kid.' He laughed when I tried running fast and tripped and tumbled and fell flat on my belly. He showed me the bridge and carried me when I had trouble getting up the steps, and he comforted me when the rattle over there scared me. I loved being his dog.

"But month after month and year after year, I got older, and I became grouchy and mean. I didn't like to be bothered.

"If there was one time in my life that I wish I could change, it was when my master met this nice girl. They spent all of their time together, and it made me jealous. I always growled at her, and he would get angry at me. One day I made him so mad he grabbed me, and I bit his hand pretty good." Louis paused for a long moment and sighed. "He yanked his hand away and it started to bleed. I was ashamed and stepped back, whimpering an apology, but I had gone too far. He grabbed me and put a leash on me, and he dragged me out the door. We walked to the park, and he unclipped my leash and walked away. I followed him, but he told me to stay. He didn't come back. I even went to his house after a while, but he wasn't there. So, I came back here to the park, and I've lived here ever since. It can get pretty gloomy at times, but you all have made my day coming here."

Louis finished speaking and they all settled down to sleep. The sky was dotted by faint stars, and a waning gibbous moon shone in the desert sky. Two hours later, Lilly woke up, feeling like something was wrong. Rex wasn't beside her. She got up slowly so she wouldn't wake up the others and jumped off the step, looking for Rex. He was sitting down in the huge metal snake's mouth, looking sad. She walked over to him and he looked at her, then looked down at the ground.

She sat down next to him and asked in concern, "Are you ok?"

He didn't speak to her for a long moment. Her worry grew until Rex burst out, "How did this happen? Why did this have to happen to us? We're still not in Alaska! We had a wonderful life, and now it's down the drain!" His tone was filled with pessimism.

"You're not in this alone," Lilly reassured him. "You have Alpha, Beta, Duke, Rosy, Louis . . ." she paused, then confidently put her paw on his and said confidently, "and me."

Rex's face turned red, and as she laughed and smiled at him, his sadness drained away.

"Would you like to go on a walk with me?" he asked.

She grinned. "Certainly."

They walked onto the bridge, and the lights on the snake's metal body were shining down on them. Rex was happy again, and so was Lilly.

"So," Lilly said, remembering his reaction to her apology the day before, "When did you learn to howl?"

He shifted uncomfortably. "Rosy taught me after she told me her story."

They got to the middle of the bridge, and it was awkwardly silent as they both tried to keep their cool. Rex cleared his throat. "So, how are you doing with this grand adventure?"

"Well," Lilly thought a moment, then answered. "This has been both fun and nerve-racking."

He laughed and they got to the other side of the bridge.

They were tired and both lay down. Rex said, "Yeah, this is a new one for me."

Lilly laughed and said, "Well, at least we're with our friends."

"That's true."

They chatted softly as they both fell asleep.

When Rosy woke up the next morning, the first thing she saw was that Rex and Lilly were missing. She went to Alpha and Beta and tried waking them up, and did the same with Duke and Louis, with no luck. So she ran to the middle of the circle and let out a boisterous howl, which woke the entire gang up quick enough.

"For a wolf, you do wake up pretty early," Louis said, disrupted from his sleep.

"That's true," she said, "but that's not important right now. Rex and Lilly are missing."

"Aww, come on," Alpha, Beta, and Duke said, annoyed.

"You're not worried?" Rosy asked.

"Sure we are," Alpha said with a shrug, "but this is hardly the first time they've done this. Last time they were gone a whole day, then showed up with a white wolf and fox. Our master was worried sick."

They all got up and searched the entire park without finding them. Just about that time, Rex and Lilly woke up, and instead of yawning, Rex let out a loud howl.

The gang on the other side of the bridge heard it and were confused, but they ran over the bridge towards the howl. They saw Rex and Lilly lying there on the other side, as relaxed as can be.

Both annoyed and relieved, Alpha snapped, "For Balto's sake, why are you two over here?"

Rex yawned. "We had an incident," and then lay back down.

Rosy shook her head and then howled again, loudly, waking up both Rex and Lilly fully.

As they walked back across the bridge together, Alpha shook his head, grumbling to himself.

"All right," Rosy said, turning to Louis, "Let's go."

Louis sighed. "All right, this way, my friends. But I still say it's dangerous."

He led them down the road to another crossroad, then sharply turned. After a little bit they came to a building boasting a big red neon light that read, "HOTEL CONGRESS."

"We're going to stop in here and visit a friend of mine," Louis said. "He might know something helpful."

The dogs walked into the hotel acting casual, including Rosy, who tried her best to act like a dog.

"This hotel looks like it's been here a long time," Lilly remarked. It was fancy but casual at the same time.

"It opened in 1918. I know everything about Tucson which I learned from my old owner," Louis said proudly.

Rex saw a young beagle with copper-colored fur and a kind face sitting on the stairs. He looked younger than Rex. Louis walked over to the young beagle with the others following close behind.

"Cooper, it's nice to see you, my friend."

"It's Copper, Louis," the beagle said shaking his head.

Rosy smiled at his name.

Copper looked over the gang. "So, you have guests. What's

going on?"

Louis's face got serious. "Where is your father?"

"He's upstairs in our master's room." Then he looked at Rosy. "Miss, I think you'll need this to blend in. I've seen you. You're the red wolf I saw on the news." A tied red bandana lay on a nearby table. Copper jumped and grabbed it in his mouth, walked over to Rosy, and slipped it over her neck.

Rex looked at her and said, "It suits you."

She smiled, then processed what Copper had just said.

"Wait, I was on the news?" she asked frantically.

"Not just you," Copper said. "The video showed gray wolves, too."

"Oh, this is bad . . . very bad," she said, her rage rising. "This is De-Vil and 'the Boss's' fault, not ours. When I see either of them or the Boss's goons, I'm going to make them pay."

They started up the stairs, "So, why are you guys here?" Copper asked as he led them down the hall. "I haven't seen you guys around Tucson."

"We're from Alaska and she's from North Carolina," Rex said. "But we got stolen by the same goons."

Copper blurted in alarm, "You got stolen by the Boss's goons? This is bad, very bad."

"What's very bad?" Rex asked.

"When the Boss doesn't get what he wants, he kills his goons. So two of his goons are probably looking frantically for you guys right now."

Copper stopped outside a room labeled "242" with an open door. They walked in and saw an older beagle lying on a bed.

"Hi, Pops."

"Hey, Copper. I see you're with Louis and some guests."

"These four are from Alaska, and this one is from North Carolina. They've all had some run-ins with the Boss's goons."

"The Boss?" The older beagle lifted his head up. Concern tightened his face. "This is bad, very bad. Oh, how rude of me—my name is Stewart. I'm Copper's father. And who might you all be?"

Louis introduced them. "This is Rex, Lilly, Alpha, Beta, Duke, and Rosy."

"It is a pleasure to meet all of you."

Their tails wagged happily. "So, do you live here?" Rex asked.

"No, me and my boy are visiting Tucson with our master. We're from Oregon." He suddenly sniffed the air. "I smell a wolf." He looked questioningly at Rosy.

"I'm a red wolf," she said sheepishly.

Then Rex asked Stewart, "So, what's the story about this cool hotel?"

"It's best known for being John Dillinger and gang's hideout back in 1934. After he and his gang robbed some banks, they hid here in this hotel, but while they were hiding, a huge fire destroyed the second floor. During the evacuation, Dillinger and his gang got caught. He was sent to jail back in Indiana, but he escaped."

"Did they ever catch him?" Duke asked eagerly.

"He got killed in an alley in Chicago, right next to a theater. The workers of this hotel say the ghosts of the people who were burned to a crisp in the fire still live here. They say this is the most haunted room in the entire hotel."

The gang stared at Stewart in shock and fear, but Louis

chuckled.

"It's just a ghost story," he said to help lift everyone's spirits.

Then Rex said, confused, "But you said the second story was burned down. How are we standing on it now?"

"Oh, later a group of people rebuilt it just as it was," Stewart said.

"Hey Pops," Copper interrupted, "these guys came here asking for our help. They are wondering if we've seen anything on the news or have any information about 'the Boss' that might help them out."

"What do you need?" Stewart asked the gang.

"They need to get to El Loco's Mansion and rescue Rosy's captured family without being caught themselves," Louis explained.

"Hmm, that will be a bit tricky . . . but I'll do the best I can to help you get your family back," Stewart said, bringing a smile to Rosy's face.

"This Boss fellow has quite the protections around his mansion," Stewart began. "First are all of his goons. They regularly patrol El Loco's mansion, inside and out."

"The goons are problematic," put in Louis, "but what I feel is even more concerning are the mansion's high walls and the protected gate that never opens to anyone except to the Boss's goons and the Boss himself. Getting into El Loco's Mansion is like finding an invisible needle in a mountain-sized haystack."

After Louis expressed his concerns, gloom and doom fell upon everyone in the room.

"Hey, don't give me those glum mugs," Louis called out. "Even though it's probably impossible, let's try our luck. Who knows, we might get lucky!"

Glum faces turned back into hopeful ones.

Realizing the afternoon was approaching, Rex said, "We really had probably get going."

They all thanked Copper and Stewart and headed for the stairs. As they left the hotel, Rosy was walking near Rex as two beautiful, large dogs passed by on leashes.

One of them said, "Ooooh, look at her with him." They both laughed snottily. "Yeah, I was thinking the same thing," the other dog said. "He could definitely do better."

Rosy heard their rude comments and that black, ominous haze came back and enveloped her. Her blue eyes turned back into vivid purple. Their master stopped at a box filled with newspapers. Rosy stopped and turned around, and the gang stopped with her.

"Are you talking about me?" Rosy said, clenching her teeth together.

The beautiful dogs smirked. "Yes."

"Don't let me ever hear you say that again," she said in a crazed frenzy.

"Don't tell us what to do. You're not the Boss over us," one of them said.

"Soon I will be," she said demonically.

Both the gang and the two beautiful dogs were startled. Rex was alarmed.

What is going on? he thought. *In a way, that's not Rosy, except that it is Rosy. But that black haze isn't her. It's almost like something is controlling her, but what?* Then it dawned on him. *Maybe her rage is controlling her? Or is it something else?*

Rosy growled at the two dogs, who shrank down,

whimpering. The master looked over and said, "Can you tell your dog to . . . c-calm d-down. . . ." Then she found herself staring at an angry red wolf and screamed, running away with her dogs. Two blocks away, she grabbed her phone and called animal control.

The black, ominous haze vanished from Rosy into thin air in an instant, and her evil purple eyes turned back to her normal blue eyes. As she came back to reality, she cowered. "It happened again. What's wrong with me? I would never say or do that!"

Her friends were confused, too, but they tried to comfort her. Suddenly there was a shout, and someone rushed towards Rosy. Animal control had pulled up and were there to take her away. Rosy darted away in a quick dash with Rex and the others followed right after her. She ran and ran, with Rex and the others following close behind. The animal control people jumped back in their truck and drove after them.

It was a desperate race to escape yet again.

Back on Mount Lemmon, De-Vil had noticed that Rosy and the dogs were gone. He swore loudly. Behind him was a wolf from his new pack, and De-Vil's rage made the wolf nervous.

"Alpha, what are you so mad about?" the wolf asked.

"Nothing," De-Vil snarled. "It's just Rosy, she seems to be getting more and more rebellious, and we can't have that."

"Why?"

"Because ever since she's mingled with those domestic filth, she's getting wild ideas," De-Vil said with disgust.

"Why is that such a problem, Sir?"

"Because if she gets ideas that are outrageous, she might learn the truth."

"What truth?"

"Nothing of your concern," De-Vil growled aggressively.

"But she's just having fun," the wolf noted cautiously.

"Fun?" De-Vil said with distaste.

"She's just having fun, for Clement's sake."

"Calm down, there's no need for this foolish nonsense," De-Vil said sternly.

"Yes, Alpha," the wolf replied, cowering slightly, "but are you sure you should get all worked up by this?"

"Yes," he said in a definite tone.

"Yeah, but in her defense, she should be able to live on her own if she wants, without you breathing down her neck twenty-four-seven," the wolf said. "She's not even originally from our pack."

"I'm just trying to keep her out of trouble," De-Vil snapped.

"Yes, Alpha, Sir, but considering your record, do you think it's wise to get all worked up about something like this?" the wolf asked cautiously.

"What are you talking about?"

"Well, another wolf shared with me that Clements had told him a story, and it worries me about what you might do when you're upset."

De-Vil turned around, looking quite intrigued. "What story might that be?"

"He told me you liked another wolf in the pack. But there was a problem; another wolf in the pack was interested in her as well."

"Oh, that story. It's just an idiotic rumor from my past," De-Vil said dismissively.

"But he told me that afterwards you did something," the wolf said nervously.

"What did I do?" De-Vil insisted.

"Well, he told me that . . ." the wolf paused, looking even more nervous than before.

"Come on, tell me! Spit it out NOW!" De-Vil demanded.

"That you . . . that you . . . killed the other wolf," he winced.

De-Vil looked furious. "You think I would kill Rosy?!"

"No," the wolf lied.

"Do you think I would jeopardize my authority and status as alpha to kill that measly wolf?" he said, raising his voice.

"Your authority?" the wolf replied, losing his own temper. "Your authority? You stole that authority when you stepped foot on this mountain! But that's not all you did!"

"What do you mean, 'that's not all'?" De-Vil asked, clenching his teeth.

"Well, after your friendship dissolved, this wolf you liked began to have strange things happen to her. At night, she heard voices—your voice. She claimed that you said 'I'm the Alpha now'—" the wolf paused, then continued, "—the same thing you said when you stepped on this mountain."

"ENOUGH!" De-Vil shouted, his voice echoing through the forest. "New decree of the Alpha. No one is allowed to speak a word of that tale, and whoever does will be sentenced to pack persecution," De-Vil uttered coldly.

This infuriated the wolf. "You're mad!" He spat at De-Vil. I'm going to tell everyone you're unfit for the noble title of Alpha." Then, to his horror, he saw the shape of a monstrous beast where De-Vil had stood. The demon had razor-sharp teeth and blood-red eyes. He stared wildly at the wolf and breathed foul winds that swept at the wolf's nostrils.

The beast spoke in a demonic voice. "I will hold this title, and no one will ever stop me. If they try, I will kill them."

The wolf cowered in fear as if he were facing a devil from the fiery pits below. Then the demon charged at the cowering wolf, knocking him to the ground. The demon swiped at the wolf, claw him across the face, then began to walk away. The injured wolf stirred. The side of his face was brutally mauled.

"Change of heart, I suppose." De-Vil's cruel voice came from the beast.

"Go to hell where you belong!" the injured wolf said spitefully.

De-Vil just walked away, his paws crunching on the fallen pine needles as the demonic aura faded. He lowered his nose and sniffed, then grinned evilly. He had found Rosy's scent.

"I'm coming, Rosy, and when I get to you and your domestic-filth friends, I will make you all pay for flouting my authority. No one will ever question my power again," De-Vil said menacingly.

He pursued Rosy's scent down the mountain.

Back downtown, the gang was still running from animal control. Rex caught up to Rosy, and she wailed woefully, "Get away from me," and ran farther ahead of him again.

"This way," Louis called, guiding them.

They ran all through downtown, past tall skyscrapers and along the freeway, still being chased by animal control. They managed to lose animal control as they all darted down into another dry riverbed. As the riverbed curved to the west, they approached a massive airport and stopped there to rest.

Rosy stayed away from the group. Rex was confused and felt sad for her. He tried to cheer her up by smiling at her, but she didn't smile back. He was worried.

But as they were resting, someone was staring at them. A man and a woman had come out of the airport with their luggage. They walked past Louis, Rex, and the gang, then the woman stopped and looked more closely at the group of dogs and then even more closely at Louis. The woman gasped in shock and stopped walking. She ran towards Louis, picked him up and wrapped him tightly in her arms, making him feel very confused. The man, who had kept walking, now stopped and looked back and saw his companion hugging a bulldog that looked a lot like his old bulldog, Louis. Instantly, it hit him like a brick. It *was* his old dog, Louis!

"Louis!" he shouted in pure joy as he ran to both of them. "Remember me?" he asked, crying tears of joy.

Louis still was confused as he looked at the man, and then at the woman, and then back at the man. Then he remembered. It was his old master and his fiancée!

"Louis, I'm so sorry I abandoned you there in the park. It was the worst mistake I've ever made in my life. Can you ever forgive me?" his master asked sorrowfully.

Louis looked at his master and began to lick his face, cheering him up. "I knew it. You are man's best friend," his master smiled, wiping away his tears. "*My* best friend," he said softly as he wrapped his arms around Louis and held him tight.

"Come on Louis, let's go home," his master said happily as

he set Louis back on the ground. The three started heading to their car, but Louis stopped and turned back to Rosy, Rex, and the gang. All of them came and gathered around him.

"Thank you," Louis told his friends. "You are the best dogs I've ever met in my entire life." He then looked at Rosy, "And you make sure these five stay close; they are true friends. Oh, and you're the best wolf I've ever met in my entire life. Don't get angry or too worked up, but surround yourself with these five and you'll be okay."

Louis then turned to Rex, "The rest of the way to El Loco's mansion is easy. Go past this airport and keep moving south until you hit an elaborate, white building with a gaudy front gate. I wish you the best of luck, and thank you for helping me," Louis said with a wonderful smile on his face as he trotted back to his master and his fiancée, who were smiling at Louis and his friends. As the three began to walk to their car, Louis bounded joyfully with his newfound owners and barked, "Thank you!"

Rosy, Rex and the gang smiled and then followed Louis's directions to El Loco's mansion by heading south, cutting across the airport. The airport was huge, and as the canids crossed a runway, they heard an airplane approaching. They ran as fast as they could down the taxiway, dodging in and around airplanes. Finally, they came to the airport's southern border barbed-wire fence. Fortunately, it was old and had an opening. They squeezed through with only a few minor scratches. They ran a few miles to the south and then stopped, staring. They had made it to the mansion.

De-Vil had gotten there first. He prowled through the

Boss's zoo, and all of the animals, even the lions and lionesses, were terrified of him.

The Boss was inside, negotiating with a buddy of his, and as they were talking, they heard something scratch at his metal double doors. One of the doors was open a little, and De-Vil barged into the room.

The Boss and his friend stared at the angry wolf in surprise, then in fear, but they had nowhere to flee. The Boss's friend was foolish and ran toward the door, trying to escape past the angry wolf. The Boss was surprised when the wolf merely moved out of his way and let him go. The Boss thought he could do the same, but De-Vil quickly moved back in front of the door and growled and glared at the Boss.

De-Vil wanted the Boss to know he had a bone to pick. He advanced on the Boss until he was backed up against the wall. De-Vil scanned the room, moving with poise and dignity, while the Boss cowered in fear. His office boasted a lot of illegal loot, taxidermy animals, sleazy magazines, and newspaper articles about the heists, devious plans, and crimes he had committed. Then De-Vil saw something that caught his evil, amber eyes. On the Boss's desk were six photos: Rex dozing off, Lilly sleeping, Alpha and Beta napping, Duke snoozing, and finally, one of Rosy in a kennel, growling aggressively.

De-Vil eased towards the Boss's desk, and the Boss frantically ran and grabbed a pistol on his desk and aimed it right at him. De-Vil looked straight at the Boss without hesitation. He had a look in his bright, amber eyes that said, "Put the gun down. I'm not your enemy."

The Boss was a little confused, but he threw the gun on

the floor. De-Vil nodded his head in appreciation. De-Vil wanted to get his message across to the Boss, so he went and grabbed the picture of Rex.

"Put that back," the Boss snapped automatically, before remembering that he was dealing with a large wolf who could attack him at any moment, and he probably shouldn't provoke him. De-Vil tore the picture of Rex into shreds, then looked meaningfully at the Boss. A slow grin spread across the Boss's face.

"You want to be partners, *lobo?* You're on. Let's capture them together." De-Vil howled in agreement.

As Rex and the gang got closer to the beautiful white mansion, they saw a large golden gate adorned with golden designs of leaves, vines, and flowers. Each pillar holding up the gate bore a large, white anaconda, its large, white coils wrapping around the pure white stone.

As the gang looked at the large golden gate, they saw two golden statues that stood on top of the anaconda pillars. On the right was a roaring lion; on the left was a roaring lioness. They looked as if to be some sort of guardians of this mansion. Strangely, no goons guarded the gate; even more strange, it was wide open.

Rex turned to Rosy, "Are you ready?"

She nodded. "You don't have to come. It's going to be pretty dangerous in there for you."

Alpha snorted. "And for you. We're going."

"All right then, let's do this."

She led the group in. They saw all kinds of exotic and rare animals. They came to a group of lions and lionesses in a huge cage. The big cats were all calm, but when one of the lions saw the dogs and Rosy, he charged toward them and fiercely gripped the iron bars. "What are you doing here? Get out of here, or you'll be like us." His voice had an African accent.

Behind him a voice with the same accent spoke disapprovingly. "Come on, Jabali, give dem a chance." The lion moved out of the way and a happy lioness came and greeted them. "Hi, I'm Moyo. Sorry for dat."

"I heard dat," Jabali said, but she ignored him and continued.

"Why are you here?" Then she looked at the six of them and her heart sank like a stone in water. "Oh, no."

"What's wrong?" Rex asked.

"Quick, are your names Rex, Lilly, Alpha, Beta, Duke, and Rose?"

"Yes. . . ." the gang replied suspiciously.

"How did you know our names?" Rex asked. "We've just. . . ."

"Dee person dat stole us and every animal here knows your names, because dee Boss says your names a lot recently, but. . . ." Then they heard footsteps and everyone froze.

All of the animals in the zoo hid in the corners of their cages, even Jabali, Moyo, and the other lions.

The gang heard a familiar, haughty tone.

"This is great, just marvelous! Look, the gang is all here." De-Vil strolled around the corner and stopped, followed by the Boss, who held a fancy wooden cane, and two of his goons, who held tranquilizer dart guns. De-Vil and the Boss's goons eased toward them.

"Run!" Rosy shouted, Rex and the rest sprinted around the

mansion, De-Vil pursuing them. They turned another corner to run but found themselves cornered behind the lions' cage.

Rex looked at his friends in despair. "Sorry guys, I guess we're caught."

"No, you not," came a voice from behind. Right behind him was Moyo and she bellowed a loud roar that startled the goons and De-Vil. Jabali added his roar, and the other lions and lionesses joined in. The goons and the Boss retreated.

"Cowards," De-Vil muttered under his breath as he looked at the roaring lions.

They stopped and glared at De-Vil with contempt. "You traitor," Jabali said coldly.

De-Vil turned to the lions' cage and saw Jabali, Moyo, and the other lions and lionesses staring straight at him. "What do you mean, my African lion friend?" De-Vil replied snootily.

"My name is Jabali. How dare you side with dee corrupt man and his minions!"

"I don't care what you say, lion. El Loco and his followers will help me achieve my goal, and no one will be able to stop us," De-Vil told Jabali arrogantly.

"You will fail," Jabali told De-Vil firmly.

"What? What do you mean, I will fail?"

"You know exactly what I'm talking about. When dee corrupt man and his minions suffer dee consequences of der heinous actions, you will not be dee arrogant wolf who is talking to me right now."

"Heh, what are you going to do about it? You're trapped behind bars," De-Vil replied mockingly.

"And if I weren't, you would be dead right where you're standing," Jabali answered in a frighteningly intimidating way. De-Vil stiffened fearfully. "Now, get out of here," Jabali ordered. "But before you leave as dee coward you are, mark my words: when dee corrupt man and his minions fall, so will you, and den we will see where your true loyalties lie."

De-Vil sprinted as fast as he could back towards the Boss's mansion.

Lilly slumped against Rex in relief. "How can we possibly thank you?" she asked, turning to the lions.

"We don't want to see you caged up like us," Jabali replied.

"Why?" Beta asked curiously.

"We have been here for over a decade," Moyo replied, gesturing at the lions around her.

"We have been away from our homes in Africa, which we miss dearly," Jabali added.

"Where are you guys from?" Duke asked eagerly.

"Me, Moyo, and dee other lions and lionesses here in dese cages are from dee Serengeti in eastern Africa. Errg, dat despicable wolf!" Jabali muttered angrily. "I can't believe he's siding with dee greedy man and his tieving minions."

"Yeah, they've been chasing after us," Rosy said, annoyed.

"But thanks for standing up for us when we really needed help," Lilly praised.

"As we said, we don't want you all ending up trapped like us in dese cages," Moyo pleaded.

"Maybe we can repay the favor by trying to get El Loco and his goons to slip up, and, as you said, 'face the consequences of their heinous actions.' It's going to catch up to them and they're going to get in trouble sooner than later," Lilly told them.

"Maybe? We will see," Moyo replied hopelessly.

Her despair made Rosy and the gang sad.

"Hey, we can promise you this: El Loco and his goons are only human, and they will make mistakes that will come back to bite them in the end," Rex said reassuringly, raising their spirits.

Rosy then asked Moyo the question she'd been wondering for so long. "Are any red wolves here?"

"Let me tink about dat. . . . Oh, yeah. They tried to bring in seven of dem a while back, but one of them flew off of dee vehicle where dey had dem. The other six I heard escaped."

"They escaped?" Rosy gasped in disbelief. "They're safe?"

"You know dem?"

"I'm the one who flew off of the vehicle! The others were my family. I'm so glad they're ok!"

They heard footsteps.

"They're coming back for you," Jabali said. "Go!"

As they took off running, they saw De-Vil, the Boss, and more goons as reinforcements coming toward them.

"Good luck!" they heard Moyo call behind them. "You're going to need it!"

They ran out of the mansion gate with De-Vil right behind them, mad as hellfire. The goons all piled into cars as the gang kept running.

CHAPTER 6

BAD TIMING

With De-Vil still hot on their tails, the gang came along some train tracks. Just then, they all heard a loud locomotive's horn and saw a diesel train approaching from behind. Rex saw a cattle car passing by with its door open and had the same crazy idea as before.

"Come on!" he shouted to his friends. "One . . . two . . . three!" he jumped into the car, and one by one, all of the gang jumped up as well, except Rosy. She was still running alongside the train.

"Jump!" Rex called. "You'll be fine!"

Rosy hesitated, then looked behind over her shoulder and saw De-Vil catching up. She jumped and Rex caught her.

"We can't let them get away," one of the goons said.

Rex looked around inside the car. Two cows in the back were staring right at him.

"Hi," Duke said pleasantly.

"Uh, this is a cattle car, not a canine car," one of the cows said.

Then the gang saw one of the car windows roll down. A goon leaned out, holding some kind of explosive in her hand, and she threw it at the cattle car. It stuck on the metal near the rear wheel, and then another explosive stuck near the front of the cattle car. Rex peeked out and saw one of the goons holding a remote-control device with a big red button, and just then . . . she pressed it. He heard a strange beeping noise and looked down. To his horror, he saw the bombs blinking that had stuck to the side of the train.

"Get down!"

He and the gang and the cows dove to the hay-covered wooden floor, then both bombs exploded and shook the whole car. Rex, the gang, and the cows all felt the train car hit the rails with a loud THUD! Sparks were flying and the damaged car was slowing the train down. The train car started to tip just as De-Vil jumped into the car.

"Come on!" Rosy screamed as the train continued to tip. The gang jumped out of the car on the side away from the freeway. They fell and hit the ground hard, then scrambled out of its way as the train car tipped over, followed by the next eight cars falling over one by one like dominoes. They stood and watched in shock, staring at the destruction the goons had caused, and realizing they were safe for the time being because the goons and De-Vil were on the other side of the derailed train.

"Good luck!" the cows yelled as they ran away.

"These guys are insane," Lilly said.

Suddenly, they heard something jump on top of the fallen cattle car. They heard growling, and then De-Vil emerged, laughing evilly.

The gang sprinted off again as he jumped off the car and took off in hot pursuit. They were running as fast as they could. Rex could feel his heart beating like a drum in his chest. They ran, and ran, and kept running, but De-Vil was slowly catching up to them.

He got close to Rex. "End of the line," he snarled, running beside him. "You and your friends are finished."

"Not true," Rex snapped back. "We're just beginning."

They veered away from the tracks, and De-Vil followed them. They ran across the desert landscape as De-Vil fumed, "You're a stubborn one."

"I'm not stubborn; I'm persistent."

"Well, that's a surprise," De-Vil said sarcastically. "You. . . ."

"Tree!" Rex abruptly yelled.

De-Vil was confused. "Tree? What tree?" Suddenly De-Vil, not looking where he was going, ran into a big green palo verde tree. The gang didn't look back to check on him; they just kept running until they were as far away from De-Vil as possible.

Finally, they slowed their pace.

"Good," Beta panted. "We lost him."

"That's good, but we need to find a place to hide," Alpha reminded them.

"How far is the smaller airport you were talking about?" Rex asked Rosy.

"It's a ways away, my friend."

Rex groaned in annoyance.

"So, where are we going to hide?" Duke asked.

"Yeah, we better find a place fast before the goons or De-Vil catch up to us," Lilly exclaimed.

They heard howling in the distance behind them.

"Let's go," Rex said.

Swiftly they again started to run. They were okay because De-Vil was a ways behind them, but they all were both nervous and cautious.

Where are we going to go? Rex thought. *We can't get caught.* He saw a mountain that looked like a sombrero hat. "Let's go to that area near that mountain over there," he called to the others as they ran. The others nodded tiredly and ran toward the small mountain.

The goons were still stuck on the other side of the derailed train. The gang ran along the tracks until they came to a train bridge. The train cars were on their sides on the train bridge, too.

They all stopped and Rex said, "One at a time." The bridge looked damaged and unstable with all of those fallen cars spread across it.

Lilly walked out onto the bridge, but she had to be careful because the train cars stretched across the entire bridge. It was thin where she was, and she heard cracking.

"This bridge is unstable," she called quietly to the others. "It could collapse at any moment if we all cross together, and we don't have all day. We have to get away from the goons and De-Vil." Lilly thought a moment. "The goons probably won't catch up, but I'm certain De-Vil will."

She carefully walked across the bridge. It was a long bridge, and even with the guard rail the drop was seriously dangerous. Lilly reminded herself that this bridge wasn't as dangerous as the avalanche they'd experienced on their trip back to Fairbanks. Finally, she got to the other side and yelled, "I'm across! Come on! We're running out of time!"

Suddenly she saw De-Vil running toward them. "RUN!" she cried.

They all looked behind and saw De-Vil coming towards them fast. One by one they ran across the faltering bridge. Rex was the last to go. Just as he began to run, De-Vil tackled him from behind.

"You're not going anywhere!" De-Vil snarled from on top of him.

"Are you sure about that?" Rex snapped. He launched De-Vil off of him and watched him hit the ground, rolling in the gravel. Rex ran onto the train bridge.

"Not today," De-Vil growled, and he ran after Rex across the train bridge.

The gang watched nervously as Rex ran as fast as he could, pursued by De-Vil. As Rex neared the end of the bridge, De-Vil was desperate to catch at least one of them, and Rex was his prime ticket. He snapped at Rex's tail. Rex flinched, nearly hitting the guard rails that could have sent him off the bridge, but he kept his footing. Suddenly he stopped, turned, and charged towards De-Vil.

The gang gasped.

"Are you crazy?" Lilly yelled.

Rex slammed his body into De-Vil with everything he had. De-Vil flew sideways, hitting the guard rails and tumbling off the train bridge. He hit the ground hard and didn't move.

Rex ran to the other side of the bridge and got off by the

others. He was panting heavily from running. Suddenly Lilly bit his tail. Rex yowled from the pain.

"What was that for?" he cried.

"You almost got yourself killed," she chided, with panic in her eyes.

They all looked where De-Vil had landed in the rocks below the bridge. He wasn't moving, but they couldn't find it in themselves to feel sorry for him. He had been trying to kill them.

Since the goons were on the other side of the derailed train and De-Vil seemed incapacitated, the gang walked quickly instead of running.

"At least we don't have to run," Rex said happily. They all nodded. They had been running all day, it seemed, but they were happy again to get out of another tight spot in one piece.

When they came up to some buildings, Rex said, "Let's get going."

"I agree," Rosy said. They sped up to a light jog. The train was still there behind them on its side, like a wall that divided the freeway from the desert and the nearby buildings. They were amazed by how long the train was.

Rex looked around as they ran. He kind of liked Tucson. He liked how it was sprawled out and was so big. He had never been in a desert before. He missed Fairbanks, pulling the sleds and those wonderful adventures he had with his master and his friends. But he sure was happy to be with his six best friends at this moment, having an exciting adventure outside of Alaska. They came to another train bridge and ran across it carefully, but it was more secure. They saw cars passing under the bridge as they crossed.

They ran for what seemed like a long while, and Rex started feeling annoyed that they had to hide from goons instead of going straight to the airport. As they ran past a golf course, he remembered back when his master would play golf back in Fairbanks with his friends and colleagues. They kept running, past shops and construction sites and a big electrical transformer station surrounded by the desert landscape. Eventually they ran past the front of the derailed train. Its three diesel engines were on their sides and people were trying to help the engineers get out. Police cars and ambulances were ready nearby, and even a helicopter was circling to land. The gang continued running, and when they passed near a few neighborhoods with tiny desert-colored houses, things started looking familiar.

Rex stopped and said, "Hey guys, look. We were here when we first arrived in Arizona."

Rosy was confused. "Wait, why were you here?"

"After we got to Arizona, we escaped from the goons at that smaller airport in Marana. We jumped on a train, but Mr. Smarty-Pants here decided to 'hop' off." He looked at Duke, and Duke chuckled sheepishly. The IHOP sign was illuminated in the distance, with the "I" light now working.

"After that, we headed straight for Mount Lemmon, though we didn't know its name yet."

The gang kept running past more shops and restaurants and tried not to get hit by cars when they crossed the busy streets. The sky was getting dark and they were all getting tired. They stopped near a large car bridge over what looked to be primarily a dry riverbed. The bridge had a mural that said "Santa Cruz River" in the middle. The mural depicted a blue winding river, some tan flat-roofed buildings that looked like houses with purple triangle-shaped mountains above and behind them.

"We have a problem," Lilly whispered to Rex. "Where are we going to sleep?"

He opened his mouth, but he didn't have an answer. He looked out over the dry river and sighed. "Let's keep going."

They left the bridge and kept running towards the small, sombrero-shaped mountain. When Rex saw an opening into the desert, he ran across the street and the rest followed. They ran through the desert, passing a few houses and crossing a smaller road as the sun began to set. The desert was eerie in the growing darkness. As the sun disappeared behind the mountain, they found themselves in the middle of the desert with not a building in sight.

They huddled close together, staring nervously into the darkness. They heard rustling and then a sudden howl split the cool night desert air.

Rosy swallowed nervously. "That's not a wolf's howl."

CHAPTER 7

MEETING THE WILDLIFE

Yellow, blue, and brown glowing eyes glittered in the distance. Then they heard growling. A group of coyotes stalked toward them, continuing to growl.

"What are you doing here? And why?" A very big coyote said in an aggressive tone. The coyotes surrounded the gang.

"Wait there! I'm coming," a voice suddenly called from off in the distance.

The big coyote shook his head in embarrassment. "You've got to be kidding me."

A female coyote came jogging up to the group. The coyote and Rex looked at each other and in unison said, "Hey, it's you!"

Everyone else looked at them in confusion.

"Do you guys know each other?" the big coyote asked.

"Yeah, he's the dog that saved Beth's son from the flash

flood over by Mount Lemmon."

The big coyote looked at Rex in surprise. "Is this true?"

Rex nodded.

The big coyote introduced himself. "I'm Raro. It's a pleasure to meet you." He introduced his friends and then got to the coyote had identified Rex. Raro said with embarrassment, "This is my younger sister, Joya. Her name is Spanish for jewel." You can call her either. She's a real gem."

Rex introduced himself and told the coyotes a brief version of their story. Then the introductions continued.

"I'm Lilly."

"I'm Alpha."

"Oh, so you're the leader of this group?" Jewel said. "So, what's your name?"

"Why do animals always think that?" Alpha sighed, annoyed. "My name *is* Alpha. I'm not the leader, Rex is. I'm more like his second-in-command," then he sighed again. "Déjà vu."

"I'm Beta and Beta is my name," Beta said bashfully.

One of the four other coyotes looked at her, then looked at Alpha and smirked. Beta blushed and frowned at the coyote.

"I'm Duke."

"Hi, I'm Rosy. I'm a red wolf. Rex has already explained what's happened to me."

As she spoke, Raro stared at her, seeming not to hear anything she said. Rosy shifted uncomfortably. Jewel looked at Raro and raised an eyebrow. She waved her paw in front of his face as he kept staring at Rosy. "Raro, Raro, earth to Raro."

Raro snapped out of his trance and swallowed, then said, "So, you don't have a place to sleep? You can sleep with our band."

The gang agreed and followed the coyotes. Rosy came up beside Rex and spoke quietly.

"Rex, can I talk to you?"

"Sure, why?"

"When I introduced myself, Raro was just staring at me. It was kind of strange."

"Maybe he was just trying to understand?" Rex suggested.

"I don't think so. It was like he was in a trance. Why would he look at me so strangely when I've just met him?"

"Maybe he likes you."

"Wait, what?" Rosy gasped. "We just met!"

Rex shrugged, "I did say maybe."

Ahead of them, Jewel smirked at Raro, then said in fluent Spanish, "Brother, I've never seen you like that. You didn't even speak to her. It's like you were in a trance." Then she saw that he was looking at Rosy again and laughed. "Ohhh, I see. You like her!"

He responded defensively, using Spanish as well. "No, I don't! It's none of your business!"

They walked until they came to a wide piece of desert far from any houses. There were a lot of coyotes, maybe twenty or thirty in all, plus other wildlife. The mother coyote Rex had helped—Beth, Jewel had said her name was—ran up to him, her cub bounding alongside her.

"Hey, you six are back!" Beth said to him. "Wait, six? I thought there were only five of you."

"This is Rosy. We met her up on Mount Lemmon." He told her a shortened version of their story.

Then she said, "I'm Beth, and this is Toby."

Rex smiled at the pup. "Oh, I remember you."

Toby grinned. "Me, too!"

"That was an amazing story," Beth added. "I'll get the band together and introduce you to the rest of the coyotes."

She gathered all of the coyotes for a meeting, then called out loudly, "Hello!" However, she was drowned out by the coyotes loud chattering. "Umm, hello," she called again, trying get their attention.

Rex lifted his head high to the indigo sky, concentrated, and let out a boisterous howl that quieted everyone.

"Thank you," Beth said to Rex. "And by the way, nice howl."

He looked at Rosy, who nodded with a beaming grin.

"Everyone, we have guests," Beth said to the others. "They're from Fairbanks, Alaska."

The gang walked to the middle of the band, and Rex introduced himself first. "Hello, everyone. I'm Rex, and I'm an Alaskan malamute. My friends and I are sled dogs, except Rosy." The gang each took turns introducing themselves.

"I'm Lilly. I'm a Samoyed."

"I'm Alpha. I'm an Alaskan husky, and not to confuse you, my *name* is Alpha; I'm not the leader."

"I'm Beta, and I'm a Siberian husky." Her voice was shy.

"I'm Duke. I'm a Greenland dog."

Rosy was nervous when her turn came. "Hi, I'm Rosy. I'm a. . . ."

A coyote interrupted her. "Wait, aren't you the red wolf that made the news the other day with those gray wolves Ren told me about?"

"Let her finish," Raro said.

She continued. "Yes, I'm the red wolf that lives with

the gray wolves. I'm not from Alaska. I'm actually from North Carolina, but then my life turned upside down and I eventually ended up here on Mount Lemmon."

The coyotes came up and greeted each of them and then went back to preparing for sleep. Jewel and Raro then introduced them all to the leader of the band.

"What an amazing story. I'm Cabezota. I'm the leader of this band of coyotes. You can call me Cabez. This is my wife, Tierra, and my two children, Raro and Joya."

"Dad, can Rex and his friends stay with us here tonight? They don't have a place to sleep."

"Sure, they can sleep here," Cabezota said. The coyotes all started settling in to sleep, but the gang just looked at each other. They didn't know where to lie down.

"You can sleep with my family," Joya said.

They went over to where Jewel's family slept. Rex and Lilly slept by each other, as did Alpha and Beta. Duke slept near a creosote bush, and Rosy slept where she could see the night sky. Jewel went to go sleep over near her parents, but she saw that Raro was sleeping over near Rosy. She went over and teased him in Spanish.

"Hey, look, it's your mate."

"Cállate," he growled back.

She chuckled, then replied in Spanish, "Okay, I'll leave you alone, but good luck. . . . I like her."

A while later Rosy woke up and opened her eyes. Almost everyone was asleep, but she saw Raro sitting there, wide awake. She got up and sat next to him.

"Hi, Raro. Are you okay? Why are you up at this hour?"

Raro was looking up at the sky full of stars and a new

moon. He looked at Rosy and said, "I'm just looking at the stars and the different constellations." Then he looked back at the sky. "I'm so sorry I didn't speak to you earlier, but you seem to be a lovely wolf." She blushed, and he continued. "Look at that one. It's called Lupus. It's Latin for 'wolf' or 'the wolf.'"

She saw its nine stars, and she was quite impressed by how much he knew. Then she saw one with three very bright stars in a row. "Hey, I know that one. I think its name is Orion."

"You're correct," Raro said with a smile. They stayed up naming constellations and chatting until they both got tired and fell asleep where they were.

Early the next morning, Rex woke up. Almost everyone was where they had gone to sleep, but he didn't see Rosy or Raro. He finally saw them. They hadn't been right next to each other when he'd gone to sleep, but he smiled to see that Rosy was warming up to Raro.

He set off for a walk. After a moment he heard, "Wait for me." He smiled and stopped. He knew who it was.

Lilly walked up. "Good morning."

They walked for a little while, then circled back to the coyote camp.

Rex asked, "Can I show you something?"

"Sure, what do you want to show me?"

He took her to where Raro and Rosy were sleeping. Lilly was astounded that Rosy was sleeping near Raro, remembering that he made Rosy uncomfortable when they met, but she was happy they were getting along now. Lilly and Rex went to where they had slept and lay back down to wait for the others to wake up.

Rex remembered back from when they had been on the train escaping the goons after they had first arrived. He turned to Lilly and said, "Hey, do you remember when you were in tears on the train when we first got here? But look at you! You're fine now."

"Yeah, look at all the fun we've had. We have gone all over Tucson and have met lots of new friends. Besides, we're with our friends."

An hour later, Alpha and Beta woke up and saw that Rex and Lilly were awake and visiting and came over and joined them.

"How did you two sleep?" Alpha asked.

Rex shrugged. "It was fine, dirt is dirt, but nothing like snow."

"Agreed," Beta and Lilly said in unison.

They talked, and after a while Duke joined them. Finally Jewel woke up.

She saw the gang sitting and talking together, but she didn't see Rosy or Raro. She walked over to the gang. "Where's Raro?"

"He's with Rosy," Rex said.

She was confused and looked around for them. When she found them still sleeping near each other, she tried to be quiet, but it was hard to hold in her chuckling. She then gave up and yelled, "WAKE UP!"

Rosy and Raro both woke up, startled.

"What happened here?" Jewel said while still laughing.

"Nothing," replied Rosy in confusion.

"Ok," she said, giggling while walking away.

Raro and Rosy got up and followed Jewel over to Rex and the others.

"How did you all sleep?" Jewel asked them.

"Pretty good," Rex said.

"Let's show you guys around."

After walking for a little while, Jewel and Raro showed the gang a place the wildlife called 'house alley.' It looked like a long alley with multiple houses on one side and only two on the other. As they got closer, they heard bickering.

"You're always blaming me for everything," a young voice exclaimed.

"At least I'm bigger than you'll ever be." The second voice was gruff and mean.

Then they saw a small dog. He was a white Boston terrier with black spots. He was arguing with a big, masculine German shepherd. The argument didn't look friendly. The small dog was near a big house with a beautiful yard, and the German shepherd was across the wash behind a smaller house.

Rex went over towards the small dog's house. It was surrounded by a long, black, metal fence. The small dog saw Rex coming over in the wash. He jumped off of the patio chair he'd been sitting on and walked to an opening in the fence.

"Are you crazy?" Jewel hissed. "Rex, we don't go that close to the houses!"

"What are you two arguing about?" Rex asked the small dog.

"Oh, we're just arguing. That ding-a-ling is always complaining about all types of things all day long."

"I heard that!"

"Shut up, Coop!" the small dog yelled, and the two started arguing again.

Rex interrupted and spoke to the Boston terrier. "What's your name?"

"My name is Charlie."

"Hi, Charlie. My name is Rex. I'm an Alaskan malamute."

"Well, it's nice to meet you," Charlie said. "What are you doing hanging out with those coyotes?"

Just then, a tall, slender boy came out of the large house. He had dark brown hair and glasses and was wearing a sky-blue T-shirt with gym shorts and flip-flops.

"Charlie!" he called. "Charlie, who are you barking at?"

"You'd better leave before my master sees you," Charlie said quickly, but Charlie's master had already seen Charlie at the fence and was puzzled to see another dog in the wash. Rex decided to make his escape.

"See you later," Charlie called as Rex ran back to the coyotes.

"What were you doing?" Jewel snapped at him.

"I was just wondering why they were arguing."

He heard her grumble angrily under her breath.

They turned at started walking back to the open desert. As they walked, Rex saw something fly swiftly over them. He stopped and to see what it was. The rest of the group stopped as well.

"Why did you stop?" Lilly asked. "Is something wrong?"

As Rex opened his mouth to speak, a tiny bird swooped down and dove straight for Rex. He ducked his head quickly. The tiny brown bird swooped back up and landed on a tall green tree that had no leaves and two large, outstretched arms. The tiny bird had brown speckled feathers and a slightly curved black beak. Rex went to put his paws up on the tree to get a better view of the bird.

"Don't touch it!" the little bird called loudly.

Rex put his paws back on the ground. "Why can't I touch it?"

"It's a cactus! They have thorns that hurt! Why would you touch it?"

Rex then noticed the small, sharp spines covering the entire cactus. "Oh. I see. Why were you going to attack me?"

"I wasn't going to attack you," said the little bird. "I'm just curious about you and your friends."

Rex was curious about the bird, too. "Ah. Well, I'm Rex. I'm an Alaskan malamute, and these are my friends, and the coyotes we just met yesterday."

"I know them," the tiny brown bird said.

Rex then asked, "What your name?"

"I'm Ren. I'm a cactus wren, one of many. Me and my kind are the Arizona state bird." She looked at the bunch and said, "Why are you six here? I've never seen you guys in this neighborhood, and it's odd that you're friends with the coyotes. Normally the dogs in this neighborhood stay away from the coyotes. And we don't usually see wolves at all, until recently."

Rex explained to Ren why they were there with the coyotes. As he was finishing up, they heard a reedy voice call out, "Ren? Ren? Where are you, Ren?"

"I'm over here, Arthur."

Rex and the others saw a bird that was much bigger than

Ren running quickly across the ground. He ran up next to the cactus. He had black and brown feathers, an oversized, dark bill, twig-like legs, and broad, black tail feathers with white tips. Strangely, though most of his head was covered with normal brown feathers, on the very top were reddish-orange feathers that looked like a flame coming out of his head. He also had interesting, blazing orange eyes.

Only when Arthur reached the cactus and Ren did he notice the five dogs, a red wolf, and two coyotes. He promptly turned to run away.

"Arthur, stop!" Rex called.

Arthur stopped, petrified by fear of the bigger animals. Rex walked up to him. "Hi, I'm Rex, and these are my friends." He then explained how they got there.

The bird had relaxed and now seemed impressed. "As Ren has stated, my name is Arthur. I'm a roadrunner, it's a pleasure to make your acquaintance." As he spoke, he ran circles around Rex. Rex got dizzy trying to follow him.

"Arthur, stop making Rex dizzy," Ren said.

Arthur stopped and chuckled.

Rex tried to walk back to the group, but he staggered before collapsing.

Arthur winced. "Sorry."

Lilly walked over to Rex and helped him up. The whole group set off together, with Ren flying overhead and Arthur running alongside them. He was a very agile bird and quick on his feet. He could run very fast, and seemed to be very nice and polite.

After a while they found a big old lizard sunning himself on rock. The group stopped and Ren perched on a nearby branch. Seeing he had company, the old lizard climbed down from his sunny rock and ambled toward them.

"Hello, Ren; hello, Arthur. How are you two? I see you're with the coyotes and some new faces today."

"Hi, Gila, how are you?" Ren said.

"It's 'Heela,' Ren. It's spelled with a 'G' but sounds like an 'H.' I'm doing good."

"How does that change things?" Ren muttered, confused, but she shook her head and introduced her new friends. "This is Rex, Lilly, Alpha, Beta, Duke, and Rosy."

"It's a pleasure meeting you all." Gila joined them as they walked down the wash.

Rex noticed Raro and Rosy walking close together. They were bonding, and he was happy for them.

Suddenly Rex heard something slither near a bush and he tensed. He took one more step and then jumped back just as a large snake struck at him with his mouth wide open.

Having barely missed Rex's face, the snake coiled back up, hissing angrily. It bared its sharp fangs and rattled its tail menacingly before it started slithered swiftly back towards a petrified Rex.

"What are you doing here? You've made a big mis-s-stake," the snake hissed in fury, preparing to strike again.

Another snake leaped out from under the dirt that had been camouflaging it. She struck at the first snake.

"Josh, stop that!" she snapped. She then apologized, "I'm so sorry. I will talk with him later. I'm Diamond. I'm a diamondback rattlesnake, like this troublemaker. His name is Joshua, but he likes to be called Josh."

"I'm s-s-so s-s-sorry," Jake said apologetically.

"That so stereotypical," Diamond said in disgust.

"But Diamond. . . ." he protested before she cut him off with a glare. He sighed. "Sorry."

As they all continued walking, Ren and Arthur came up to Rex.

"Hiya," Arthur said with a beaming grin.

Rex looked over, "Oh, hi, Arthur and Ren."

"So, you're from Alaska?" Ren asked.

"Yeah."

"Do you miss it?" Arthur asked.

"Yeah, I miss it, but Arizona is actually pretty nice, too."

"Can I ride on your back?" Ren asked Rex. "My wings need a rest."

Rex nodded and she landed lightly on Rex's back.

She rode on Rex for a while, which didn't bother him at all. As the afternoon wore on, Ren and Arthur left, then Diamond and Jake, and finally Gila. The dogs, Rosy, and the coyotes went back to the band and rested.

"What an amazing day of exploring the area," Rex sighed.

They all talked as it got late. The sun was going down over the mountain. Its golden rays stretched out like heavenly paths with red, orange, and yellow painting the bluish-purple sky and clouds.

They all went to sleep in the same sleeping arrangements as the night before. This time, Jewel didn't tease Raro, because she noticed how happy he was with Rosy.

Rex had a dream. He was with Lilly, Alpha, Beta, Duke, Rosy, Raro, Jewel, Ren, Arthur, and an unknown grayish-brown bird. They were on the mural bridge they had crossed the day before.

He heard explosions. The buildings on either side of the bridge were crumbling and blown up. Two goons stepped out of an empty public bus that spanned a gap in the bridge between the opposing lanes of traffic. De-Vil was there, causing havoc and chaos. Rex and his friends were fighting De-Vil and the goons on the bridge. The Boss was there, also; he lit sticks of dynamite and threw them at the bridge, which blew up, breaking off a large section of the bridge. Rex felt terrified for himself and his friends. He heard the sound of raging water, and looked and saw a flash flood coming right at them. Another large piece of the bridge broke off and plunged into the raging river.

"Lilly!" he cried, looking around for her.

"Rex, watch out!" Lilly cried just before De-Vil tackled him onto the hard concrete. De-Vil's fangs were bared; he was foaming at the mouth, his eyes crazed and blood red.

Rex woke up with a jolt, waking up Lilly as well. He stood for a moment and then took off running into the desert. Lilly ran after him, afraid and confused.

Rex panted as he ran, shaking from the dream. *What was that? It felt too real to be a dream, but....* He slowed his pace, his mind spinning.

Lilly ran and finally caught a glimpse of Rex between some bushes. She ran over to him. "Are you okay? What happened?"

"I had a horrible dream." He was still shaking. "It was like ... it was actually happening. You were there, and everybody else. It felt so real. Not like a dream." He thought back on his dream and fear tensed the muscles in his throat. He tried to speak, to explain the dream, but he could only choke out the words, "Explosions . . . the bridge, the river . . . goons, De-Vil, El Loco . . . so much chaos." He gasped and shuddered. "Horrible."

"It was just a nightmare," she reassured him, putting a paw on him to calm him down. She stayed close to him as they walked back to where they had been sleeping. Lilly let Rex sleep closer to her because she knew he wasn't okay. She fell asleep. Rex lay awake, one thought circling in his mind. "That wasn't a dream; it wasn't a nightmare; so what could it have been?"

Rex finally fell asleep, exhausted, but then he heard a voice yelling demonically, "JOIN ME, OR EVERYTHING YOU KNOW AND EVERYONE YOU LOVE AND TRUST WILL BE THE DEATH OF YOU!!!!!"

Rex sprung awake and looked around, but he didn't know who said it, and no one else seemed to have heard anything. He settled in closer to Lilly and thought, *Why is this happening to me? This is so strange. This has never happened to me before.* Finally, he managed to doze back to sleep.

In the morning they all woke up and began visiting.

Rex went over to Jewel. "What's for breakfast?"

"Prickly pear fruit."

Rex was intrigued by the notion.

"Do you want to come and help me get some?"

"I'd be glad to."

She led the way to search for some prickly pear cactuses. As they walked, Jewel noticed the scar on Rex's shoulder. "What's that from?"

He looked at it. "Before my friends and I were snatched

from Alaska, we went on a dog sled trip. One night Lilly and I were outside and had a skirmish with a timber wolf. I fought him, but he bit me deep there on my shoulder. I fell and was bleeding pretty heavily. Lilly took care of him and came to my aid. The scar has been there ever since."

"Lilly seems very important to you," Jewel observed. "How long have you two been friends?"

"Lilly is very important to me, and she knows it. I first met her when my master was younger, so I've known her for a long time . . . since my childhood."

"Wow, you are good friends," Jewel said in awe.

"I have had the most amazing travels with her. She has been my inspiration, and we are really close."

"Do you like her?"

He nodded. "Yeah." He wasn't embarrassed by admitting the truth this time. "I've had a crush on her since the day we met, but I try to keep those feelings inside. I don't want her to know. If she doesn't like me the way I like her . . . oh, this is foolish. You don't want to hear all of this."

"Yes, I do, and it's not foolish. You just stated why, and it doesn't seem foolish at all to me."

They kept walking. *Yeah, Jewel is right.* Rex thought. *Lilly has been my best friend as long as I can remember. I help her and she does the same for me.*

Jewel and Rex found a large patch of prickly pears. The cacti had a whole bunch of pads shaped like ping-pong paddles, green and spiny, small and big, thick and thin. The fruit grew on the tops of the pads. The fruits were small, oval-shaped, and a shade of magenta, and there were a lot of them. Jewel looked around for something to use to get the magenta fruit off. She found a long cactus rib that had belonged to a withering cactus whose green spiny exterior had rotted and fallen off, exposing its woody ribs.

"This'll do," she said happily, grabbing the long cactus rib in her mouth. "You'd better stand back; this might get messy," she advised Rex, who did as she asked.

Jewel held the long cactus rib in her mouth like a baseball bat and swung it toward the magenta fruit. She whacked off fruit after fruit until a good number were scattered on the ground.

"Can you help me gather some of these prickly pear fruits?" Jewel dropped the long cactus rib onto the dusty ground. Rex nodded. "Be gentle with them; they're a bit prickly," she said, gathering the fruit in her mouth.

Rex grabbed the rest of the small magenta fruits. *Jewel was right, they are a bit prickly,* he thought as he carried the tiny prickly fruits back to the camp.

While Rex and Jewel were gone, Duke was trying to amuse himself, but he was alone and bored. He went over to where Alpha and Beta were talking in the shade of some bushes.

"What are you two talking about?" he cut into their conversation.

"Ugh . . . Duke, can't you take a hint?" Alpha said.

Duke was confused. "Uh . . . no?"

Alpha was irritated. "Can you leave us alone? Sheesh!"

Duke's head drooped, and he walked away, dejected.

"Alpha!" Beta said in shock.

"What?" he said defensively. "He's always disturbing us!"

"You could have been nicer to him," she said sincerely.

Alpha felt ashamed.

Duke looked for someone else to talk to. He saw Raro talking with Rosy and he walked over to them, feeling unhappy.

"Oh, hi Duke," Rosy said pleasantly when he got over to them. "How are you doing?" He didn't say anything, and that worried her. "Are you okay?"

"Yeah, I'm fine. I just got yelled at."

"By whom?"

"Alpha."

"Oh yeah, that Alpha seems like a strong fella," Raro said. "Why did he yell at you?"

"Alpha and I are good friends, but he gets mad at me when I barge into conversations, which is a bad habit of mine."

"You can talk with us," Rosy said with a smile. "Come sit down."

Duke sat down, feeling much happier.

Lilly sat alone, pondering what had happened last night with Rex. *Ok, Rex had a nightmare. But normally in Alaska when he would have a nightmare, he would wake up and then calm down. This time he ran willy-nilly into the desert and he could barely talk about it.* She remembered what he had managed to say. *"Explosions . . . the bridge, the river . . . goons, De-Vil, El Loco . . . so much chaos. Horrible." Ok, De-Vil is De-Vil, and the goons are the Boss's goons. El Loco is obviously the Boss. The bridge could be either the damaged train bridge where Rex knocked De-Vil off or the bridge we crossed a couple days ago. But he spoke of a river, as well as horrible chaos and explosions. I understand the first few, but the others have me stumped.*

It sounds like he was trying to describe his nightmare, a nightmare about the Boss and his goons; but why was he so upset? Then she had an epiphany. *Wait! Maybe Rex felt the dream, or nightmare or whatever it was, and it was real, at least felt real to him. I need to get Rex to tell me what he saw.*

She saw Rex and Jewel coming back with the fruit and got up to meet them.

"We got some prickly pear fruits!" Jewel called around the fruits in her mouth. "Get 'em while they're ripe, but be careful—there are tiny spines on its skin."

They all gathered around, and Jewel and Rex dropped their magenta fruits to the ground.

After everyone had eaten breakfast, Rex sat alone while the others talked or explored the desert nearby. He thought about what had happened last night and the words he heard afterwards: *Join me or everything you know and everyone you trust will be the death of you!* Whoever or whatever had said it had sounded demonic.

As Rex lay there, suddenly he was lost in thought.

He saw himself lying on the road of the destroyed bridge. Lilly stood next to him, watching things unfold. The wildlife he met the day before and the gang were watching also. He felt pain throughout his entire body, and he could taste blood and dirt in his mouth. His vision was blurred, and the only thing he could see was the public bus straddling the gap in the bridge. On top of the bus, Rex saw a wolf and a person wearing fancy white clothing. He smelled dynamite mixed with ash and dust. The bus started to slip, and the wolf attacked the man in the fancy white clothing, pinning him down on the roof of the bus.

"Wait, wait, wait! You can't do this! We're partners!" he heard the man gasp in a cowardly tone.

"Do you think I would be a partner with you?" the wolf snarled like a demon.

The man seemed shocked that the wolf would talk to him like that. Though he was in pain, Rex heard all of the animals talking but couldn't quite understand what they were saying. They said a name and then "actually spoke to." But as he struggled to hear anything else, a surge of pain shot through his entire body. Suddenly another explosion rocked the bridge, making the bus shift more and more until, finally, it slowly slid off the bridge into the raging river below.

As he fell, the man yelled in Spanish, "So this is my punishment for life!"

As the wolf plunged down with the bus, he roared, "I'M NOT DONE WITH YOU ALL. I'LL BE BACK!"

Rex came back to reality with a gasp. "It happened again!"

A few animals nearby heard him.

"What happened again?" Alpha asked.

"Nothing," Rex choked out. The others looked at him strangely and went back to what they were doing.

Lilly padded over to Rex. "Are you okay? You've been acting strangely."

Rex turned to her with fear in his eyes. "The same thing happened again as last night, only this time I was awake. I had another glimpse of the bridge and bus with all of its smells and I felt like I was there."

"It happened while you were awake? Tell me exactly what you saw last night and just now."

He told her every detail.

Lilly shook her head. "I'm not sure what it all means. Hopefully it's just the stress of the last few days working through you and it will go away soon."

"I hope so."

They all spent the rest of the day relaxing with the coyotes, then settled in for another night. Almost everyone had fallen asleep.

Raro was lying down with Rosy. She was bashful and quiet. "Hey, are you okay?" he asked her quietly. "You're quiet tonight."

She didn't answer at first, just watched the daylight sink below the horizon with its bright and beautiful colors. When it started getting dark, she asked him, "Do you think I'm a monster?"

"What? Of course not!"

She didn't look at him.

"Why would you think that?" Raro asked, concerned.

"I don't know . . . over the past several days, I've had these violent outbursts and I say hurtful things. I violent things that I would never say or do when I am myself. It's terrifying—I hear an ominous voice in my head that almost forces me to say and do these awful things," Rosy muttered nervously. "It makes me feel like I'm an impulsive and violent monster."

"Rosy, I don't think you're a monster. You are the most pleasant, kind, pretty, intelligent, funny, and caring animal that I've ever met, and that's saying a lot."

His kind words filled her entire body with warmth and joy. He was one of the kindest and most honest animals she had ever met, too. She felt something she hadn't felt in months.

Wait. Why am I feeling this way? Do I like Raro? No, I already like Hunter, though it's been so long since I've seen him. But they're very similar . . . kind, happy, intelligent, nice, handsome, and brave. Stay focused, Rosy! I guess the only difference is that Hunter is a Mexican gray wolf and Raro is a coyote.

Suddenly her confusion and frustration burst out. "Oh my, this is so crazy! I had a perfect life until those crooks took me and my family. I then met my scientist friends and got stolen again. I meet Hunter, the pack splits up and we have to leave each other. Again, off on another adventure when we came to that mountain and De-Vil turned into a traitor! But then I met Rex and his friends. . . ." she ranted on.

Raro patiently listened as Rosy spilled her frustration. Then with a sincere voice, he reassured her. "It's fine, it's fine. As you said, there were some great times and awesome memories, but you can't always have those good times in life without experiencing their opposites, like anger, strife, sadness, and pain."

She calmed down and looked over at him.

Their eyes met, and Raro spoke softly. "If no one will defend you, I will."

Rosy smiled and laid her head down, slowly drifting off to sleep. *I hope this works out.*

Rex couldn't sleep. He was being tortured by that same sentence. *Join me or everything you know and everyone you trust will be the death of you!* He was scared. Then he remembered a song his master's parents would sing to his master as a kid when he was sad or scared. Later in life, the master would sing it to all of his dogs when they were sad or scared. Now Rex sang it softly to himself.

The Spirit of Alaska, let her winter winds rage.
But it won't hurt as it drifts over the sky,
Where the northern lights dance,
Where its bright colors shine.
Where the wolves run across the tundra
And the fish swim in the icy turquoise rivers.
Where the courageous mountaineers climb and scale
The towering and treacherous mountains.
Where the Natives lived long, long ago,
And their descendants now live today.
Where the lucky men with their courageous dogs
Brave the winter storms to find their riches of oil and gold
Beneath the icy, snow packed rocky ground.
Where the spirit of the wild
And courageous people and animals live and survive.

As he was singing, Lilly heard him and opened her eyes. She saw Rex quietly singing the song, and she felt happy. He sang it twice more then drifted off to sleep. Lilly chuckled softly, not wanting to wake him, then quietly she started singing the song to soothe him with her own soft voice.

As she relaxed and fell asleep, both were unaware of the eyes watching them from the shadows.

CHAPTER 8

ACTING CASUAL

The following morning, Lilly woke up and noticed Rex snug up against her. She whispered in his ear, "Wake up, sleepyhead."

He woke up to her kind and lovely face. He started humming "The Spirit of Alaska" again, and Lilly hummed along with him. Alpha woke next and heard them humming the tune he fondly remembered. Alpha didn't just hum it with them, he sang it. They were surprised, because Alpha didn't sing too often.

The Spirit of Alaska, let her winter winds rage.
But it won't hurt as it drifts over the sky,
Where the northern lights dance,
Where its bright colors shine.
Where the wolves run across the tundra

And the fish swim in the icy turquoise rivers.
Where the courageous mountaineers climb and scale
The towering and treacherous mountains.
Where the Natives lived long, long ago,
And their descendants now live today.
Where the lucky men with their courageous dogs
Brave the winter storms to find their riches of oil and gold
Beneath the icy, snow packed rocky ground.
Where the spirit of the wild
And courageous people and animals live and survive.

His singing woke Beta. She opened her eyes, annoyed, but when she heard the tune, she settled down and sang with Alpha as Rex and Lilly joined in with the words. Duke woke next and started singing, too.

When Raro and Rosy woke up and heard singing, they investigated and saw Rex and his friends all singing.

"What are you guys singing?" Raro asked at the end of the song.

"'The Spirit of Alaska,'" Rex replied. "It's a song our master used to sing to us."

"Can we sing with you?" Rosy asked.

"Sure."

"Will you teach us the words to the song?" Raro asked.

Rex taught them the words, saying them instead of singing them. The friends sang it together in laughter and glee. Jewel woke up to the cheerful tune and walked over to where the others had gathered.

"What are you all singing?" she asked them, laughing.

"THE SPIRIT OF ALASKA!" they all shouted in joy. All of

the coyotes and wildlife in the area heard them yell.

She laughed again. "Ok, I'll leave you all to it."

After another breakfast of prickly pear fruit, they all walked toward the house alley and could hear Charlie and the German shepherd bickering, as before.

"Long time, no see!" They heard a familiar voice call overhead. "How have you guys been?"

Ren fluttered down to land on Rex's head as Arthur zipped out of the bushes.

"Can we join you guys?" Arthur asked.

They all nodded.

"So how have you all been?" Ren asked.

They all responded with "fine" and "good."

As they continued toward the house alley, Ren heard all of them humming "The Spirit of Alaska."

"So you were the ones who were singing that pleasant tune earlier this morning!" she said. "Arthur and I heard it before breakfast."

As they came to some taller bushes, Rex wandered in close to them. As he was about to put his paw past the bush, Jewel yelled, "Don't go past that point!"

He pulled his paw back. "Why?"

"It's our boundary," she said firmly. "We don't pass it, and that goes for you, too."

"Boundary? What boundary?"

"The boundary that keeps us safe. We can't cross over to where the humans are. We might be seen or hurt by them. They think we're the enemy."

Rex shrugged. "You can't, but we can. We're domestics; you're feral," he stated mildly. Jewel squinted her eyes and growled at him, and he was taken aback, wondering if he'd pushed her past her limit.

"Just let it slide," Lilly said to both of them.

They turned to keep walking, but Rex was curious about what was beyond the bushes, and he was irritated. He knew Jewel was trying to protect him, but he and his friends from Alaska were domestic animals. They could roam freely, unlike his wild friends the coyotes. Rosy was in between, because she was wild, but had been around humans enough to act like a dog when she needed to.

Abruptly, Rex turned and ran through the bushes.

"You've gotta be kidding me," Jewel said.

Lilly and the other dogs followed after him. They found themselves on a quiet, winding neighborhood road.

"Why did you do that?" Lilly asked. "Jewel told you not to."

"We're domestic, Lilly. We can come here, just like I told her."

"You provoked her," Lilly said wryly, "and I saved your tail."

He nodded in agreement. "Thanks."

Suddenly, they saw an Australian shepherd with copper fur, a white underbelly, and blue eyes sprinting toward them down the road. She stopped right in front of them. Jewel, Raro, Rosy, Ren, and Arthur watched carefully from back behind the bushes, where they wouldn't be spotted.

"Howdy y'all!" the Australian shepherd greeted them. "I'm Bandit."

They were a little unsure about this new dog, but Rex introduced himself. "I'm Rex, and these are my friends."

Bandit grinned. "Well, it's nice to meet y'all. We don't see many dogs like you around here."

"Yeah, we're actually from Alaska," Rex explained, "but we got kidnapped by the Boss's goons."

"Alaska?" she asked in shock. "Y'all are from Alaska, and you say y'all done got stolen by the notorious Boss? That's horrible!"

"Where are we?" Rex asked her.

"You're in Casanova Estates, the most pleasant place y'all have ever been."

"Who lives here?" Alpha asked.

"Lots of people, dogs, cats . . . all sorts." She pointed to Charlie's house. "Like, Charlie lives over there up on that rise." Then she looked further down the road, "And that there house is where I live with my masters." Now she looked past Charlie's house. "And behind Charlie's house you have Coop . . . or Cooper. I don't rightly know what they called 'im, but that's where he lives." Then she looked at a long, tall brick wall. "And behind that there wall is where Napoleon and Anna live." She turned and looked at the gang. "Would y'all like to take a stroll with me?"

The dogs nodded and followed Bandit down the road. She noticed that Rex walked close to Lilly and that Alpha did the same with Beta.

"Do you four like each other?" she asked.

Both Rex and Alpha became red-faced and said in embarrassment, "No, we're just friends."

Lilly and Beta also blushed and said, "Yeah, just friends."

"Oh, I am so sorry," Bandit apologized. "Please forgive me."

"It's ok," they all said.

Duke was a little ahead of them, being a little crazy as usual.

"Is he always like this? Or is this here new behavior?" Bandit asked.

"He's always been like this," Rex laughed. "He's been this crazy since the first day we met him."

Duke ran faster, not looking where he was going.

"Ah, mister, you should look where you're goin'!" Bandit called. "If you're not careful, you're goin' to run into a jumpin' cactus! It's not pretty when you run into one of them."

But Duke wasn't listening, and he ran right into one. His side was promptly covered in fine, furry, barbed cholla spines, and he whimpered in pain.

Bandit winced in sympathy. "Owww. That there's got to hurt—but you mess with the bull, you get the horns."

They all went over to him, and he was like a copper pin cushion covered in cactus.

"Are you okay?" Bandit asked.

"No," Duke moaned in pain.

"I'm sorry you're hurt, but you can't run around willy-nilly like that. You're hurt on account of you not listening to me. You just kept runnin,' and look what you done got yourself into."

"Hey," Rex protested, "You don't have to be so harsh."

"Harsh?" Bandit snapped. "You reckon I'm harsh tryin' to keep your friend out of trouble? You don't even know the meanin' of harsh. I been harsher, but your friend needs a lesson. You want him to get into more trouble?"

"Duke is Duke," Rex snapped back, proudly defending his friend. "And that's that. A lecture won't change him."

"Well, I reckon you better be careful," she warned. "Who knows if he's the kindest dog in the world or a crazed lunatic."

Rex was appalled. "You miss, are as stubborn as a bull, but you don't even care," he said, his voice rising.

"Do you know what manners are, Mister? You're talkin' to a lady! Give me the respect I deserve!"

"Oh, excuse me for my lack of manners, Miss," he said, his voice dripping with sarcasm.

"You'd better watch your mouth, Mister. You're barking up the wrong tree, and it's not gonna be pretty," she snarled.

"Stop it, both of you!" Lilly yelled.

"It's none of your business!" they both yelled back.

Lilly's kind nature was cracking like a dam about to burst. "I'm about to blow a fuse," she warned in a low voice.

"What'd you say?" Bandit stopped arguing to ask. "I didn't hear you. You gotta speak up."

"Oh, sorry; don't mind my manners," Lilly said snottily with a dash of sarcasm. They all stared at her. "You're acting like wolves! Jeez! Can't you two just get along? I don't know you very well, Miss, but you are very stubborn, and I would advise you to keep your temper in check. You both are acting like idiots, but, ugh! You were fine at the start, and Rex, I expect better of you!"

"I'm sorry, Lilly," Rex said to her with his head hung low. He had just been scolded by one of the nicest dogs in the world.

"Yeah, sorry Lilly. I do need to work on keeping my temper under control," Bandit also said shamefully.

"I forgive you both, but one thing that would put me in a better mood right now is you two forgiving each other. I wasn't the one who was in the argument," Lilly said calmly.

"Well, I'm sorry, Rex," said Bandit. "We done got off on the awful wrong foot or paw . . . but I consider you a friend, same with your four friends there. Let's get Duke some help."

"Yeah, I forgot about that," Rex chuckled sheepishly, looking at Duke. "Can you stand up?" he asked his friend.

"I'll try." Duke slowly stood up and eased himself into a walk as they all continued down the street.

"Hey, Lilly," Bandit said quietly, "I really am sorry about that earlier. I can be too darn stubborn and a little harsh, but it was on account of me tryin' to warn your friend Duke. My temper can be awful bad, but I mean well. I was wonderin' about something, though. Remember when I done said, 'Do you like each other?' Do you like Rex?"

"Yes, I like Rex. I've liked him since the first day I met him," she said softly so Rex wouldn't hear.

"I won't tell a livin' soul, I swear it."

"Thanks," Lilly said appreciatively.

"That's what friends are for."

They came around a corner and walked down a street that ended as a cul-de-sac.

"Hey, look there! Some new neighbors have done moved into the neighborhood." Bandit was looking at a one-story adobe-style house with a moving truck in the driveway. "Wait," she suddenly said, looking at her new friends in confusion. "If y'all are from Alaska, then where have y'all been sleeping? I saw y'all come outta those bushes back there."

"Yeah, we actually have been sleeping with some coyotes up the wash," Rex told her honestly.

"Do you reckon I will believe that hogwash? Cause that there is the most made-up story I've ever heard in my life."

"I'm telling the truth. I also have a friend named Rosy.

She's a red wolf."

"Stop lyin', Mister. You think I'm dumb?"

"I'm telling the truth! Why don't you believe me?" he pleaded with her. "C'mon, back me up, guys."

"He's not lying," Lilly said. "He would never lie."

"And how do I know you're not lyin' to me, too?"

"Neither Lilly nor Rex are lying. I know both of them, and they wouldn't lie about this. Besides, I was there, also," Alpha told her.

"Ugh! Now I know all three of you are lyin' to me," Bandit said in annoyance.

"They are all telling the truth!" Beta said boldly.

"Are y'all just makin' this here up, or are y'all just messing with me?!" she yelled loudly, thinking she was being played. Dead silence followed her outburst. "So y'all *was* lyin' to me," she said in anger.

"THEY'RE NOT LYING!" They all turned to stare at Duke. He calmed down and spoke to Bandit. "I know you think I'm the stupid and crazy one of the group, but they wouldn't lie. Why won't you believe us? We told you that we're from Alaska and were stolen by some goons, and you believed us—but you won't believe that we slept with our coyote friends and that we also have a red wolf as our friend? We've slept up on Mount Lemmon, run across both Marana and Tucson, been chased by an evil gray wolf named De-Vil and the Boss's goons a few days ago, and you still don't believe us?"

They all watched Duke in shock.

"Okay, I believe y'all now," Bandit said, overwhelmed.

"Finally!" Rex said in relief.

"Yeah," Lilly, Alpha, Beta, and Duke said in in unison.

Bandit asked them one more time to make sure. "So, the things y'all done told me are true."

"One hundred percent true," Rex said.

They kept walking and weren't paying much attention while in the middle of the cul-de-sac they heard a loud car horn honk right behind them. They looked and saw a car speeding right toward them and they all scattered. The car was an old tan-and-white 1976 station wagon. It parked in front of the adobe house with the moving truck in its driveway.

"The varmint who is drivin' that there car has a lot of nerve," Bandit said, annoyed.

"Well, we *were* walking right in the middle of the road, so it makes sense that cars could come up behind us," Alpha said logically.

The driver door swung open and a tall, slender man in his forties got out. He had dark brown hair and brown eyes and wore a fashionable dark suit and tie. His glasses and neat apparel made him look as sharp as a tack.

"Looks like a businessman," Alpha murmured.

The passenger door swung open next and a beautiful woman stepped out, also looking to be in her early forties. She had a rosy face and long brown hair. Graceful and poised, she wore a red blouse with a medium-length black skirt.

The back door opened and a teenage boy climbed out. He had shaggy, dark brown hair and wore a dark blue t-shirt with gray gym shorts.

"He looks hip," Duke said appreciatively.

Right behind the boy, and in the middle of an argument with him, was his younger teenage sister. She had long brown hair and was wearing a simple, sky-blue t-shirt, blue jeans, and a silver necklace with a polished vibrant green stone pendant.

"I like her," Lilly said. "She looks smart, modest, and dignified."

"So, this here must be the family that's movin' in," Bandit said quietly.

"Yeah, they look happy." Rex said with respect.

Suddenly Duke began to sway side to side, then abruptly, he collapsed.

"Duke!" Lilly cried. The dogs all started barking frantically for help, not knowing what else to do.

The teenage girl heard them barking. "What's that?" she asked her brother.

"Just some stupid dogs," he said, shrugging.

She looked back to the cul-de-sac and saw five big, barking dogs gathered around another big dog lying on the ground. "Oh my gosh, that dog needs our help!"

She ran to the dog with her brother close behind.

"He's unconscious. What's he covered in?" the boy asked.

The girl knelt next to Duke. The other five dogs pressed in closer, whining in concern.

"I'm going to help your friend," she reassured them.

The dogs eased back, trusting her.

"Mom, Dad, come help us!" she yelled urgently to her parents.

The parents saw the commotion in the cul-de-sac and hurried over to them. "Get a blanket," the father called to his wife when he saw the unconscious dog. She quickly grabbed one out of the station wagon and followed him.

"Come on, kids, we need to help this dog," he said as his wife handed him the blanket. They each took a side of the blanket, laid it down, and carefully slid Duke onto it. They gently lifted him up and walked towards their house. "Careful," the father said as the mother let go of the blanket with one hand to open the front door. They walked in and let Rex and the others follow. The house was filled with moving boxes. The family carefully lifted the blanket holding Duke onto the dining room table.

"What do we do?" the boy asked his parents.

"We pull them out, one by one," his father told him frankly.

"Won't that hurt him? And what are these things all over this dog?"

"They're cholla spines," the daughter said.

"What?" her brother asked confused.

"It's a type of cactus with super-fine barbed spines," she said, rolling her eyes at him.

"Now you're just making up words."

"It's a real word, ding-a-ling."

"Ok, nerd."

"I told you not to call me that!"

Rex and the others listened to them bickering as their father tried to touch one of the cholla spines.

"Ow! That hurt! Can you two please pipe down?" he snapped.

"Told you it would hurt," the brother muttered before both kids fell silent.

The dad looked around and then opened one of the moving boxes. "Ah yes, these will help." He pulled out some oven mitts. He then grabbed some needle-nose pliers that were lying on the counter from hanging pictures earlier.

The daughter had started checking the other dogs' tags. She went over to Bandit first. "Hey, this dog lives just around the corner from us!"

"Is that so? Maybe we can take her back to her owner after we're done," the father said as he carried the pliers back to Duke.

Then the girl checked Rex's tag. "What?" she muttered. She then quickly checked Lilly's, Alpha's, and Beta's tags. "How in the world . . . ? Dad!"

"What?" He was focused on Duke and carefully eased his mitted hand on the fine cholla spines. There were dozens of them caught in Duke's fur.

"I don't think we'll be able to return all these other dogs today."

"Why not?" he nodded at the oven mitt in satisfaction. "It just might work."

"Because these other four dogs are from Fairbanks, Alaska."

"What?!" The whole family stared at her.

Her dad took off the oven mitts and check all the tags himself. "She's right," he said to his wife. The wife and brother checked the tags, too, as the father looked at Duke's tag as he lay on the table. "This one's from Fairbanks, too."

They stared at each other. "What are they doing here in Marana?" the son asked.

The dad rubbed his forehead. "I don't know, but we've got to focus on helping this one right now." He went back to Duke, placing the oven mitts back on his hands and gently laid them on two clusters of the cholla spines. "Maybe it's good he's unconscious. This is going to hurt."

He wiggled the spines around a bit, while pushed slightly, and then yanked away, pulling most of the cholla spines clear out of Duke's skin.

"OW! THAT HURT!" Duke roared in English as he woke up. He shut his mouth quickly, but he'd already made the mistake.

"Duke!" Alpha snapped, then shut his mouth quickly, too.

"Really, Alpha," Beta said in disappointment, then she realized she'd just made the same mistake.

"Nice going, Beta," Lilly snapped, then flushed.

"Seriously, guys?" Rex said in frustration, then flinched. He looked to Bandit, but there was only an empty spot where she had previously stood. She had bolted out the open front door.

The family stared at them all with their mouths wide open before the brother spoke.

"Did those dogs just talk?"

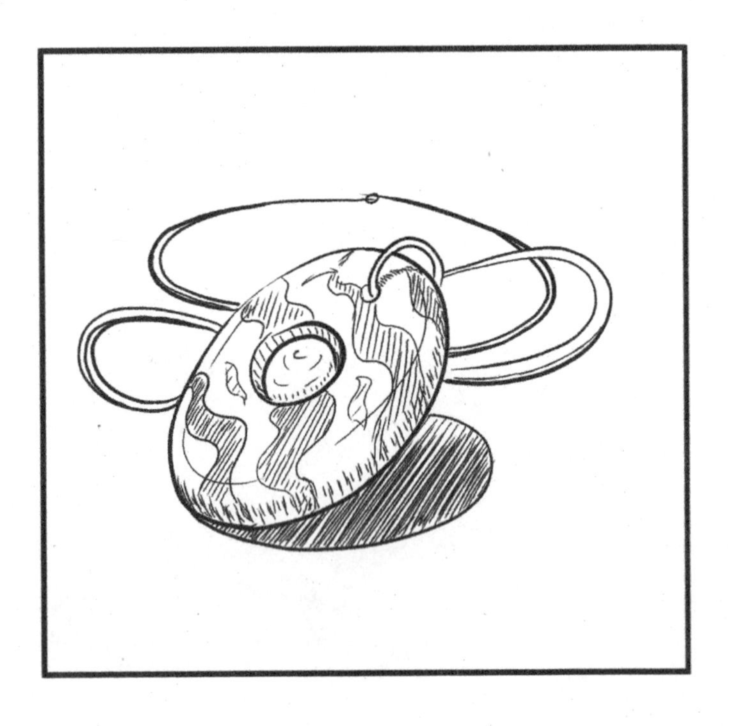

CHAPTER 9

UH-OH! THE SECRET IS EXPOSED!

"Nooooo," Rex said, trying to keep the secret. The whole family stared at all of them, speechless. Rex chuckled sheepishly.

Suddenly the mother fainted and her husband caught her. She woke up on the couch a few minutes later and said, "I had the strangest dream! There were dogs in our house, and they were talking!"

"Mom, that actually happened," the daughter said. The wife looked around and saw Rex and the others.

"You can talk to us. Is this some kind of secret we cracked wide open?" the father asked the dogs.

"Ok," Rex said reluctantly. "Hello, um . . . I'm Rex. I'm an Alaskan malamute, and these are my friends."

"Hi! I'm Lilly. I'm a Samoyed, and it's a pleasure to meet y'all." Then she caught herself. "I mean, you all. Sorry."

"Hey, I'm Alpha. I'm an Alaskan husky. How are you guys doing?"

"Um, hi, I'm Beta." Her voice was barely audible.

"Is she ok?" the father asked.

"She's a bit shy," Alpha told him.

"Hi, I'm Duke! I'm so sorry for what I have gotten you into, but thanks for taking care of me. It means a lot."

"You're welcome," the daughter replied, wide-eyed.

"I'm Matthew," the father said. "We're the Smiths. This is my wife." He put his hand on his wife's shoulder.

The wife, now sitting up on the couch, smiled kindly at the dogs. "Hi. I'm Emerald, but you can call me Emma." Rex and the others nodded, so she continued. "These are our son and our daughter," she said, looking over at her children.

"Hi, I'm Jade," the daughter said warmly. "It's nice to meet you all."

"Hey," her brother said, giving them a relaxed nod, "I'm Samuel, but you can call me Sam."

Then the father asked them the question they had been waiting for. "How can you talk? And why are you here? How did you get here?"

"This has to be a secret," Rex said seriously. "You can't tell anyone about this, or everything will turn into chaos. Do you promise?"

Matthew turned to his family. "Ok, Smiths, we have to keep their secret. Do we promise?"

"We promise," the family said in unison.

"Can only you guys talk?" Jade asked the dogs. "Or can other animals talk as well?"

Rex sighed, really not wanting to talk about the logistics,

so Lilly explained.

"Well, you're going to be shocked, but it's not just us who can talk. Every animal on earth can talk like humans, but what language they speak depends where they live. We're from Alaska, so we can speak American English, but a coyote from Mexico would speak Spanish. Animals can also learn different languages, just like humans."

"So every animal can talk?" Sam asked.

"Yes," Lilly answered. "Dogs, cats, bears, wolves, coyotes, birds, insects, lizards, fish . . . all kinds. They can talk."

"Wow, that's amazing!" Jade said in awe. "We will keep your secret with our lives."

"But why don't animals talk to humans?" Sam asked.

"Because of the law of nature," Rex sighed regretfully.

"The law of nature?" Jade asked, intrigued. "Wait, is that when dogs had to survive a long time ago up North when it was primitive and dangerous? They had to listen to their master, and if they bit their master they got hit in the head with a club, teaching them not to do it again?"

"You're probably thinking of the law of club and fang from Jack London's novel, *Call of The Wild*," Emerald corrected her.

Rex replied, slightly annoyed. "I mean it's the law of animal nature. It's what all animals follow: feral, domestic, carnivore, herbivore, omnivores . . . we all obey. It might not seem like a big deal if just one human being finds out, but then the person can't hold it in and tells his or her friends and acquaintances, and they tell their friends and acquaintances, and on and on. Then people would expect animals to act like them, but animals aren't the same. Eventually, no one would know the difference between the law of human nature and the law of animal nature. It would become chaotic. Some days animals might act like humans and humans like animals because they don't know the difference between who's the logical one and who's the instinctual one. It's better we keep things separate and clear."

Jade nodded in agreement.

"Ok, we'll keep your secret," Sam agreed. "But if you're from Alaska, how did you get down here to Arizona?"

"We're sled dogs," Rex explained. "We haul cargo to towns and cities around Alaska. One time we went to Nome, where Balto and his teammates delivered the much-needed serum back in the day. It was amazing!"

"Who's Balto?" Sam asked, confused.

"He was a famous sled dog," Jade explained.

"Let's get back on track," Lilly suggested. "Just after our last trip, which was its own adventure, we had gotten home to Fairbanks with our master when we were stolen by some strange men. They tranquilized us and we woke up here. We found out later that they were goons sent by the infamous 'Boss.'"

"The who?" Sam asked confused.

"He's the head of an organization that steals exotic animals."

"Are you talking about El Loco, the criminal animal lord?" Jade asked Lilly.

Lilly nodded.

"El Loco?" Emerald asked Jade in confusion.

"He's the guy whose entourage got busted for trying to steal animals from the Denver Zoo," Jade replied.

"Did you live in Denver?" Rex asked.

"No, we lived in a small town near there called Annville," Matthew explained.

"Why did you guys move?" Alpha asked.

"I got a promotion at my job," Matthew replied with a beaming grin.

"Called it," Alpha muttered.

"Let's get back to your story," Emerald said.

"So . . . you're saying that you got stolen by José 'El Loco' Tonto's henchmen?" Jade asked, and the gang all nodded.

"How did you get away from them?" asked Sam.

"We managed to escape nearby at that small airport and jumped on a train. We eventually ended up on Mount Lemmon."

"How did you get back here in our neighborhood?" Jade asked.

"We had a run-in with some Mexican gray wolves up on the mountain and had to run away," Rex explained. "Although, we made friends with a red wolf, Rosy, who was with them. Her family had also been taken by the Boss's goons. So we headed to his mansion just south of Tucson to see if we could find or help them."

Duke cut in, "At the mansion, we found out that we had another enemy. He tried to attack us and we had to take off running again. It was scary but exciting!"

"Another enemy?" asked Emerald.

Rex nodded grimly. "A sick and twisted, evil, Mexican gray wolf named De-Vil. Apparently, he's now working with the Boss."

"Rex fought him off," Alpha threw in, "and we eventually ended up nearby in the desert. This is where we met some coyotes that live in your area. They showed us this neighborhood, and we had just made friends with your neighbor's dog, Bandit, prior to meeting you all."

"Wow," Matthew said to the dogs. "You've been on quite a journey. If you'd like, you can stay here with us until we can find a way to get you guys back home to your master. First, let's get the rest of the cactus out of your friend and then finish getting our stuff off the moving truck."

They got every last spine out of Duke's side, and by the evening had the rest of their boxes and furniture off the truck, into the house, and more or less stacked in their appropriate rooms.

Jade and Sam collapsed on the couch while Rex and the others rested on the carpet nearby. It was getting late.

"I'm tired. I think I'm going to lie down," Jade said sleepily.

"Ditto," Sam said.

"Us, too," Rex and the gang agreed, yawning.

Emerald stood between two doors and said to them, "Boys to the right, girls to the left."

As Jade and Sam went to their new rooms, Rex and Alpha tried to follow Lilly and Beta into Jade's room. Emerald redirected the boys to join Sam and the girls to join Jade. Rex, Alpha, and Duke follow Sam into his room. It was a bit bigger than Jade's bedroom. Rex looked around Sam's room. His queen-sized bed was messy and his sheets were hanging off the bed down to the carpeted floor. A heap of dirty clothes was piled next to his closet and a tower of cardboard moving boxes were stacked on each other precariously.

Sam went to one of the boxes and opened it up. He pulled out a large red-and-orange cloth banner. He grabbed some thumbtacks from the box and tacked the banner on the wall. The background of the banner was all red; an orange X went from each corner of the banner to its center. In the middle, a knight in shining silver armor was astride a brown, armored horse that was rearing back. In his right gauntlet, the knight held a long lance with a soccer ball impaled on its end; in his left gauntlet, he held a large red shield painted with an orange, roaring lion. Under the knight and horse in bold letters were the words ANNVILLE KNIGHTS.

"Sleep anywhere you like, except my bed. Capisce?" He ran and leaped like he was trying to fly, body-slammed face-down on his bed, and lay motionless.

Rex began looking for a spot to sleep in the mess around them. "Hey Sam," Duke whispered. "Where can we sleep?"

"Anywhere but up here," Sam muttered sluggishly.

"Come on, let's get some sleep," Rex said sleepily to Alpha and Duke. They each found a spot on the carpeted floor and quickly dozed off.

Jade opened her door and let Lilly and Beta in first, then closed the door behind herself. She flipped a switch and light filled the dark room. Lilly and Beta looked around. A ceiling fan spun above them, and purple gem-like orbs hung at the ends of the fan cords, glittering in the light. Jade's room was small and the walls were a sky blue—but what stood out most in the room were her colorful curtains. They were every color of the rainbow, and during the day, as sunlight shone through them, each color would fall vibrantly across the floor in a beautiful vertical pattern.

"Your curtains are very pretty. They remind me of the

rainbows I've seen in Alaska," Lilly told Jade.

"Yeah, they also remind me of the northern lights," Beta smiled.

"You're right, I see it," Lilly said, staring at the colorful curtains.

"Good eye, Beta." Jade grabbed the two rainbow-colored curtain panels and closed them with a flip. "Yeah, I got them for my tenth birthday. You should have seen my face—it was like I got a rainbow for a birthday present."

Jade grabbed her backpack, set it on the desk in front of the window, and opened it up. It was filled with books, binders, and things from school. She pulled out a laptop and set it on the desk. Jade then opened two neatly labeled moving boxes filled with books of all colors and sizes, and put them alphabetically into her small white bookcase until it was filled.

"Wow, that's a lot of books," Beta said looking at the book-filled bookcase.

"Yeah, I've collected them over the years. I love books. They have a wonderful way of conveying facts and knowledge, but I really love how they tell stories. History books are my favorite."

Jade continued to organize the rest of her room. She plugged in her alarm clock on a nightstand, next to a dark brown lamp with a blue shade. Next to the lamp was a golden hourglass and a carved wooden camel figurine that had designs like of leaves and flowers all over it. Jade then unpacked three rolled-up posters, unrolled them, and taped them up on the wall. The first poster depicted the famous painting of General George Washington with his men crossing the Delaware river. Under the picture were the words "Perseverance and spirit have done wonders in all ages. - George Washington, First President of the United States of America and General." The second poster depicted the famous painting of Napoleon crossing the alps on his intrepid steed and words that read, "Impossible is a word to be found only in the dictionary of fools. - Napoleon Bonaparte, French General and Statesman." And the last one depicted Lao Tzu, an old, bald sage with white hair on the back of his head and a wispy white beard and mustache. He was dressed in a yellow silk robe and wore a calm, wise look on his face. The poster read, "Being deeply loved by someone gives you strength, while loving someone deeply gives you courage. - Lao Tzu, Chinese Philosopher."

Jade jumped down from her bed, reached into a large box, and grabbed a roll of double-sided tape and a plastic container filled with white plastic stars that had a greenish tint to them. One at a time, she grabbed a star and a tiny piece of tape and placed them all over her ceiling until the container was empty. Jade, Lilly, and Beta looked at the ceiling covered in plastic stars as Jade yawned and said, "Sleep anywhere you like."

She grabbed a book from her bookshelf and placed it on her nightstand, and then looked at Lilly and Beta and asked, "Wanna see something magical?"

"Yeah," they chorused.

She turned off her light and her room was flooded by darkness—except for the green plastic stars glowing on the ceiling. They were clustered in constellation-like patterns, making the room look like the night sky.

Lilly and Beta gazed in wonder at the glowing stars as Jade opened her closet and pulled out a yellow nightgown adorned with white daisy flowers. She got into her nightgown and then snuggled down into bed. Lilly and Beta lay on the floor nearby, but Jade said, "Come on, guys, you can sleep up here with me."

They were hesitant at first, but then jumped up and settled comfortably on her bed. Jade turned on the lamp on her nightstand, grabbed her book, and opened to where her bookmark was. She slowly read through the pages for several minutes.

"What are you reading?" Beta asked curiously.

"Oh, it's one of my favorite books of all time. *Call of the Wild* by Jack London. It's a real page-turner. Since I was little, I've been interested in learning about the world around me and the things in it. So naturally, I love to read about lands far from Annville that had interesting upbringings and histories. Myths and legends are my favorites, and how civilizations and groups of people come to be and interact," Jade explained. "But I really love to read just about anything I can get my hands on," she said, chuckling. "When I was in elementary school back in Annville, I was known as the 'Bookworm Bullet' because I would run as fast as I could to the library to see what new books were there that I could read. I basically read every book in that small library. If I wasn't at the school library or the Annville public library, I was reading books at home that my parents had collected over the years. When I was twelve, I was looking for a new book to read." Jade looked down at the book she was reading and smiled. "I found this book and read it. I couldn't stop reading it. It was the most interesting book I had ever read in my life. The perilous adventure of Buck, the pampered pooch of the blazing South who turns into a king of the wild great white North. Honestly, Jack London is a true storyteller. The way he portrays the Klondike Gold Rush in the Canadian Yukon Territory is phenomenal," Jade told them with excitement.

Jade turned to her new friends eagerly. "What is Alaska really like?"

Lilly's face twisted as she and Beta thought.

"It's home," Lilly said nostalgically.

"It's wonderful," Beta exclaimed with happiness.

"Every day was a new adventure with our master on our trips," Lilly told Jade. "Denali and the national park it sits on are the crown jewel of the Alaskan wilderness, but Alaska itself is the crown where the jewels rest. There are so many places in Alaska that tourists and nature enthusiasts would give an entire arm or leg to see," Lilly explained.

"Have you guys ever been to Canada?" Jade asked them. They both shook their heads.

"We haven't been to Canada, but our master has," Beta told Jade.

"We have been close to the Canadian border on several of our trips," Lilly added.

Jade opened her mouth to say something, then closed it quickly. Lilly and Beta both noticed and looked at each other.

"Is everything all right?" Beta asked, concerned.

"Yeah, you looked like you had something to say," said Lilly.

"Do . . . do you guys miss Alaska?" Jade asked them.

"Yes, we miss it a lot. It's where we were born and it's

where we were taken in by our master," Lilly said. "Arizona is an interesting place, but it doesn't have the same deep nostalgia for us like Alaska."

"Sorry! I . . . I was just wondering what Alaska was like. I didn't want to get you both homesick," Jade quickly apologized.

"It's okay, you were just being curious." Lilly reassured her, making her worried expression melt away.

"But in all seriousness, I promise that my family and I will help you guys get back to Alaska in any way that we can."

"Thank you," Lilly said thankfully.

"You're welcome. Helping someone out is always a pleasure."

Jade closed her book, placed it on her nightstand, and turned off the lamp. As darkness filled the room, the green plastic stars on the ceiling glowed brightly.

"Let's get some sleep," Jade said as she got under her covers.

Lilly and Beta shifted on the bed to get in a comfortable position.

"Goodnight, you two," Jade said.

"You, too," Lilly and Beta replied, and in moments they were sound asleep.

In the morning, Jade woke up with Beta and Lilly's faces in view. She yawned and stretched, then gently tossed her covers, which brushed the dogs' noses and woke them up. Beta and Lilly yawned.

"How did you two sleep?" Jade asked.

"Pretty good."

"Yeah, I slept like rock," Lilly said pleasantly.

"Well, good."

Lilly and Beta stood up and stretched, then jumped off Jade's bed and gracefully landed on the floor. Jade got ready for the day in a turquoise dress with the green stone pendant silver necklace and dark green flat shoes.

"What's the occasion?" Lilly asked, intrigued.

"Church," Jade told them.

"Oh," Lilly said, realizing it was Sunday. She thought back to her master. He didn't have a specific religion, but she knew he believed in God. All of his travels with his dogs were treacherous, but he and his dogs always came out safe and alive. His office was God's domain—the wilderness, where wild animals lived and survived, and where tall pine trees grew; where canyons, valleys, gorges, and ravines ripped the earth's crust, and mountains towered and loomed over the beautiful Alaskan landscape.

"That's a pretty necklace you have there," Beta said to Jade, looking at the vibrant green stone.

"Oh, thank you," Jade replied.

"What kind of stone is it?" Lilly asked.

"It's jade." She smiled down at the pendant. "It used to be Mother's. She was wearing a bracelet with this stone on it when I was born," she touched the stone, "so she named me Jade. For my eleventh birthday, she gave me this necklace with the stone I was named after."

"In ancient Chinese culture, and even still today, jade is believed to be the shed tears of dragons that fall to earth from the heavens, hardening along the way and falling into riverbeds." Jade opened the door and they walked into the hallway.

Sam was dressed for church as well and was tucking his shirt into his pants as the Rex, Alpha, and Duke followed him out.

"You look nice," Jade said approvingly, eyeing his vibrant blue and red striped tie.

"Thanks," he said.

Lilly went to Rex. "How did you guys sleep?"

"Fine."

"Just fine? I slept great," she said with a chuckle.

"Sam had us sleep on the ground. He said, 'sleep anywhere you like except my bed, capisce?'" He mimicked Sam's voice.

She winced. "Jade let us sleep up on her bed with her."

"Yeah, it wasn't the best," Rex said in low voice. "Don't get me wrong, you and I both know we've slept on uncomfortable Alaskan ground in subzero conditions," he explained to Lilly as she nodded in agreement. "He's . . . just not the welcoming type."

"I feel your pain," Lilly said sympathetically. "But cheer up, my friend," she smiled. "Sometimes bad things happen to good people, but if we change our mindset into a positive one, what wonders may abound!"

They followed Jade and Sam with the other dogs into the living room and saw Emerald in a long, dark blue dress and black heels, and Matthew in a sharp gray suit.

After breakfast, Matthew turned to the dogs. "We're going to church, so we'll see you in a few hours." The gang heard their station wagon leave the driveway.

"So, what do you guys want to do?" Rex asked the other dogs.

"Maybe we can explore the neighborhood a little bit more and try to get in touch with Bandit," Lilly said.

At first, they couldn't find a way out of the house, but Duke managed to paw open the latched handle of the back door and they took off, leaving the door opened slightly. They slipped out into the backyard and saw an artificial turf lawn, a swimming pool, and, luckily, a gate that was slightly open.

As they ran down the cul-de-sac, they saw Bandit out on her morning stroll.

"Hello, Bandit, how've you been?" Rex asked.

"Oh, it's you. How have y'all been?"

"Good! We've made friends with the family that helped Duke out yesterday," Lilly told her.

"Oh, thank goodness," Bandit sighed in relief. "I was sweating like a sinner in a church in there." Then she wheeled toward Duke. "Speakin' of *Duke*," she said, sneering at him. "You must be a half-wit! You done gave away our secret and busted the law of animal nature!"

"The Smiths promised not to tell anyone," Rex told her.

"Do y'all trust 'em? I've met some people who blabber when they hear something. They say they'll keep a secret, but they can't. I'm just sayin'."

"Well, the Smiths are not like that. They're going to help us get back to Alaska."

"Do y'all believe that returning to Alaska is y'all's fate—that it's inevitable?" Bandit looked skeptical. "I'm not stopping y'all, but it will take some time. And what about the Boss and De-Vil? Y'all can't be spotted, or they'll be after you. It's a risky bet."

"Bandit? Where are ya, Bandit?" Off in the distance, a

young girl's voice called out in a Southern accent.

"Oh, sorry, my master is callin' me. I got to go, but darn good luck on tryin' to get back to Alaska." Bandit turned and ran back toward her master.

The dogs went back to the Smiths' house, closed the gate behind them, and squeezed through the back door. They all lay down and talked and rested until they heard the front door open.

"We're home," Jade's voice sang out as Sam dashed into the hallway. "Stop running in the house, Sam," Jade snapped.

"Make me, nerd," he taunted.

She charged after him like a furious bull down the hallway.

"So, what did you all do this morning?" Matthew asked calmly, walking into the room.

"We just went on a stroll with Bandit—the other dog that was with us—and then came back here."

Matthew nodded and went to change out of his church clothes. Sam came out of the hallway wearing an "Imagine Dragons" t-shirt and gym shorts. He slumped down on the couch with his cell phone in hand. Jade came out in a bright green t-shirt with a purple skirt. She had a polished red wooden violin in her left hand and the bow in her right. She put her chin on the chinrest and lifted the bow, stroking the strings. She was a skilled violinist, and when her bow touched the strings, she made the most beautiful music they had ever heard.

Rex and the others enjoyed the music, just lying there and watching her graceful movements as she played.

"Wow, I'm impressed!" Lilly said when Jade had finished. "You're a great violinist. Simply amazing!"

"Thanks! It's very fun to play," Jade said as she began a new song.

Rex and the others were impressed at how she could play and talk at the same time. After she had played her beautiful and soothing music for a while, she gently put down her violin and bow on the kitchen counter, got a glass of water to drink, and then set her empty cup in the sink.

As the dogs were chilling, they heard tapping on the front window near the door. They all turned to look and saw a bird sitting on the windowsill.

"It's Ren!" Lilly said.

"Could you open the door?" Rex asked Jade. "She's a friend of ours."

Jade opened the front door and let Ren fly in. She was startled when Arthur ran in past her feet. Ren flew over to Rex and landed on a coffee table near him.

"Who are they?" Sam asked, looking at Ren and Arthur.

"Oh, Sam and Jade, this is Ren the cactus wren and Arthur the roadrunner. Ren and Arthur, this is Jade and Sam."

Ren and Arthur both looked shocked. "Did you just talk to humans?!" Ren asked the gang, shocked.

The gang realized their mistake.

"Oh, it's not what it looks like. . . ." Rex began. "Please don't tell anyone. They're our only way of getting back to Alaska," he desperately begged.

"You can't, it's against the law of animal nature," Arthur said frankly, then turned and ran for the door, followed closely by Ren.

"Jade, shut the door!" Lilly yelled. Jade slammed the door shut.

"Girl, please open the door," Ren pleaded with Jade.

"I'm sorry, little birdie, but I can't do that," Jade replied.

"Let us out now!" Ren demanded.

"Nope; we're trying to help them get home. Don't you care about them?" Jade asked. "They're our friends. Can't you help them, too?"

Ren sighed. "I can't believe I'm saying this . . ." she said reluctantly, "but we'll help by keeping our beaks shut."

"Thank you so much," Jade said gratefully.

"Now, why are you two here?" Lilly asked.

"I'm sorry to be the bearer of bad news, but I've got some bad news," Ren said nervously.

"What is it?!" Lilly asked anxiously.

"Rosy told me the Boss's goons are getting close to your whereabouts. I was flying over near the river bridge on Cortaro this morning, and I saw them patrolling for you."

"Oh, this is bad. Very, very bad," Rex said, pacing back and forth. The other dogs looked at each other worriedly.

"Unfortunately, I have more bad news."

The dogs all stared at Arthur now.

"I was talking to some quails who live near that bridge. They said they saw a gray wolf lurking around the dry riverbed under the bridge."

"De-Vil!" the dogs all gasped. Sam and Jade just looked at each other.

"But he fell!" Beta said anxiously, looking at Alpha.

He leaned his shoulder against her to comfort her. "He must have survived the fall."

"I'm sorry," Ren said softly. "We shouldn't stay here very long."

Jade opened the door and Arthur called out, "Goodbye and good luck!" Ren flew out behind him.

That night they all went to bed in the same sleeping arrangements as before. Jade sat talking on the bed with Beta and Lilly.

"What's your favorite color?" Jade asked.

"My favorite color is white," Lilly said.

"Mine is blue," Beta offered.

Jade smiled. "Mine's green."

After talking a little longer, Lilly sighed. "Rex is probably super-stressed right now."

"You two seem to be good friends."

"Yeah, we're friends," Lilly responded, distracted by her thoughts.

Jade noticed her distraction. "Do you like Rex?"

"Yes," Lilly said, embarrassed.

"You don't have to be embarrassed about it," Jade said with a smile. "We all have feelings. I think it's kind of sweet you like him. He seems like a sweet and funny guy." Jade turned to Beta. "So, who do you like?"

"Alpha," she said honestly.

Jade tilted her head thoughtfully. "He seems like a brute, but that can be a good thing."

"He can be as angry as a beast to others, but he's very sweet and kind. He's a softy on the inside," Beta said with a smile.

"Just don't tell them we like them," Lilly said.

"I promise," Jade agreed before turning off the light to go to sleep.

In Sam's room, a similar conversation was taking place.

"So, what's your favorite food?" Sam asked the boys.

"Mine is probably cheese," Rex said.

Alpha yawned. "Mine is some good old red meat."

Duke wagged his tail. "Mine is prickly pear fruit."

Sam looked at him, confused.

"Oh, we had it in the desert with the coyotes," Rex informed him.

"Well, mine is pizza," Sam said with a smile.

"Do you think Lilly and the others are okay?" Rex asked Sam. "Just asking."

Sam grinned. "Why, do you like Lilly?" he nudged Rex.

"Yeah, I do."

"Really? I was actually just joking, but that's cool." Sam looked over at Alpha. "Who do you like?"

"Beta."

"Cool, she must be a lucky girl to have you as a friend."

"Thanks."

Now Sam nudged Duke. "Do you like anyone?"

"Nah, I'm not really into anyone at the moment," Duke answered.

"Do you promise not to tell them?" Alpha asked.

"I promise," Sam said, and turned off the light.

Only a few miles away, under the Cortaro bridge, a pair of sinister eyes lurked in the darkness. A gray-brown quail was suddenly snatched from the air and pinned to the ground.

"Don't eat me," the quail begged.

"I'm not going to eat you," a voice snarled, ferocious teeth snapping near the quail's head. "I need information. Tell me where those Alaskan dogs and the red wolf are." The shadowy head licked its chops. "Otherwise, I *will* eat you!"

The bird cowered. "I don't know where they are!"

The teeth snapped closer.

"But I'll try to find them!" the quail said hurriedly. The paw released and the bird flew frantically away to do the beast's evil bidding.

Back at the Smith's house, everything was quiet as they all slept. Suddenly Lilly whimpered and shifted on the bed.

She was at an unfamiliar park with Rex, the gang, and the Smiths. Abruptly, they heard screaming and explosions, and the air started to smell of sulfur and dust. Chaos surrounded them, with people running everywhere and bumping into them. The gang and the Smiths ran to a nearby bridge and saw a chubby Hispanic man dressed in all white clothing. He was holding sticks of dynamite. Suddenly he lit their fuses and threw them.

BOOM!

Lilly gasped and darted toward the bridge, only to slam into Jade's bedroom door. She looked around, dazed. The dream had felt so real. Her ears were still ringing from the explosion.

"What on earth?" Jade turned on the light, and she and Beta looked at Lilly sprawled on the floor.

"Are you ok?" Jade asked, concerned. "What happened?"

"I need to talk to Rex, immediately!" she said without hesitation.

Jade looked at her closely, then nodded slowly. "Ok." She opened the door for Lilly. Lilly squeezed through the door and it shut behind her. The light in Jade's room went out, leaving Lilly in the pitch-black darkness of the hallway. She heard footsteps and froze. A low growl sounded—not a dog growl.

Oh, no. Please don't be De-Vil. Please, please, in the name of all things that are good and just . . . don't be De-Vil.

A pair of bright, almond-brown eyes appeared at the end of the hallway, staring right at her. Lilly yelped and backed up against the wall. She wanted to run but was petrified with fear. She whimpered. Strangely, as the eyes approached, her fear faded, and she felt a familiar warm presence, pleasant and assuring. She knew it wasn't going to do her any harm.

"It's ok. It's just me."

Lilly breathed a sigh of relief at Rex's voice. "Why are you awake at this hour?"

"I was feeling a bit peckish, so I was going to get a midnight snack. Why are *you* up?"

She chuckled sheepishly. "I was actually coming to talk to you. Remember those dreams you had? Just now I had one and it was so real." She then told him all about her dream.

Rex sighed. "That's how I felt when I had mine. Now you know what I'm going through. But why were you yelping and whimpering when I was coming toward you? Did you think I was going to hurt you? You know I would never do that."

"I know. I actually thought you were De-Vil."

"What? Why would you think that?"

"I heard a low growl, and no one in this house growls like a wolf, so I assumed it was De-Vil. You don't growl like that, though. Did you hear a low growl? Maybe it was just the air conditioner."

Suddenly Rex's stomach made a low growl like the one Lilly had heard. They both laughed.

"Guilty. Guess it was me."

"You know, it was interesting. I was so afraid with you creeping so quietly toward me, but once you got close, I just felt . . . comforted, even though I didn't know it was you quite yet."

"I was actually trying to keep quiet when I heard you whimpering. I didn't want you to think of me as a threat."

"It was actually quite nice and comfortable. I thought you were an angel."

Rex looked at her. "What do you mean by that?"

She realized what she had admitted. "Oh, nothing. I'm probably just tired." *I need to think before I say things around him.*

"Let's go to the kitchen. I still need a snack." They both chuckled again, remembering the growl that had frightened Lilly earlier.

They went into the kitchen but didn't find anything that looked good.

"Should we go back to our rooms?" Rex asked as they paused in the hallway.

"What if we sleep on the couch together, like old times?"

Rex smiled. "I like the sound of that."

They padded over to the couch in the family room and lay down.

As they slept, Lilly heard someone say, *"Do you think you can beat me? I am a wolf! I am way stronger than you! You are pets—pampered and weak and unable to survive."* The voice paused, then yelled, *"YOU'RE NOTHING!!!"*

Lilly jolted awake, looking around for the source of that voice. She saw only Rex, and he wasn't a sleep talker.

He lifted his head. "You ok?"

She settled in closer to him. "Yeah, I'm ok."

They both laid their heads back down, and Lilly thought in the darkness, *my life will never be the same.*

In the morning when Jade and Beta woke up, they were surprised not to see Lilly in the room. Sam, Alpha, and Duke were also surprised that Rex wasn't there when they woke up. They all walked out of their rooms searching for the dogs.

"Do you know where Lilly is?" Jade asked Sam.

"No. Do you know where Rex is?"

"Not a clue."

"Let's try to find them together," Beta said. "They would likely be sleeping together."

They found them fast asleep on the family room couch.

"Wake up, you two!" the other dogs yelled.

Rex and Lilly opened their eyes. "We're up!" Lilly said crankily. "We're up, just shut your traps."

"Yeah, what she said." Rex said just as grumpily.

"Why were you two on the couch?" Sam asked.

"Oh, I forgot, I have some business to attend to," Rex said.

"What kind of business?" Jade asked.

"Nonya."

She was confused. "Nonya business? Oh, I get it. That was clever . . . and kind of rude at the same time."

Sam folded his arms. "Why won't you tell us?"

"Again, nonya business." Rex didn't want to speak of what had happened between him and Lilly. It was special, even if they didn't know exactly what it was. Besides, telling the others could just complicate things.

Jade turned to Lilly. "Come on, you ran into my bedroom door last night. What's up?"

"It's really none of your concern." Lilly said firmly. "End of discussion; just let us rest."

The others looked at each other and backed off. They weren't sure what was going on between those two and didn't know if their irritation was just a little flurry or a full-on blizzard of rage. Either way, they didn't want to make it worse. Soon, Rex and Lilly were resting on the couch, Alpha and Beta were chitchatting, and Duke was being his normal self. Jade was practicing her violin and Sam was watching TV.

The quail De-Vil had threatened flew through the desert, trying to find Ren. Finally, he saw her perched on a low-lying branch of an ironwood tree. In his nervousness, he flew down way too fast, crashed into the ground, and rolled in the dirt.

"Hi, Ren, how are you doing today?" he greeted her politely while shaking the dust and dirt from his feathers.

"Good, Torpe, I'm doing good," she smiled at her friend.

"Hey, I need to ask you something."

"What's on your mind?"

"You know your Alaskan dog friends? Do you perchance know they live?"

"They live at the house at the end of the cul-de-sac over there, by where those two dogs argue all day." Ren looked at him curiously. "Why?"

"Uhh. . . . Anyways, thanks for the info," he shifted nervously.

"Don't mention it."

"See you later, Ren," Torpe called as he flew away.

"Happy flying," she shouted back. Oddly enough, she saw him fly southeast instead of northwest towards Rex and the others. "That clumsy Torpe," she said, chuckling before flying off herself.

Back at the Smith household, Lilly was thinking of ways to cheer up Rex. He was glum and she knew they were both still tense. Every idea she came up with didn't sound like a good option, until one golden idea popped into her head.

"The Spirit of Alaska," she began to sing in her soft, angelic voice, "Let her winter winds rage. . . ."

Rex smiled as she sang. When she finished, the other dogs cheered by barking and Sam and Jade clapped their hands excitedly.

"Wow, you're a good singer!" Jade said in awe.

"Yeah, that was amazing!" Sam agreed.

"It was nothing, really," Lilly said, blushing a little.

"You sang like an angel, Lilly!" Rex said, shaking his head in amazement. "It was just. . . ." He trailed off, trying to find a word to describe her singing, but he had so many he could say to her he couldn't choose just one. "I really can't put it into words. It was just simply wonderful."

She blushed even harder. "Well, thanks Rex, that's very kind of you."

Her feeling of contentment suddenly evaporated and she felt a dark weight, like something bad was going to happen. Not now, but soon. She waited a moment until the others went back to what they were doing, then leaned in close to

Rex. "I need to talk to you," she whispered.

"Why?" He looked at her face and frowned. "What's wrong?"

"Just follow my lead."

"Please excuse us," Lilly said politely to everyone in the room before jumping off the couch and going to the entrance of the hallway. She looked back at Rex and gestured with her head for him to come. Rex jumped up and followed her.

"What is it?" Rex asked as soon as they were alone. "Another dream?"

She shook her head. "No, it's not like the dreams . . . or whatever they were. It's more like I felt something. I felt like something really, really bad is going to happen."

Rex looked alarmed. "Now?"

She shook her head. "Not right now, but soon."

Rex looked grave. "That's not good."

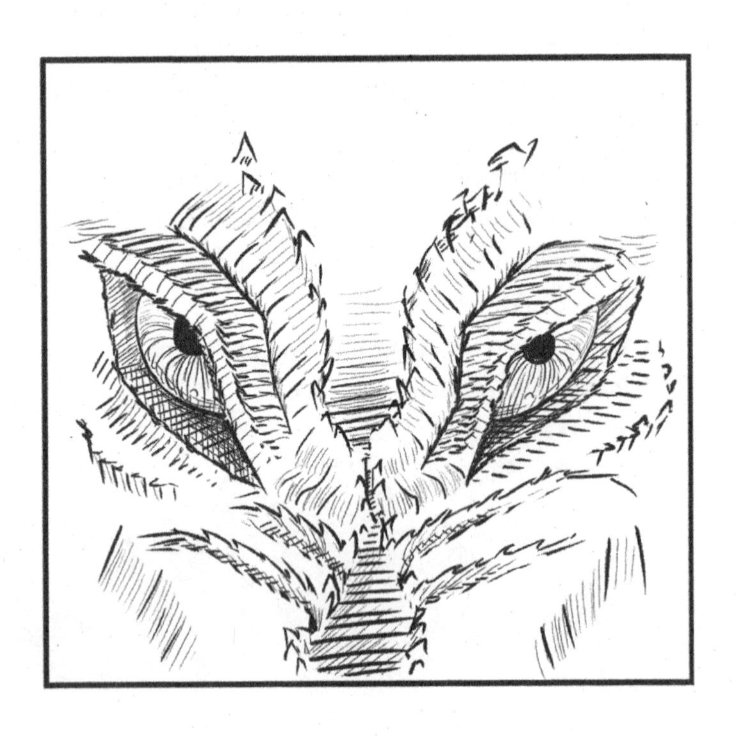

CHAPTER 10

ON THE DOWN LOW

Torpe perched on an apartment building's fence, close to the Cortaro bridge.

"I'm going to break Ren's trust," he sighed to himself. "I hope she'll forgive me."

A dark, shadowy figure was lurking under the bridge. Torpe took a deep breath. "Okay, let's get this over with," he said regretfully.

He glided down and landed on a rock near the base of the bridge, but he didn't see De-Vil. It was eerie. He heard something rustle behind him—but when he turned to look, he saw only the shadow of the bridge. A twig cracked to his other side. As he turned, De-Vil sprang out of nowhere, right in Torpe's face.

"Miss me?" he snarled menacingly.

"No," Torpe answered coldly.

"Oh, that's hurtful from my new henchman. Or should I say hench-bird? I'll call you that from now on, 'hench-bird Torpe.' I like . . . it has a nice ring to it." He said it was like Torpe's name was in lights. But in Torpe's mind, it was more like his name was in prison search lights.

"There is no way in heck I'm doing that."

De-Vil wasn't listening. "From now on, you're my new hench-bird."

"Are you deaf?" Torpe squawked. "I will never join your posse! You're sick and twisted and I would rather die than join you!"

Suddenly Torpe was pinned to the ground by De-Vil's paw. "Is that a request?" De-Vil whispered menacingly. He pressed down until Torpe's eyes seemed to bulge out.

"They're in. . . ." Torpe choked. "Ugh! I can't breathe!"

"Tell me where they are!" De-Vil's eyes were crazed. "Or I'll make the next word you speak your last!"

Torpe was too panicked to understand as he gasped for air.

De-Vil leaned in even closer to make Torpe understand. "You can tell me where they are and live . . . or you can choose not to and die. Choose wisely."

Torpe closed his eyes in defeat, still choking. "They're . . . at a . . . neighborhood . . . called . . . Casanova . . . Estates."

De-Vil flicked Torpe against the rock he had been perched on. He hit the ground and gasped for precious air.

"Why thank you, hench-bird. You're so helpful. Now, where is Casanova Estates?"

Torpe didn't speak.

De- Vil smacked him against the rock again. "WHERE IS

CASANOVA ESTATES?"

Torpe got up slowly to his feet and hung his head. "I'll show you. Follow me." He flapped his wings to take off, only to feel something biting at his tail feathers. He squawked in pain, freezing when he realized his tail feathers were between De-Vil's teeth.

De-Vil threw Torpe to the ground. "You fool! We can't do that."

Torpe winced in pain. "Why not? Isn't sooner the better?"

"We'll strike at night," De-Vil snarled. "That's the best time."

Torpe shuddered at the thought of being at the mercy of the wolf's temper all day. "How long will that be?"

"Patience, Torpe, patience. Good things come to those who wait," De-Vil said with a malevolent smirk. His eyes blazed evilly.

Torpe looked across the desert toward the dogs. "I'm sorry," he whispered, then tucked his head under his wing to wait.

After a few minutes, Torpe raised his head and risked a question. "Why are you so mad and mean?"

"I'm not mean; I'm just direct."

"You must have quite the bone to pick with those dogs. What did they do to deserve your wrath?"

"It's not the dogs; I could care less about the dogs . . . well, that's not true. I would like to kill everyone single one of them!" De-Vil said growling, "But what I really want is that red wolf named Rosy."

"What's so important about her?"

"Since we are here just waiting for it to get dark," De-

Vil sneered, "let me tell you a little bit about myself and how I got here.

When I was younger, I befriended the kindest wolf I had ever met in my life. Her name was Charis.

De-Vil smiled fondly.

We became best friends and were inseparable. As we grew up and spent time together, our friendship started becoming more than just a friendship to me. The time we spent together made me more and more infatuated with her. She was kindhearted and understood me better than anyone else did. She introduced me to one of her friends.

De-Vil's face grew somber, and he continued in a low, melancholy voice.

His name was Chrys. Chrys was a fun-loving wolf. He always had a smile on his face and a spring in his step. I was pretty good friends with both Chrys and Charis. The three of us spent time exploring valleys and forests and just having adventure after adventure. We grew up together and our friendships became strong. But that all changed on the day Chrys came to me bouncing with enthusiasm and told me he was going to ask Charis to be his mate.

De-Vil let out a regretful sigh.

After he shared that information with me, I began to fill with jealousy and rage and told him he shouldn't ask her. He asked why and I explained to him that I had liked her way before he had. He definitely was not too pleased with me and that statement. He yelled at me, accusing me that I was being selfish, crushing his moment of happiness, and that I should be happy for him instead of being a self-centered jerk.

With a tinge of regret in his somber voice, De-Vil continued.

As we argued, I was getting angrier and angrier by the minute. My anger boiled over and I began to growl, scaring Chrys. He backed off with his tail between his legs, pleading that he was sorry and for me to not be so angry.

Tears began to fall from De-Vil's amber eyes, recently hard and unmoving, but now weak and fragile.

I stalked towards Chrys, snarling and fueled by jealousy and rage. He was petrified and pleaded for me to stop, but I was filled with so much anger I ignored his desperate cries and continued toward him. H-he pleaded again for me to stop and told me that he would do anything if I would just calm down and stop. A-and I told him to d-d-die.

De-Vil's voice became unstable with emotion.

I-I dug m-my claws i-into his neck, and he flopped on the ground, wailing and gasping in agony. . . . Then I clenched my sharp teeth into his blood-soaked gray neck and shook.

Torpe gasped in horror as De-Vil sobbed.

After all of the bloodshed and panic, Chrys's lifeless body lay on the ground. My mind rushed frantically like a raging river, twisting and turning at every anxious thought. His dead green eyes were unblinking, mocking me as if staring right through me from the beyond.

I drug his dead carcass as fast as I could, looking for a place to hide him. That was when I found Mud Cave. I hid his body far into the cave and beneath the mud, for fear it would start to smell. I covered the bloody trail with piles of dirt and rocks and then sprinted over to the river to wash the blood and mud off of my face. Even though I had washed Chrys's blood from my face, I felt like the blood was still there.

Days passed, and I tried acting as normal as I could. One day, I was greeted by two wolves from the wolves' council. They told me Clements needed to talk with me. I told them I would come and find him. As I walked up to Poplar Point, my mind was coming up with all types of anxious thoughts. I walked into council area and found Clements looking over the amazing view of the valley below. I walked up to him nervously, and he asked me how I was doing. I told him I was fine.

I asked Clements why he needed me, and he told me he needed to discuss a very important matter. I was trying to stay calm, but at the same time, anxious thoughts were flooding my head. He noticed my nervousness and asked me if I was really okay. I told him I was nervous; he replied it was okay to be nervous. I again asked him why he wanted to talk with me. He replied that he had noticed my skill in giving advice to other wolves in the pack and asked if I would like to join the wolves' council as his head counselor.

De-Vil paused, shook his head, and laughed.

I was nervous that someone might've found Chrys's carcass in the depths of Mud Cave, but no—he wanted me to be his head counselor, of all things.

De-Vil paused once more as a wicked grin spread across his face.

Then my mind started racing. If I became Clements' head counselor, I could gain his trust, and when the problem of "Chrys has been murdered" arose, I would be on his good side and divert the attention from myself. So I agreed. Clements was delighted and said my helpful advice would better assist him and the counsel in making better decisions for our pack.

After meeting with Clements, I walked back to Mud Cave and checked on Chrys's body. Even buried in the mud, his rotting carcass gave off such a horrid stench, and his unblinking eyes filled me with shameful guilt. I walked out of the cave, washed the mud off my fur in the river, and began walking with all kinds of thoughts buzzing around in my head.

I walked to my favorite spot on a high hilltop, overlooking the lower part of the valley. I heard someone walking up to the hilltop behind me. Without moving my head from viewing the valley below, I told whomever it was to go away, but they kept approaching, so I quickly turned my head and shouted at them to leave me alone!

De-Vil paused for a few moments, and a glum expression spread across his face.

It was Charis. She had a surprised look on her face because I had just shouted at her. She asked why I was so snappy, and I told her I didn't mean to be so curt with her; I had thought it was someone else. She noticed something was wrong and asked if I was okay. I just told her I was tired, but asked how she was. She said she was okay and had been walking through the woods, but had I seen Chrys? I tried to stay as cool as possible, but it was quite hard. I wanted to tell her what had happened, but I couldn't or didn't dare, so I told her no, I hadn't seen him. I redirected the conversation by telling her Clements had appointed me as his head counselor and the newest member of the wolves' council. Charis was beyond ecstatic and congratulated me over and over, but I didn't receive her congratulations, and she asked what was bothering me. I told her nothing was wrong, but she knew something was definitely wrong.

De-Vil's head began to sink lower.

Charis sincerely asked me if I was okay. I couldn't speak, which made her even more concerned. She told me I could tell her anything because we were best friends. I then asked her, if she had done something unforgivable, what would she do? She paused and thought long and hard. She told me if she had done something unforgivable, she would be truthful and accept the consequences of her actions. She asked me why I would ask such a question. I told her inaudibly that I had killed Chrys. She didn't hear what I said and asked me to repeat it.

De-Vil stopped. His eyes closed in shame.

I asked her, what she would do if she lost a close friend? She didn't seem to understand and asked what I was trying to get at.

Every thought and emotion raged in my head like an unstoppable flood. Charis was waiting for my answer. I felt as if a ton of boulders were pressing down on me and I couldn't hold it in anymore. I yelled out in agony, "I k-k-killed Ch-Chrys!"

She was shocked by my words and simply asked why. I broke out in tears, telling her I had killed him because of her. She backed away with a frightened look, as if I were a savage beast. I began to walk towards her saying that I had liked her ever since we had first met. I told her she was the kindest and best wolf I had met in my life and asked her to be my mate.

De-Vil paused and sighed.

Her face showed neither joy or happiness. She screamed at me, saying she would never be my mate—ever. My heart felt as if it were tumbling downhill like a large boulder. She told me that what I had done was a cruel act of selfishness over a blinded and foolish fantasy. I felt like at that moment, my soul had been tainted by envy and anger, as well as Chrys's blood.

Charis began to walk away in a huff, and I asked her where she was going. She told me over her shoulder that she was going to tell both Clements and the wolves' council what unspeakable and unforgivable act I had done to Chrys. As she was leaving, my fear-driven mind spiraled out of control. My head raised, my amber eyes flashed scarlet, and I growled one word forcefully: "DON'T!"

She stopped, turned around, and asked me what I had said as her beautiful blue eyes widened with fear. I told her in a dangerously murderous tone that she couldn't tell Clements or anyone else, or she would end up like Chrys.

De-Vil began to cry.

All of my negative feelings were buzzing around in my head. I began to yell and threaten her in deplorable ways that I would hurt her if my unspeakable act got out. My mind was numb to any signs of second thoughts or regret, and my mouth was shrieking foul words and ideas as Charis cowered in fear. The beast inside of me told me to press on, telling me stalk and prowl towards her as if she were my prey.

Tears streaked down De-Vil's face. "My next victim!" he howled remorsefully.

The beast filled me with violent adrenaline, making me scratch and bite her to . . . hurt . . . her. The beast and I backed her into some large boulders. She screamed and yelped. The beast made me tell her that no one would hear her and that she was out of luck.

De-Vil's amber eyes looked like they were being crushed under all of this guilt.

The beast made me into an unfeeling and cruel monster who wanted to kill her because she was going to tell Clements. Clements in turn would tell the pack I was a menace, and I would ether get banished or killed for my heinous crime.

I loomed over Charis as she cried profusely and pled for me not to hurt her—that whatever I was going to do to her wasn't going to make things right or bring Chrys back.

The beast told me she was trying to distract me so I would have pity on her and spare her. It urged me to kill her, because she would be a witness against me if I let her live.

De-Vil paused for what seemed like a long time.

I hesitated, and the beast began to roar at me that I was weak and that if I didn't kill Charis, she would be my downfall. As the beast yelled at me to commit, I looked into Charis's blue eyes that were petrified with fear and reflected on when we first met.

I was alone and resting on that very hilltop, gazing over the river and surrounding forest. That's when she popped out of nowhere and made me jump straight up from the grassy ground. I snapped around to see a beautiful wolf with light gray fur and sky-blue eyes who greeted me kindly and asked what I was doing.

A crinkle of a smile sprouted from De-Vil's mouth.

I told the blue-eyed wolf I was looking at the surrounding forest. She plopped down right next to me and asked if she could join, too. "I'm Charis; it's nice to meet you," she said in a bright, peppy voice, a warm smile on her face. "What's your name?" she asked, her sky-blue eyes looking eagerly at me.

As I came back to the present and gazed into Charis's frightened eyes, I started to reconsider the horrible words the beast was screaming for me to afflict upon her. "I'm De-Vil," I spoke aloud, "and I will not kill my friend!"

I collapsed to the ground, sobbing, and Charis came up to me and asked if I was okay. I told her that I was not. She asked me what was going on and why I didn't look like myself. She described how I looked monstrously evil and that my kind amber eyes were a bright blood-red. My mind thought back with guilt to Chrys's blood splattered all over my face and my mouth after I had brutally bit into his neck.

Charis pleaded with me that we both go to Clements and tell him what had happened; she pointed out that would've been what Chrys wanted. I nodded, sniffing a bit, and got up. She gave me a happy grin; I smiled back.

We began walking down the hill towards Poplar Point. Charis told me everything was going to be okay because Clements was wise and would help me. As we walked, I heard the coarse voice of the beast snarl at me, saying I was being led to my demise. I pushed back at the voice and told it I was going to make things right by confessing my wrongs to Clements, as Charis had urged. The beast snidely told me that Charis was foolish in telling me to get help from the happy-go-lucky simpleton. I told the voice to go away and leave me alone. The beast sinisterly told me he would never leave me until my death, which sent shivers down my spine.

I glanced at Charis and saw that she looked worried. I asked if she was okay. She replied that she was fine, but I knew better. The beast whispered to me that she was worried about herself getting tied up in the murder of one of her best friends. I told the voice that wouldn't be the case and that Clements was usually pretty lenient.

We eventually arrived at the entrance of Poplar Point. My heart was racing. I looked at Charis nervously. She gave me a sympathetic smile and told me everything was going to be okay and that she wouldn't abandon me. In the back of my mind, the beast continued to whisper that if I confessed, I would be considered a threat to the pack. That thought made me extremely nervous.

We walked into Poplar Point. Its towering cottonwood trees loomed over me, like they knew of my heinous act. The council members were conversing with each other and Clements was sitting down among them with a smile on his face. Charis nudged me and I cleared my throat as loudly as I could, but my nervousness made it quite difficult and it wasn't that loud. Charis cleared her throat quite a bit more loudly and caught all of their attention. Every wolf's neck turned in our direction, and I felt as if all of their gazing eyes could see into my tainted soul.

Clements looked up at us with a jovial look on his face. "De-Vil, Charis, what a wonderful surprise. What brings you two here today?"

The beast surged horrible and gruesome thoughts in my mind of things that would happen to me if I told Clements and the council that I had killed Chrys in cold blood for Charis.

"Come on De-Vil, tell them," Charis said under breath. "Sorry, he's a bit nervous," she said more loudly to Clements and

the council. "Come on," she urged quietly, as she glanced at me with an assertive stare.

The beast told me, "Kill her! She's a scheming traitor!" I shot back and told him she wasn't.

"Come on!" Charis repeated in annoyance. I glared at her sharply and her sky-blue eyes filled with dread.

"No!" I growled back.

"Are you two alright?" Clements asked.

"He's just very nervous to tell you that he . . . ."

I cut her off with a glare.

"What? I'm trying to help you!" she said irately as she turned to confront me.

That's when the beast in me smiled deviously and began to laugh hysterically. It laughed and laughed unceasingly and I asked it why it was laughing. It didn't answer my question but only said, "Tell her what you think." It was malicious and cold.

That's when all hell broke loose.

De-Vil paused with a sigh, then continued.

My tongue that had been bound down with fear was now loosened, and I shrieked out angrily, making the birds in the tall cottonwood trees fly away.

"Holy skies! Will you just shut up?" I shouted at Charis angrily. "I don't want to tell them! Can't you get that through your thick head? I'm trying to survive here, and telling them all won't make anything better than it already is.

Her face was shocked. I looked around and saw the stunned faces of the council members. Murmurs and whispers moved through the crowd of wolves like the wind rustling through tall grass. Even Clements, the amicable alpha himself, was completely dumbstruck.

I came back to reality and realized what I had done. I looked up at the tall cottonwood trees and just stared as everyone else was silent and shocked at my outrageous behavior.

"De-Vil . . . ?" Clements and Charis both began to say before I ran away from what I had done.

"De-Vil!" Charis shouted behind me. I ran as fast as my feet could take me and just wanting to be alone. "De-Vil, stop!" She shouted again behind me. I looked back and she was gaining on me. I began to sprint even faster, trying to lose her as I wove through the trees. I looked behind me again to see if she was still chasing after me, and she was, just like a predator after its prey.

"De-Vil, watch out!" I heard her shout urgently, and as I turned to look forward, I ran straight into a tree . . . head-first.

My head throbbed and I could feel my mind pulse inside my skull. Charis caught up to me as I lay on the ground, now sobbing from pain. Then the beast came back and reminded me that Charis would be my downfall. Charis compassionately asked if I was okay and I quickly told her that I wasn't. I tried to stand up, but my legs were like swaying twigs. I tried again and managed to stand up, shaking. I told her that the pain from running into the tree was painful, but not as painful as the guilt from killing Chrys. She reassured me that everything was going to be okay. I asked her if she actually thought that murdering my own friend is okay. She didn't reply, and that's when the beast really got hold of my aching heart.

She was about to speak but the beast, having a rejuvenated hold upon my heart, loosened my tongue even more than it had at Poplar Point. "Maybe your assumptions are false! I'm trying to . . . t-to survive as my reputation and life are on the verge of collapse!" I yelled at her.

"De-Vil, this isn't you. This isn't the excitable, caring wolf I met up on our favorite spot," she said, looking at me like I was some sort of monster.

"I am Clements's high counselor! Do you think he would ever trust me again if I told him I had murdered Chrys? Killing my best friend because of a jealous rage when Chrys stated he was going to ask you to be his mate?" I spewed out angrily.

"What did you say?" she asked in total seriousness. I then realized what I had just told her and begged, "Charis, please, let me. . . ." I began to tell her but she cut me off with an astonished look.

"De-Vil. . . . What were you thinking? You should have been happy for Chrys asking me to be his mate," she scolded. "He wasn't saying that he was going to take me away from you, he was just going to ask me to be his mate. And if either of you had asked, I would have happily agreed," she added.

My ears perked up quickly and my face filled with joy.

"No," she said firmly. "I cannot in good conscience be your mate after all of this. I cannot be bound as a mate to a friend who brutally slaughtered Chrys because of jealousy."

My heart shattered into hundreds of pieces, leaving my previously loosened tongue stiff and rigid like stone.

"Kill her," the beast snarled coldly. "Kill her or she'll be your downfall. She has insulted you, crushed your heart, and if you don't kill her, she will be the herald of your doom." The beast forcefully shoved this gory idea into my thoughts. I didn't think killing her would make anything better so I countered the beast. Big mistake. It stalked, circling around me, and then suddenly

lunged toward me, baring its blood-stained and razor-sharp teeth and giving me a deadly stare with its scarlet eyes. "KILL HER OR SHE WILL BE THE DEATH OF YOU!!!" it bellowed demonically.

I was about to yell back at the scarlet-eyed beast when I saw something that made my eyes widen and stopped me in my tracks. In between the trees and just behind Charis stood Chrys. His body was a misty silver, like the full moon's rays, and his green eyes shone like two small, green apples. I could see the other trees, rocks and underbrush through his misty silver outline, as if he were made out of mist. His neck was stained vivid scarlet where I had struck his final blow.

"De-Vil," he spoke.

"Chrys?" I asked dumbfounded, "W-what are y-you . . . you doing here? Y-you're . . . d-dead." I spoke to Chrys's vaporous silver ghost.

"I'm here to warn you of someone who will be your downfall," he told me.

"O-of her?" I asked Chrys's ghost anxiously while looking over at Charis, who looked confused.

"No, I'm warning you of a newcomer who will come to this valley and will uncover what you've done."

"Who?" I asked nervously.

"Beware; the newcomer's color is that of a beautiful red flower blooming in the spring." His green eyes turned into a radiant golden color like the sun at noonday. "One who will come to this valley and befriend one whose eyes are brown like a mighty oak and another whose eyes gleam like the sea. Beware of the maroon foreigner from the east and these friends, because they will be your downfall as they uncover your misdeeds from the

muddy depths."

"W-who? Tell me, tell me!" I begged.

"Beware of the newcomer," he told me again.

"Tell me!" I pleaded, but he just kept whispering, "Beware of the newcomer." He turned around and began to walk away, still whispering, "Beware of the newcomer."

"Tell me! Tell me! Tell me!" I again begged, but he kept walking away, saying, "Beware of the newcomer."

"Tell me! TELL ME, CHRYS! TELL ME WHO THIS NEWCOMER IS!" I yelled out.

Chrys's warning lingered in my mind as wild and frantic thoughts about what just happened began to flood into my mind.

"What was that?" Charis asked in utter bewilderment.

"Nothing," I weakly said.

"Something definitely just happened there," she said with a surety. "Were you . . . t-talking to . . . Chrys? Isn't he dead?" she asked, confused.

"I guess? Probably? I think so," I replied with uncertainty.

"You're not sure?"

"I don't know. I've been hearing a wrathful, disembodied voice telling me to do horrible things. I heard it when I . . . I kil . . ." I stopped, exhaling unsteadily, ". . . I killed Chrys, and for some reason, that ire-filled voice makes me do whatever it wants, like I'm its host. I was arguing with it, and then I saw what I thought was the ghost of Chrys."

Charis was confused. "What just happened with Chrys's ghost?"

"He was warning me of a newcomer coming to this valley."

"What did he tell you?" she asked, and I explained his

puzzling prediction.

"A rose," Charis said.

"What?" I turned to her.

"A beautiful red flower that blooms in the spring sounds like a rose; they start to bloom in the springtime," she explained. "And whoever this newcomer is will be friends with Hunter, the son of Robert and Shira, as well as Aqua, the daughter of Tiberius and Doris."

"How did you figure that out?"

"It was simple. If you look around at your surroundings with the purpose of finding something, you will get the answer you need."

"Do you know who this newcomer is?"

"No," she shrugged. "But whoever they are, they will be the color of a rose and will come from the east to uncover your murderous dealings," she told me as I looked to the east. "Wait? Where is Chrys?" she asked. "Where is his body?"

"You figure it out if you're so smart," I told her snidely.

She stopped and thought for a few minutes and then her face filled with dread. "You put him in Mud Cave. Th-that's a t-terrible place to hide a body."

"And I guess you have experience with hiding bodies?" I asked her sarcastically.

"N-no, but someone will find out sooner rather than later."

"No one even goes out to Mud Cave hardly. Mostly because of its long tunnel and the hassle of trekking out and cleaning the mud out of your fur in the river." I explained.

"Who knows. Yes, Mud Cave is quite secluded, but that doesn't mean wolves or other animals will won't go in or near it."

"But the timeline of when this supposed newcomer will come

into our valley wasn't stated. They could come in a thousand years," I told her.

"Or they could come tomorrow. We don't know, only Chrys's ghost knows," she refuted. "And even if this newcomer doesn't come soon, they will come and expose you for what you've done. Chrys's ghost's prediction talks about this newcomer becoming friends with Hunter and Aqua, a.k.a. the adventure duo who love to explore any and every new place they can find. What are you going to do when they befriend this newcomer? They'll become unstoppable."

Not if I have anything to say about it, *I thought, and the beast smiled.*

"We can make things right if you tell the truth, and it will make you feel better. I will stand by your side every step of the way."

"So that means you're going to be on my side?" I asked.

"No, I'm only helping you with confessing to Clements and the wolf council."

"Kill her," the beast whispered in my ear sinisterly.

"No, I will not!" I said defiantly.

"Come on, De-Vil! Holding in the guilt will do you no good, and if you don't confess now, Chrys's blood and body will be a witness against you," Charis said, sounding annoyed at my stubbornness.

"Do you know what I am going through right now?" I shouted. "I killed my best friend. Nothing will make that better. His ghost came and told me of my downfall."

She seemed taken aback. "I'm trying to help you, De-Vil," she said seriously.

"You're trying to rat me out," I countered.

Charis let out a frustrated sigh. "De-Vil, I'm really trying to help you out, but if you don't help in this process, swift justice will come upon you."

"I can't confess. They'll banish me for the slaughter of a fellow packmate, or worse, they'll execute me."

"I'll try my best to persuade them to do neither."

"You don't get it! NOTHING IS GOING TO MAKE WHAT I'VE DONE ANY BETTER, CHARIS!" I shouted at her as the beast gripped my tainted soul. I began to walk away in a rage.

"DE-VIL! YOU COME BACK HERE RIGHT NOW!" Charis shouted; her tone was inflamed with vivid anger.

"Holy skies!" I said as I turned toward her. "This is exactly what I expected. The beast told me that if I told anyone my little secret, I would be met with opposition."

"De-Vil, do the right thing. Do it for Chrys's sake. You can make things right if you confess," she begged.

"No, I will not," I told her adamantly.

She began to leave, and I asked her where she was going. She looked at me as if I was a new wolf she had just met. I was about to tell her I was sorry for everything, but she cut me off before I could say anything and glared at me angrily.

"I hope you're happy with yourself," she snarled.

Her words were rough and jagged like rocks on the edge of a cliff. She left quickly without saying another word. I stood there dumbfounded.

Tears began to fall from De-Vil's eyes.

I had just gotten rid of another friend. One I killed mercilessly and the other I just pushed away. I began to sob my eyes out, surrounded by trees who witnessed and heard everything that had unfolded. My tears fell to the earth as my head hung down in shame.

"You made a big mistake," someone said.

I looked up, sniffing a bit, to find Chrys's misty silver ghost standing in front of me. I stumbled back, stunned to see him again.

"What? Have you seen a ghost?" he asked with a smirk on his misty silver face.

"No," I said, trying to act like everything was alright when in reality, nothing was.

"What are you doing here—coming to tell me more vague riddles and clues?" I asked suspiciously.

"No, I've come back to help you," Chrys's ghost replied.

"Help me?" I asked, confused. "What about your prediction? Isn't that pretty telling of my downfall?"

"Maybe, if you want to interpret it that way."

"Why would you want to help me? I killed you."

"You have to reconcile with Charis," he said urgently.

"What? Why?"

"Because the only way to truly face your fears and confess what you've done is in getting her help," Chrys's ghost explained.

"I can't! She wants me to confess to the wolves' council, but I don't want to leave this valley that means everything to me. I want to do what is right, but every idea leads me to a fate of banishment and living with my tainted soul and being tortured by my misdeeds." I stopped suddenly, my face filling with dread. "Or they will k-kill me if they find out what I did to you."

"Then you have to do what's right," Chrys's ghost replied.

"I can't," I told him with a fearful whisper.

"You can. I believe you can, and now you have to believe in yourself that you can, too," Chrys's ghost encouraged me with firm conviction.

His words bounced around my mind like echoes in a cave. They filled me with guilt and, unfortunately, seething anger. This is when the beast came back.

"Who is this?" he asked. "Is that Chrys?" It answered its own question before I could. The beast began to growl. "I thought you killed him," it snarled.

"I'm as shocked to see him as you are," I replied.

The beast began to yell and scream at me. It told me that I shouldn't listen to Chrys's ghost, because he is dead in the muddy depths of Mud Cave, and that I'm going insane.

Chrys's ghost noticed my distress. "De-Vil, are you okay?"

"Yeah, I-I'm fine," I told him but my shaky voice must have said otherwise.

"Come on, tell me what you are feeling," he said sincerely.

"I'm scared. Every path I look at leads to disaster and my inevitable doom. Charis doesn't trust me because I choose not to avenge you." I shivered. "But how can a-avenge you if I was the one who k-killed you in the first place?" I cried out.

He looked at me with a fond smile, making the beast angry. "Why is he smiling?" the beast growled.

"You just have to believe in yourself and take a leap of faith," Chrys's ghost told me genuinely, which filled my tainted soul with warmth and clarity.

The beast didn't like this and began to fight back against Chrys's goodness.

"I'll try," I told Chrys in a huff, and his smile widened even more.

"I know you can," he said, smiling back at me.

He began to walk away and my mind began to be flooded with thoughts of worry. I began to panic. "Don't go!" I frantically called out. "I need y-y-your help!"

Chrys's ghost turned around, his misty silver face toward me, and looked just like his kind, happy self before his demise.

"De-Vil, I will always be with you. Please just gather your courage and do the right thing," Chrys's ghost told me. His apple-green eyes were filled with joy, and he had his familiar smile on his face.

As he began to leave, his misty silver body moved like a wavy, silvery cloud. His green eyes looked at the surrounding forest, the same forest he would run around with me and Charis in our adventures. One question was still bothering me. His body began to vanish, but I yelled, "Wait! I have one more question I need to ask you before you go." My voice shaking, I asked desperately, "Are you real?"

"I am as real as you make me out to be," Chrys answered vaguely. His lips curled into a tiny smile.

"No!" I cried out. "Please tell me if you are real or not," I asked desperately. "Please, please Chrys! Tell me if you are real!" But as I asked, his body vanished.

His face, smile, and green eyes that were always filled with happiness were engraved into my mind. I walked slowly back home with Chrys's warning still in my mind.

It seemed like after that day passed, my life began to go downhill. I reluctantly went to Poplar Point for the wolves' council, because my absence would invite suspicion due to my outburst towards Charis in front of Clements and the council.

As I entered Poplar Point, Clements welcomed me, and it

seemed like every eye of the council was now on me. That scared the living daylights out of me. The council was discussing various things happening throughout the valley. I was silent and looked at the tall cottonwoods looming over me. It felt like the tree knew what I had done, and my outburst had just occurred the day before, making me even more nervous.

I looked down the line of wolves, and my eyes met Clements's. He was looking right at me. His face did not have its normal, jovial expression; it seemed quite the opposite. That's when I got even more worried. My mind was spewing nervous thoughts and I just knew Clements knew something. I looked away from him as my mind began to swirl with fear and panic.

The council continued talking about all types of things related to the valley. I didn't pay any attention. All I could think about was how to find a way out of this tricky situation I was in. I couldn't keep my thoughts straight as the meeting dragged on, and it was getting dark. Clements finally concluded the council meeting and thanked every wolf for their attendance and contributions to the discussion.

As everyone was leaving, I tried joining a group of wolves walking out, but Clements called out that he needed to talk to me. I was scared out of my mind and turned around, trying to hide my fear. He was about to speak, but I blurted out, "Clements, I'm so sorry. I should have told you sooner. I— ".

"It's okay, I understand," he said warmly. "It must be hard carrying all of this weight by yourself. I promise I will help you bear this burden."

When he said that, my heart skipped a beat out of its fear-driven symphony.

"You will?" I asked in shock.

"Yes. The title of head counselor is a big step, and I chose you because your intellect will help our council with decisions that ultimately help the pack. But I chose you above every other wolf because I feel you will follow your heart in making right decisions."

That's when the beast snapped back. "Lie," he whispered in my ear.

This I did, instead of coming clean and facing my consequences.

I went to the wolves' council meetings often and contributed, hoping that if a wolf or another animal found Chrys's carcass, I wouldn't be a suspect. I clearly was evading my problems. I would show up early for the meetings and talk to the other members of the council, getting to get to know them, but mainly trying to put myself in a good light in their minds and make my angry outburst a distant memory.

Rowan and Willow were elected into the wolves' council. They were a happy young pair and brought so many agenda items to discuss because of their daily walks and interactions throughout the valley. Time passed and I quickly became known around the valley as Clements's second-in-command.

A problem arose when Chrys's parents came to Clements and told him that Chrys had been missing. I tried to remain calm and act just as concerned as Clements was. He told me to run throughout the valley as fast as I could and howl for the members of the council to get to Poplar Point immediately.

I did just that: I ran throughout the whole valley, howling and yelling to any council member in earshot that we were having an urgent meeting and to go to Poplar Point straightaway.

After notifying the valley, I swiftly checked that Chrys's carcass was still where I had left it. And it was, continuing to rot and smell absolutely horrible. I dragged his rotting carcass deeper into the bowels of the cave, just in case. I then cleaned myself up and sprinted as fast as I could back to Poplar Point, arriving out of breath and panting.

"Ah, De-Vil, there you are. We were wondering when you would arrive," Clements greeted me. Every member of the council was there, waiting patiently for me to get back. As I was walking towards Clements to take my seat next to him, my heart stopped abruptly, making me halt in my tracks. Right next to Clements were Chrys's parents, both looking worried and distressed.

Shocked, I said, "Oh . . . hello Rue, Susan. . . . It's nice to see you two." As I spoke to them, I was tried my hardest to stay calm and not show my fear.

They both looked very worried, especially Susan. Her black eyes were filled with dread. Clements reassured both of them that the council would help find their son.

"We just want to find our boy," Susan cried out.

"Yes, we just want him safely back," Rue said glumly.

The council started to ask Rue and Susan questions, trying to get information and clues about when Chrys had gone missing so they could formulate a plan for his search. After a lengthy discussion, the council decided to have wolves search the greater valley area for any clues about Chrys's location. Rue and Susan were both so very grateful to Clements and the council for offering their assistance to find their lost son. Clements concluded the meeting and thanked the council for their help and insights.

As members of the council began to leave, Chrys's parents

and I stayed behind. Rue and Susan thanked Clements and me for our concern and assistance, which made me quiet and a bit squeamish.

After Rue and Susan were gone, I looked over at Clement and he had a warm smile on his face. "See that, they have hope, and that's a wonderful sight," he sighed.

"Hey Clements, can I ask you something? It's been bothering me for a while now."

"Sure, what's on your mind?" he replied in his usual helpful way.

"H-how do you know what to do in times of crisis . . . being the alpha and all?"

"Hmmm. . . ." he uttered as he thought. "I find that clearing my mind of doubt and worry is a good first step." He paused. "I also think of myself just as an ordinary wolf; nothing more. I'm honored when the wolves of the council and pack hold me in high regard and look to me, their alpha, for help," he explained. "But as I have said before, I'm just an ordinary wolf." Clements chuckled. "I am fortunate to have been elected to my position, but there are plenty of others that could be in my position. Oh, and one more thing: don't forget who you truly are in your mind; but most importantly, in your heart," he said sincerely.

"Thanks, Clements. I really needed that."

"You're welcome. Helping a fellow wolf is always a pleasure," he told me, grinning.

We both began to walk away but the beast told me to ask Clements another question, so I did. "Hey, Clements, can I be one of the first to help search for Chrys? He is one of my best friends, and I want to find him as much as his parents do."

"Sure, but be sure to not overexert yourself, we'll find him

eventually."

"Okay, I'll let you know what I find tomorrow." I called out as we split paths and he headed back towards his home.

"Good, I can't wait to hear what you discover," he said cheerfully.

I ran as fast as I could back to my home where I found my parents resting. I told them how Clements had a special assignment for me to do this night. My mom seemed worried and told me to be careful, but my dad only told me to come straight back to our home when I was done.

I walked normally so as to not arouse the suspicion of wolves on their nightly strolls. I finally got to Mud Cave's entrance and sprinted down its long cavernous tunnel, only to be confronted by Chrys's ghost, standing in front of his rotting carcass.

His misty silver body was surrounded by what looked like a glowing moonlight-silver halo. His blood-splattered neck was a fiery scarlet, like a small flame, and his green irises were hidden behind his narrowed eyes as he glared at me intensely.

"What's with that look?"

"You hypocrite," he uttered with pure hatred in his voice.

"What?" I asked, confused.

"You heard me. You haven't reconciled with Charis, you haven't discussed any of this with Clements and the council, and you're leading my parents and others along when I'm actually rotting down here in Mud Cave." Chrys's ghost glowered at me.

"How am I going to tell them?"

"You need to go and find Charis. She'll help."

I groaned, "I don't think you're aware, but Charis and I aren't really on good terms at the moment."

"Yeah, because not only are you not being honest with

Clements, the council, and my parents, you're not being honest with yourself." He paused and looked at me like I was a stranger instead of a best friend. "Your aura has changed. It used to be friendly, but now it's . . . anxious and disturbed," he said.

"I have not changed," I retorted back.

"You definitely have. Before you killed me, you were happy and carefree, but now you look like some wolf that's scared someone is about to shout, 'Hey everybody, I've found something horrible near Mud Cave!'"

"Have you been following me?" I asked.

"Pretty much," he answered. "What do think I've been doing—just roaming about the forest? Turn around and go get some sleep, and when you wake up, go find Charis," he advised.

I just jumped in the mud, which squished underneath my paws.

"De-Vil, you need stop! You need to be honest with yourself, because you're only digging yourself into a deeper hole. Once you dig too deep you won't be able to escape. Do you really want it to be that way?" Chrys's ghost pleaded.

"I have to! I have no other options left!" I told him.

"I knew it; you're too stubborn to care."

I began to trudge through mud, trying to find Chrys's rotting carcass. I eventually found it by the smell, and oh, was it awful. Parts of his body had been eaten away by maggots. His green eyes were still open and staring at me with a haunting look that sent a shiver down my spine.

But I was committed to my task. I took his gray tail in my mouth and began to drag the carcass deeper into the cave. After working for a couple of hours, I finally found a deep hole in the bowels of the mountains.

"Push it in," the beast whispered. "Push it, then you won't have to face any more of this nonsense from your dead friend."

So I did. I pushed my best friend's carcass off into the deep hole, where it fell into the darkness below until I heard a distant . . . thud.

I turned around and ran as fast as my feet could carry me out of Mud Cave. But even at its entrance I could still smell the rancid odor of Chrys's remnants. I was a little nervous, but I reassured myself that caves weren't the most pleasant-smelling places in the valley. The smell would probably go away with time, and no wolf would search and go that far into the cave or even to that deep hole.

As soon as I got out of the cave and back to fresh air, I ran to the river and washed my mud-covered body clean. I then slowly walked to my home, where I slept through the rest of the night like a rock.

The next morning, I found Clements sitting on a tall hill. I went to him and we exchanged greetings. He asked me how my quest in finding Chrys had gone. I told him I'd gone around the lower half of the valley but hadn't found him or any traces of him anywhere. Clements told me not to worry; he was going to address the pack about Chrys's disappearance and use volunteer wolves to scour the valley and beyond for any clues or traces of him. I smiled and he smiled back.

I stayed with Clements that morning, and we were joined by some members of the council who asked for more information about Chrys, his disappearance, and the planned search for him. Clements announced that he would address the entire pack at noon about a fellow wolf that had gone missing. At the appointed time, Clements, myself, and other wolves of the council gathered the wolves of the pack into a nearby field.

I stood next to Clements and other fellow council members when he began. "My fellow wolves, I have dire news to share with you. One of our fellow wolves, Chrys, the son of Rue and Susan, has gone missing," Clements told the pack.

As he explained how search parties were going to spread out and search for Chrys, I scanned the crowd for Charis. I found her sitting near her parents. She was looking around through the council and wolves until she found me. We met each other's gaze and she gave me an urgent look, as if to say, "Tell them, please just tell them!" I looked away and turned back to Clements, who was about to end his speech.

"Don't you worry, we'll find him. If you want to help, get with a member of the council that will be up front." When he was done speaking, I told him I needed to go and talk to someone. He smiled and said, "Go on ahead."

I went over to talk with Charis. She was startled as I approached and asked how I was doing. I told her everything was good, to which she made a curt remark of how could I be doing good with Chrys being gone. This scared me at first, but my fear quickly turned into anger. We began arguing about Chrys and what should or shouldn't have happened. It escalated to the point that other wolves began to notice our intense quarrel. I decided to end it by turning around and walking away.

Afterwards, Clements came to me and asked what my fight with Charis was about. I told him it was nothing, we were just disagreeing on something. He told me that a little fighting or quarreling is natural and shows that she cares for me. He did, however, warn that fighting can cause doubt and destroy friendships. I smiled and thanked him. He told me to go and get some rest, which I did.

As months passed by, the pack searched everywhere: every cave, river, creek, and hill in the valley, leaving no stone or boulder unturned. With all of this effort, not a single clue about or trace of Chrys was found.

Clements gathered all of the wolves who helped in the search to communicate to Rue and Susan what they had found. The news was too much for Susan—she couldn't stop sobbing, and clearly, Rue was distraught.

Clements began to speak. "Chrys was a good wolf, and his memory will not be forgotten." Clements's voice was thick with emotion. "He will be remembered among his fellow wolves who have lost their lives, just like him."

Wolves began to give their condolences to Rue and Susan. I looked for Charis in the crowd and found her with a furious scowl on her face. All of this had been weighing on me. After the meeting I ran to Mud Cave, where I hid and cried for some time. After a while, I was able to compose myself, and I went back to my home and rested.

What I didn't know then was that some wolves who overheard my argument with Charis began to be suspicious and started spreading rumors about me. I became more and more defensive when they would come up and ask me if I had killed Chrys. They spewed information like, they knew what kind of wolf he was and that he would never have run away. They were always met with an angry wolf who told them loudly that I would never kill my best friend . . . ever.

Many months passed and my reputation held firm, even with the suspicions and allegations from some wolves. One afternoon I was at Poplar Point with Clements and the council, discussing matters of the valley and the pack, when in the middle of our discussion, Charis interrupted Clements and said she needed to talk to me immediately. I ignored her, but Clements agreed and told me go with her, which I did, reluctantly. After we got away from the immediate area, she began to run, and I followed her. We ran deep into the forest. I asked her where we were going, but she would only say, away from prying eyes and ears.

We came to a secluded part of the forest, and I was finally able to ask her what was so important. She told me she had talked with Chrys's ghost and was in shock, along with me. I asked her what he had said. She told me that while he was sitting in the plane between existence and nonexistence, he would hear bits and pieces that didn't really make sense. He heard the words "I am the alpha now," and something about a blue comet. He said that on the night when a blue comet would cross the night sky, a foreigner from the east would arrive with the beauty of a red spring flower.

She again pleaded with me to share the truth and be honest with not only the pack but myself. If I didn't, Chrys's ghost's prediction would come true, where I would be exposed and lose everyone's trust and would be either banished or killed. She said the truth was more important than my reputation and title, and to think of all the lives I was hurting—Rue and Susan, Clements, the council, not to mention our own friendship being torn apart.

I told her I couldn't, but she already knew that and said I had changed. She began to leave. I told her to stop, but she just ran away. Time passed from our talk deep in the forest, and when I would see her around the valley, she wouldn't even talk to me.

One night, I was sleeping, when I felt the bright moonlight shining on my face and it woke me up. I opened my eyes and found it wasn't the moon at all; it was Chrys's misty silver ghost. I was startled and asked, "What are you doing here?"

"Tonight," he said with ominous fervor, as his green eyes glittered and the scarlet bloodstain on his neck glowed brightly.

"Tonight? Chrys, what are you talking about?"

"You have to go to Clements and tell him of what you've done," he ordered.

"Why?"

"Because if you don't, my prediction will come true. The sign will be that when the blue comet passes across the sky, a foreigner from the east will come. She will have the complexion of a beautiful spring red rose and will uncover what you've done."

He suggested that I go to Clements right away and accept my punishment.

"But he's asleep," I said.

"That doesn't matter. Go now so that he might have some compassion on you. Because if he just finds out... you will be on your own," he said matter-of-factly. "Additionally, your fate be will sealed due to your inaction if the blue comet streaks across the night sky." Chrys's ghost began to fade away, and he looked right at me with a kind smile on his misty silver face. "Come on, De-Vil, I know you. You're my best friend, and I don't want you to suffer more from your unfortunate mistake. You can be the wolf again that you once were." He began to fade away faster.

"No, not again! Chrys, I need you. I need you! Please don't go!" I frantically called out. I could only see his misty silver face and his compassionate green eyes.

"Do the right thing, De-Vil. Do the right thing and all will be okay." His face faded away and I began to cry uncontrollably. I raised my head to the night sky and just howled.

Eventually I composed myself and stopped crying. I gazed up at the beautiful night sky with its many stars and bright silvery moon. That's when it happened—a bright blue speck began to fly across the darkened sky. I wished I could have done something to stop this from ever happening, but when I looked again, the blue comet was gone.

I went to sleep, trying to forget everything that had happened that night. Many months passed by and no one but Charis knew I had killed Chrys. I am known by the wolves who respect me as Clements's venerable head counselor, but some wolves call me Clements's illegitimate devil's advocate behind my back.

One day I heard from a few wolves on the council that Hunter and his friend found a red wolf that had come from far away. I first saw and was introduced to Rosy when her friends brought her to see Clements. I saw her beautiful rose-colored coat and noticed she was pretty friendly with Hunter. I kept my eye on her from a distance and saw that she also befriended Aquamarine, but all was well because Rosy, Hunter, and Aquamarine had no reason to go near Mud Cave. I wasn't worried, but I still kept a close eye on them from time to time.

They did, however, end up down in Mud Cave, and I continued keeping a close tab on those three after they had meddled down there. I eventually broke them up when I sold my plan for the pack to Clements. It was to split the pack in half and take them far away 'for their safety.' I wanted to get at least half of them, especially Rosy, away from the pack and away from Mud Cave.

"This is how we got to the greater Tucson area, Torpe. Sorry for such a long back story."

"I'm just sitting here waiting. We have nothing but time," Torpe said. "But that is quite the story. You sure screwed everything up," Torpe smirked.

"Yes, I did, but get that smirk off your face before I permanently rip it off," De-Vil snarled.

As the sun was starting to set, Sam moaned. "I'm bored, and I'm sick of unpacking."

"Ditto on that," Alpha muttered.

"I'm bored, too," Beta admitted. Rex and Lilly nodded in agreement, and Duke just shrugged.

"Can't we go somewhere?" Rex asked.

"How about the park?" Beta offered. "Can we please go to a park?"

The other dogs all perked up, their eyes all staring imploringly at Jade.

She smiled. "The park sounds nice. Maybe we could go to a dog park tomorrow morning. I'll look one up."

The dogs were ecstatic. Alpha and Beta sat together, excitedly talking.

"Remember the last time we went to a dog park?" Alpha said eagerly.

"It was before our last trip to Anchorage," Beta said wistfully. "It feels like a lifetime ago. The Fairbanks dog park was always one of my favorite places to go with our master."

"That was the life," Alpha sighed nostalgically. "Pulling the sled, the dog park, all the other dogs. . . . It was all so much fun."

"Do you think we'll ever get back to Fairbanks?" Beta laid her head down and nuzzled closer.

"I hope so. But even if we don't . . . it wouldn't hurt to have a life here in Arizona with our new friends."

"It's a nice place here in Tucson, or Marana," Beta agreed. "And at least we're together."

Alpha rested his chin on her head. "Yeah." He looked around contentedly at his friends.

Rex was practically bouncing off the walls, he was so excited about going to a park. Lilly smiled fondly. The stress had been hitting him hard. Her own smile fell as she remembered her dreams and impressions. Rex noticed.

"What's wrong?"

"I'm excited to go to the dog park, but . . . we're in hiding. It would be bad if either De-Vil or the Boss's goons saw us there."

Rex grew sober. "I agree, it would be a disaster. We'll have to be on full alert when we go to the park. I would almost say we shouldn't go, but. . . ."

Lilly nodded in agreement. "Look at us," she gestured to the excitement that filled the house. The gang was like a group of grounded fireworks that were about to take off into an explosive frenzy. "We need a break."

"We'll be all right," Rex said confidently, trying to loosen up the tension in his shoulders as he remembered what they could face. "We'll be careful."

They settled in with smiles and watched Duke's antics.

"I hope Rosy is okay," Rex said unexpectedly.

Lilly looked at him, hoping his concern wasn't more than

concern.

Suddenly Rex chuckled. "Why do I have to be worried? She's got Raro, and he'll protect and take care of her."

Lilly smiled in relief. "They seem like a nice couple."

"They do," Rex agreed, settling in closer.

"Bedtime!" Jade suddenly called. Lilly and Rex looked at each other regretfully, then followed the brother and sister into their rooms.

As Rex, Alpha, and Duke settled themselves on the floor next to Sam's bed, he surprised them.

"Hey, do you guys want to sleep up here with me?"

"Wait," Rex said in confusion. "Didn't you say. . . ."

Sam cut him off before the dog could finish. "I know what I said the first night," he admitted regretfully, "but this is my final offer. Take it or leave it."

The dogs immediately jumped up onto Sam's bed. It was nice for them. Sam wouldn't admit it, but it was nice for him, too. He liked to have company, but he kept that information to himself, because he didn't want them to know he was a softy.

Torpe looked at the night sky, dotted with stars as if Van Gogh's *Starry Night* had been painted across the sky. He tried to forget that behind him, in the shadows under the bridge, lurked De-Vil.

"Now," the wolf growled, emerging from the dark.

De-Vil and his 'hench-bird' Torpe silently crossed the road unseen. They went through the desert wash, careful not to be spotted by coyotes or other desert wildlife. Torpe knew Cabezota had decreed that if anyone saw De-Vil, they would take him to Cabezota to be executed. And there was no knowing if he would hold Torpe responsible as well.

Torpe's stomach dropped as the 'house alley' came into view. Torpe led De-Vil through the neighborhood, right to the Smiths' front door.

De-Vil pawed at the door, trying to find a way to open it. Torpe perched miserably on the front windowsill, wishing there was something he could do to stop all of this. But what could a quail do against a demonic wolf?

Suddenly, in his tiny little bird brain, a light bulb went on. There was something he could do. It was drastic, but it could mark him as a good animal and De-Vil as the villain.

As De-Vil kept trying to open the front door, Torpe grabbed the largest rock he could carry and flew up into the air. De-Vil was too frustrated with the door to notice.

Torpe flew high and then dive-bombed the front window like an air force fighter jet. He let go of the rock, which flew like missile, shattering the large glass window with a CRASH!

The security alarm went off and glass covered the family room floor.

De-Vil turned to Torpe murderously. "What the H-E-double-hockey-sticks was that for?" he snarled.

"Justice," Torpe said, dignified. "I was right, you are a maniac! I'm going to tell Cabezota and the coyotes what vile things you've done, and you will finally face the consequences of your actions."

"I'll kill you first!" De-Vil snarled, lunging at him, but Torpe was quicker this time. He flew far away from De-Vil, and he intended to stay far away.

De-Vil was as mad as hellfire. He cursed Torpe with foul

language of every kind.

Matthew sprinted to the front room to see what was causing the security alarm to go off. He was shocked to see the front glass window completely shattered. His shock turned into fear as he looked outside of the shattered window and saw a shadowy creature staring back at him with glowing red eyes. Matthew grabbed an umbrella that was leaning on a cardboard box.

The creature stalked toward the wide-open window, giving Matthew a deathly glare.

Matthew was petrified with fear. He ducked down behind a chair with the umbrella in his tightly gripped hand.

The creature was getting closer and closer, and then suddenly, loud squawking could be heard off in the distance.

Matthew peered over the chair to see if the creature was still there; it wasn't. He heard the sound of bushes rustling and something running away on the cool night desert ground.

Matthew slumped down to the floor, his eyes wide with fear, as Emerald, Sam, Jade, Rex, and the gang came running into the front room.

Emerald turned on the light and everyone gasped in horror. There were glass fragments everywhere and a rock sitting on a now-cracked coffee table.

Then they saw Matthew, slumped on the ground with an umbrella in his hand. Emerald rushed over to him. "Matt! What happened?!" She placed a hand on his petrified face. "Are you ok?"

He didn't speak for a moment, which made everyone nervous. His expression said he had just seen something utterly horrifying.

"I-it tried to c-come into th-the h-h-house," he stuttered in shock.

"What tried to get in?" Jade asked.

"I-I don't k-know, but it was a huge sh-shadowy creature with glowing r-r-red eyes," he explained, his body still stiff with fear.

"Wait—did you say the shadowy creature had red eyes?" Rex asked.

Matthew nodded stiffly.

"Why?" Emerald asked Rex.

"Because it sounds familiar."

"How so?" Lilly asked.

"Rosy told me about a shadowy creature with scarlet eyes that stared at her from high up on a ridge."

"You mean De-Vil came here?" Alpha and Beta both said fearfully.

"But how would he have thrown that rock? Canines aren't good rock throwers," Duke asked, confused.

"I don't know how, but he got very close and almost got in the house," Rex replied direly.

"I thought De-Vil had amber eyes," Lilly said.

"He does, but Matthew's description of this mysterious creature was very close to Rosy's description of the beast she saw up in the valley," Rex explained.

"Who do you think it is out of the two?" Lilly asked.

"I don't know," Rex said. "It's probably De-Vil, with him hunting us down and all, but the beast Matt saw and the beast Rosy saw are very concerning."

"Ok, Smiths, we are all going to sleep in our room tonight,

and we'll stay there until the sun rises," Emerald told everyone.

So the Smiths and the gang walked down the hall to Emerald and Matthew's room. Rex looked up at Matthew, who was walking rigidly and clinging to Emerald's arm. He had a haunted look on his face.

As they entered the master bedroom, Rex noticed a nice, king-sized bed. On the wall above the bed was a family crest. It was red with a hammer and clamped tongs crossing each other. On the top it read in golden letters: *"SMITH FAMILY,"* and at the bottom of the shield it read in silvery letters: *"Throughout life, we forge our souls."*

Emerald helped Matthew to their bed and then closed and locked the bedroom door.

"Ok, we are all going to sleep in here together. Jade, you and Sam go into our closet and get out a couple blankets." Jade and Sam came back with a couple blankets and got into the king-sized bed with their parents. Rex and the others settled down on the ground, circling the bed.

"Mom, can we say a prayer before we go to bed?" Jade asked.

"Sure," Emerald said with a smile. So Emerald prayed for their safety and well-being and their much-needed sleep. Then they all lay down to sleep.

"Lilly, Lilly!" Rex whispered.

"What?"

"Let's sing 'The Spirit of Alaska.'"

"Okay," she said, and they both began to sing. The peace of the song filled and surrounded the house.

Everyone woke up rested in spite of their anxious night before. Rex got up first and charged for the living room, beating the others and lying down just in time to see Lilly make a graceful entrance into the room. She lay right next to Rex, careful to choose a spot free of broken glass. Beta briskly followed her in and lay down on the floor, quietly, as usual. Duke bounced in happily after her and lay near a floor lamp. Alpha was slow to enter, and his expression was a bit grumpy, but he lay on floor with Beta as usual.

"How are you doing this morning?" Rex asked Lilly.

"Good, how about you?" she said fondly.

"I have great news!"

"What is it? Don't leave me guessing," she laughed.

"Sam let us sleep in his bed with him! Prior to all of the commotion, at least."

"Wow, that is good news. Good news indeed." She smiled.

He smiled back. "You look wonderful today, Lilly."

She looked at him surprised. "Why, thank you Rex, that was very kind of you."

A few minutes later Sam walked in wearing a blue t-shirt, tan jeans, and socks. Jade wasn't far behind him, wearing a pink t-shirt with blue jeans.

As they ate breakfast and waited for the planned time to go to the park, Rex could only think about how to get rid of De-Vil, the Boss, and his goons, which in turn would help Northwest Tucson stay safe.

The group was gathered in the living room again.

"I'm bored," Alpha moaned. "Can we go to the park yet?"

Emerald walked in wearing a purple blouse and black jeans, and Matthew came in with a gray button up, long blue khakis, and business shoes. He kissed Emerald on the cheek as she said to the dogs, "The park sounds nice. Maybe we'll go at 11:00. I saw one on our way here and I think you all will like it." She smiled at them, as the dogs all sighed. "Well, back to unpacking for me." She left the room. Matthew's phone started to ring and he left as he was answering it.

"I'm going to get some fresh air," Rex said.

"I'll come with you," Lilly responded, and the other dogs followed.

They all went into the backyard and inhaled the hot, dry Arizona air. "Arizonan air is way different from Alaskan air," Alpha said, huffing and puffing.

"Arizona is hot," Beta added.

"No kidding!" Lilly agreed.

"We've got some time to burn. Let's go see if we can find our friends in the desert," Rex said.

Torpe was flying around trying to find everyone to tell them everything about the previous day's craziness and what he had learned about De-Vil, his past, and his plan. He frantically searched the desert, flying as fast as he could to find them.

Torpe was done helping De-Vil with his insane plans, but he was also nervous about his friends finding out that he had helped De-Vil, who was planning to murder Rex, his friends, and the family.

Finally, he saw Rosy's bright, reddish-brown fur reflecting the blinding desert sun. Her colors differed from the greenish-brown desert below and she stood out easily. He could see the pack of coyotes and Rex and the other dogs gathered in a loose group.

Torpe was nervous—could he make the animals understand that he hadn't assisted De-Vil of his own free will? Torpe decided he would explain that he threw the rock through the window, triggered the house alarm, and alerted Rex and the others that De-Vil was on the Smiths' doorstep.

Torpe swooped down to where everyone was resting and visiting on the desert ground. They all seemed anxious, especially Rex and his friends, from what had happened the previous night. *Should I tell them?* Torpe thought nervously. He landed on a low-hanging branch and saw that Ren and Arthur were there also.

"Oh, Torpe, you're here," Ren said as she noticed him land.

Everyone looked at him, and he felt so guilty, but why? He did save Rex, his friends, and the new family from the murderous clutches of De-Vil. He was mostly nervous that they might be hostile toward him for helping De-Vil in his evil plot. He didn't mean to do it; it wasn't intentional; it had only happened because he was under the cruel and vicious control of De-Vil; he had had no other choice!

"So, Torpe, what brings you here?" Ren asked. "You flew in pretty quickly. Is there something you want to tell us?"

"Yes, there is something I have to tell you all," Torpe replied quickly. Everyone's head perked up, and the animals all looked at him with interest.

Torpe shifted his wings nervously. "I know some things about De-Vil."

"WHAT?!" everyone said in shocked unison.

"You know things about De-Vil?" Lilly asked him slowly, amazement in her voice.

He nodded.

"Then tell us!" Jewel exclaimed.

Torpe felt even more uncomfortable. All eyes were on him, expectant. Torpe took a deep breath. *Ok, let's get this over with. The sooner I tell them, the sooner I can get it off my conscience. You're going to be alright. Just tell them,* Torpe told himself.

He began and told them everything De-Vil had told him under the bridge. He told them of De-Vil's two best friends, Charis and Chrys, and how his infatuation with Charis sent him into a jealous rage, leading him to kill his friend Chrys. He explained in great detail how De-Vil hid Chrys's rotting carcass deep in the tunnels of Mud Cave, and how he spent months trying to cover up his murderous crime, even after Clements had appointed him as his head counselor and given him a seat on the wolves' council. He described how Chrys's misty, silvery ghost came regularly to De-Vil, encouraging him to do the right thing and confess, but De-Vil refused. And how Chrys's ghost predicted De-Vil's eventual demise from an 'eastern newcomer that was like a beautiful red spring flower, or a red rose.' He also explained how De-Vil had brought half of the pack to Mount Lemmon to split up Rosy, Aqua, and Hunter, and that was where he had met the 'domestics,' as he sinisterly called the gang.

Everyone was astonished at the detailed information and malevolent plan De-Vil had for them.

"He's not going to stop until we and anyone against him are dead," Rex said slowly.

"That sounds about right," Lilly replied glumly.

"What should we do?" Beta asked.

"We have to stop him," Alpha answered. "It's the only thing we can do."

"But where is he?" asked Duke.

They all looked at Torpe, but he just shrugged his wings.

Rosy had been quiet while Torpe told them everything. It was because of De-Vil that she had been torn away from her new pack. Seething anger coursed through her whole body like a raging fire. He had taken everything from her, and now he was going to murder her and her friends!

"That good-for-nothing, selfish LIAR!" Rosy snarled, her tone full of bitterness.

"It's ok, Rosy. We will find a way to get rid of him," said Raro in an attempt to comfort and calm her down.

"NO!" Rosy shouted. "We have to find him and kill him." Her tone was still filled with stinging anger. "Even if I have to do it myself."

At this, everyone was astounded and concerned. Rosy was the happiest, least- confrontational wolf they had ever met, but after her outburst, they now all looked at her like she had just told them she was going to side with De-Vil, her worst enemy.

"We'll find him," Raro replied sincerely. "And he will face the consequences of his actions."

Ren was considering everything Torpe had told them, and one thing didn't make sense. "Hey Torpe, I have one question for you," she said.

Everyone looked back at Torpe and he started to get even more nervous. "What is it?" he squeaked out.

"How do you know all of this about De-Vil?" Ren asked curiously. The others nodded in agreement.

Torpe shifted his wings nervously. "What do you mean?" he choked out. They all continued to look at him, and he felt more and more nervous by the second.

"Torpe, are you alright?" Lilly asked with concern. "You look nervous."

"No, no, I'm fine, I'm fine." he replied quickly. *Should I tell them?* Torpe thought. He felt like a huge boulder was slowly crushing him. *Will they see me as their friend if I tell them the truth, or will they see me as an enemy like De-Vil? I just want them to understand.*

"Do you know what else doesn't make any sense?" Rex asked. "Who threw the rock through the Smiths' window? De-Vil couldn't have, and even if he could, why would he? It woke us all up."

Torpe broke into a sweat. *It's now or never.* "I heard he had an accomplice."

"He did?" Arthur asked in confusion.

"But how do you know that?" Ren asked.

Torpe hesitated, then squeaked, "I was his help." He gasped in relief at finally coming clean.

"What!" the grouped exclaimed all at once.

Torpe looked down in shame.

Ren stared at him, appalled. "You did what?!"

"I helped him," he admitted again.

"You helped him? Torpe, you stupid, clumsy bird! He is our friends' enemy! Why in the world would you help him? He's trying to kill them!"

"I know, I know," Torpe said, ashamed. "But he would have killed me if I didn't help him." Then he paused and looked up. "I did help them, though."

"Wait, what?" Ren said, confused.

"I was the one who saved them," he told Ren.

"What? You saved us?" Rex asked. Then it all made sense, "You're the one who threw the rock that shattered the glass and alerted us!"

"And drove away De-Vil, I might add," Lilly said, smiling at Torpe.

"It all turned out ok," Beta agreed.

"See, I'm on your side," Torpe told Ren. "But I've learned that De-Vil must be stopped no matter what, before it is too late."

"Thanks for sharing all of this information with us," Rex said. "It truly shows what kind of wolf De-Vil is, and he's still out there."

"Hey, when are we supposed to go to the park?" Duke asked.

"That's right, we probably should head back to the Smiths' house," Lilly said.

Everyone agreed to gather again later, and the gang headed back to the neighborhood.

When they all got back to the Smiths' backyard, Duke ran straight to the pool and jumped in.

"That's our Duke," Alpha said, laughing. "If you can't beat it, enjoy it!" Alpha dove in after him. His head popped out, shivering a little bit. "Come on in, the water is fine. Well, I should say, kind of cool, but you'll get used to it."

Beta took the opportunity to beat the heat and jumped in with a splash. Rex and Lilly weren't far behind, jumping into the pool at the same time and making an even bigger splash.

Lilly splashed some water at Rex with her paw. "Ah, this is nice, isn't it?"

"Yeah, just like old times up in Alaska, swimming in the refreshing rivers and lakes," Rex replied as Lilly smiled in agreement.

Suddenly Jade poked her head out the back door. "What are you all doing?"

Rex gave her an odd look. "Isn't it obvious? We're swimming."

She shook her head and went back inside.

While they were swimming, Matthew and Emerald heard a knock at their front door. They answered it to find a nicely dressed, middle-aged woman with brown hair. She held a small potted cactus and wore a bright smile on her face.

"Hello, you must be the Smiths. I'm Penelope Peters, but you can call me Penny. I live just over there, in one of the houses up on that small rise." She gestured with her free hand.

"Hi, I'm Matthew. It's a pleasure to meet you, Penny."

"I'm Emerald, but I go by Emma. It's nice to meet you."

"It's nice to meet you both," Penny said with a smile. "Maybe you can come over to our place and meet my family." She handed the potted cactus to Emerald.

"Smiths," Matthew called out, "we have company."

Jade and Sam charged in and stood beside their parents.

"This in our 14-year-old daughter," Emerald said, gesturing to Jade.

"Delighted to meet you. I'm Jade."

"And this is our 15-year-old son," she said as she put her hand on Sam's head.

"My name is Samuel, but I go by Sam. Nice to meet you."

Penny smiled. "I have a son that would love to be both of your friends. His name is Scott, but he goes by Scottie." Jade looked intrigued.

They all heard splashes from the pool, and Penny looked confused. "Who's swimming?"

"Our dogs," Jade replied.

"Dogs?" Penny sounded surprised. "You guys have dogs? I never saw dogs when you were moving in."

"Yeah, we have five dogs," Jade replied. "Their names are Rex, Lilly, Alpha, Beta, and Duke."

"Our family has a dog, too," Penny said cheerfully. "His name is Charlie." Penny suddenly noticed the shattered glass. "Oh my goodness! What happened here? Your window is completely destroyed!"

"We don't really know," Emerald lied. "Maybe it was some hoodlums who think it's funny to vandalize other people's property."

"Oh, no, what an awful welcome to the neighborhood. I promise you, I've never heard of this happening to anyone in our neighborhood. I do have to go, but I hope you'll come over and visit." Penny said goodbye and left.

Jade went to the back door. "You almost blew your cover," she told them in a critical tone. "Now at least one of our neighbors knows you're all here."

"Oh, sorry," Alpha replied with a slight tinge of rudeness. "We were just having fun."

Jade left in a snit.

"Nice going, Alpha," Rex said, a little perturbed at his friend's behavior. "One of your best works yet."

A while later they finished swimming and all got out, shaking themselves dry. Jade came out with towels and in a better mood.

"What are the towels for?" Rex asked her.

She came to Rex and started drying him off. "My mom is a stickler for keeping the house clean, and I would feel bad if you guys got in trouble for getting the floors wet." She then dried off all of the other dogs.

After being sufficiently dried, they all went back inside and tried waiting patiently. After what seemed like forever, the clock finally struck eleven, and Jade shouted, "Mom, it's eleven o'clock! Time to go to the park!"

"Okay, Jade," Emerald called from back in one of the rooms.

A few minutes later, everyone was ready to go. Emerald grabbed a bag of frisbees, soccer balls, and other fun things to do at the park. They all got into the station wagon and headed out.

The dogs could barely contain their excitement as Matthew parked the car.

"This park is huge!" Duke called out gleefully as he ran.

"It's only a little bigger than the Fairbanks dog park," Beta laughed.

Sam threw a Frisbee and Beta raced after it. As it glided down, she jumped up and caught it in her mouth and then ran back and gave it to him. He handed it to his sister and grabbed a soccer ball and threw it for Duke to chase. Jade threw the frisbee to Rex and the others while Emerald and Matthew sat on camp chairs and watched.

None of them noticed a woman walking past and definitely

didn't hear as she pressed her earpiece's talk button and said, "This is Goon Twenty-six. They're at Crossroads Park. I repeat, they're at Crossroads Park. We've got them."

As soon as the Boss got the news, he headed to his goons' break room at the mansion. They were all playing video games. He slapped his lead goon right on the back of his head.

"What are you burros doing? Goon Twenty-six has just spotted the dogs at Crossroads Park up off of Cortaro Road. Let's move, you boneheads!" The goons all ran to get their equipment and climbed into the cars that were heading for Crossroads Park.

Back at the park, the dogs and the Smiths were just enjoying time together. Jade threw the frisbee as hard as she could. Rex went racing after it, but suddenly he was distracted by a bad presence. He forgot about the frisbee and his feet kept running. The others were confused because the frisbee had already landed on the ground, but Rex kept running like he was following a phantom frisbee. He slammed headfirst into a chain-link fence and hit the ground.

Lilly cried out, "Rex!" She raced to his side with the others close behind.

"What was that about?" she asked frantically as she reached him. "Are you ok?"

He slowly got to his feet. "Ow. That hurt."

"Why did you keep running? It's like you were following something." Lilly's eyes were worried.

"I don't know. Was I really?" Rex was still dazed from hitting the fence.

"Yeah," Alpha agreed. "You're acting like those times recently when you said, 'It happened again,' back in the desert."

The other dogs nodded in agreement.

Rex and Lilly shared an uncomfortable look and started to pant nervously. Rex felt the guilt of keeping both his and Lilly's secret pressing down on him.

"Okay. I'm going to come clean. You all know Lilly and I have been acting a little strange lately. . . . Let me explain why."

"Rex, what are you doing?" Lilly whispered.

"I'm telling the truth. I can't live a lie."

She nodded as he took a deep breath and continued. "Lilly and I have had these weird dreams . . . premonitions . . . or whatever they are, but they seem and feel . . . different. These dreams feel super real, and we can also feel when bad things are going to happen. That's what's been going on these past few days." Rex felt all of his guilt melt away and he breathed a sigh of relief. He smiled at Lilly, who smiled back, feeling the same.

Beneath the nearby Cortaro bridge, De-Vil paced back and forth, thinking of his next move toward slaughtering Rex and his friends. Suddenly, he heard familiar voices. He slipped from the shadows of the bridge to see who it was, while still trying to stay hidden. The Boss and his goons were climbing out of their cars on the other side of the bridge.

The Boss lit a stick of dynamite and threw it near the edge of the bridge, then ran for cover with his goons.

BOOM!

Everyone at the park jumped, then turned and looked toward the bridge and saw smoke rising. Lilly huddled close to Rex as people screamed and fled to their cars. The gang ran towards the bridge, determined to see what had just happened.

When they got there, the bridge was empty except for a man dressed in white clothes standing on the opposite end. José, the animal Boss of Tucson, threw another stick of lit dynamite, blowing up an even larger part of the bridge.

Lilly was slammed with déjà vu. "I've seen this before!" she gasped.

"That's my cue," De-Vil said menacingly as he watched part of the bridge crumble down to the dry riverbed below. He cracked his neck from side to side and snarled, "It's go time," as he stalked towards the dogs with a sinister smile on his face.

CHAPTER 11

DESPERATE TIMES CALL FOR EXPLOSIVE MEASURES

Lilly stared in horror at the scene. "Rex!"

He turned at the urgency in her voice.

"Do you remember what I told you about those dreams I had?"

He nodded slowly and looked back at the bridge. "Yeah, one was about a bridge . . . and explosions."

"I think that dream was a premonition."

"That makes total sense. Unfortunately, we have a bigger threat to take care of." He turned to the rest of the dogs. "Come on. Let's end this."

He started running toward the middle of the bridge, the other dogs in tight formation behind him, just like in their days pulling sleds.

The Boss saw them coming. "Get them!" he shouted to his goons.

Two goons ran toward them with tranquilizer dart guns. The dogs huddled together and growled fiercely at the goons, baring their teeth. They were relieved when the goons turned and ran away in terror, but their relief was short-lived. Someone else was growling aggressively right behind them.

The dogs all turned around slowly.

De-Vil stood there, his lips twisted in a malevolent smile. "You guys are dead."

Torpe flew toward the dust and smoke hanging in the air from the explosions, anxious to see what was going on. When he saw the Boss shouting orders in Spanish to his goons, Torpe almost flew away—but then he saw the dogs racing toward the bridge . . . and De-Vil creeping up behind them.

"Oh no! They're in trouble! I have to tell the others."

He flew as fast as he could to the desert wash, looking desperately for someone who could help. To his amazement, all of his friends were coming toward the explosion they had just heard.

When he dove down and landed next to Ren. "Where are Rosy, Raro, and Jewel?" he gasped urgently.

She looked at him strangely. "Why? I think they are right behind me."

"Rex and the others are in trouble."

"What! You should have told me that first! Come on!"

They flew off looking for Rosy, Raro, and Jewel. Torpe and Ren flew above and to either side as Arthur ran below.

"I see them!" Torpe shouted, banking to the right.

The three birds met up on the ground in front of Raro and Rosy.

"What's wrong? You all look scared," Rosy said, dread biting at her stomach.

"Rex and the others are in a heap of trouble."

Ren looked between the two of them. "Where's Jewel?"

"I don't know," Raro said firmly. "But if they're in trouble, we'll need all the help we can get."

Just then, Jewel showed up, and they all took off to save their friends.

Rex, Lilly, Alpha, Beta, and Duke huddled together as the bridge was being blown to smithereens around them.

"How are we going to get out of this one?" Alpha grimly asked Rex.

"This might be it. With the goons on one side of us and De-Vil on the other. . . ."

Just then, the cavalry arrived!

The dogs whipped around to see Raro leading Rosy, Jewel, Torpe, Ren, and Arthur straight to them.

"Oh, thank goodness," whispered Beta.

"All right!" Rex said like a military general. "Torpe, Ren, and Arthur, you take care of the Boss and his goons while the rest of us take care of De-Vil."

The birds did everything they could to stop the Boss and his goons. Ren and Torpe flew into and pecked at their faces and pulled at their hair. Arthur ran between their legs, tripping them up, and then the three of them turned around and took off with their equipment and explosives.

Rex, the other dogs, the coyotes, and one red wolf faced De-Vil, standing shoulder to shoulder.

"Eight against one, De-Vil. You've lost this one," Rex said

firmly.

"Do you think you all can defeat me?" De-Vil laughed cockily. "I'd like to see you weaklings try."

"Maybe not," Rex said bravely, "but we'll go down fighting."

De-Vil lunged forward, snarling at them. Rex and the gang began to circle De-Vil, growling and snarling. Rex and Lilly struck first. They both lunged at De-Vil, biting and scratching.

De-Vil clamped his jaws on Lilly's collar and threw her aside like trash before being tackled by an angry, growling Rex. He smacked Rex in the face with his sharp claws, catching him off guard. Rex stumbled back, his face bleeding.

Lilly got up and was joined by Alpha, Beta, and Duke. All of them began to walk toward him, snarling. De-Vil's amber eyes were filled with malice and rage. Lilly and Alpha charged at De-Vil, snapping and biting as they went in. Alpha grappled with De-Vil, baring his teeth, but was shoved down to the hard pavement.

Lilly tackled De-Vil and clawed at him ruthlessly before being knocked hard in the head by De-Vil's headbutt. She stumbled back, shaking her head and whining in pain. Beta and Duke both charged at De-Vil, trying to overpower him, but were easily tackled to the ground.

Rosy and Jewel began to circle De-Vil as he was baring his teeth. Jewel charged and jumped at him, snapping and biting, before being shoved to the ground. Rosy attacked and tackled him to the ground. "You egotistical maniac," she growled.

"Aw, what a harsh thing to say," De-Vil said sarcastically. "You really should be a little nicer. . . ." he began to say. "Weakling!" he uttered sinisterly as his eyes flashed scarlet.

Rosy was caught off guard and forcefully thrown, hitting the pavement hard. De-Vil stood up and shook the dust off of his black fur. "As I said, did you all really think you could beat me? I am more powerful than all of you because I know how to achieve my ends."

Rex and Lilly frowned as they looked at De-Vil. He leered murderously at them and their friends, standing tall in his lofty pride.

Rosy stared at De-Vil with pure hatred. He was the wolf who ruined her life and the lives of the other wolves from her new pack. He tore her from Hunter, Robert, Clements, and the other half of the pack all because of his stupid infatuation with best friend, Charis, which led him to murder his other best friend, Chrys.

De-Vil was within the reach of her fangs and claws, which pulsed with her unrelenting anger.

De-Vil noticed Rosy's death stare. "Has no one told you that staring is rude?" he sneered.

"You're one to talk," she muttered angrily.

"What did you say?"

"You ruined my life." She growled at him aggressively.

"No," he countered. "You ruined *my* life. MY LIFE!" He shouted.

Rosy let out a loud exasperated shriek. "YOU RUINED YOUR OWN LIFE!!!" "You. . . ." she began to say angrily but was visibly shaking with anger. "Y-you're so hellbent in your pridefulness, thinking I am the one who caused your life to fall apart, when in reality it was *you* that caused your life with Charis and Chrys to fall apart." She growled.

"My life fell apart because other forces caused it to." De-Vil was about to defend himself further, but Rosy cut him off.

"And you with your deceptive plan, ominous scarlet eyes, and your weird evil powers."

"I don't have powers," he replied frankly, which shocked Rosy.

"Y-you . . . you don't . . . you don't have any powers?" she asked him in confusion. "What about when I saw you looking creepily at me with your scarlet eyes? You have amber eyes, so why did you have scarlet eyes then? And what about my dream with you before I knew it was you, what about that?"

"You think I'm supernatural?" De-Vil replied slowly in confusion. "I'm just a wolf, nothing more, I'm just very smart, or 'deceptive' as you put it. You must've eaten a mushroom or something in Mud Cave before I was looking at you."

Rosy looked at De-Vil with a look of contempt. "Chrys was right," Rosy began angrily. "You are a hypocrite."

De-Vil growled at her. "Watch it, you red fleabag."

"You watch your mouth!" Raro snarled, stepping forward. "Or I'll gladly shut it for you."

"Oh, I'm so scared," De-Vil laughed.

Raro cracked his head from side to side. "You should be." His muscles tightened. "For Tucson and Marana!" He lunged forward, tackling De-Vil. He shoved his muzzle forcefully into De-Vil's face. "You're a disgrace, and a complete joke to the entire canine family."

Just then, Raro howled in pain as De-Vil's fangs clamped onto his leg. He collapsed, his leg bleeding and De-Vil threw him off to the side and stood.

An empty city bus pulled up, and two goons jumped out.

Rosy began to cry, nuzzling at Raro. Suddenly, a black,

ominous haze engulfed Rosy's entire being, and her kind, blue eyes turned dark purple.

"Rosy?" Raro asked nervously, looking up at her as she pulled back.

"Shut up!" she snapped at everyone, but they didn't listen. "Shut up!" Something in her seemed to burst. "Shut up! Shut up! Shut up!"

"Rosy, are you okay?" Rex asked. He then noticed the black, ominous haze and her purple eyes and breathed, "Oh, no."

"SHUUUUT UUUUP!!!!!" This time it was a loud, piercing, demonic cry.

The battlefield froze, from De-Vil, Rex, and the other dogs to the Boss, his goons, and the birds still tormenting them.

Rosy began to speak in tongues somehow, which sounded strange to Rex, like a record player playing in reverse.

"Sih ttel." She paused, then slowly continued speaking. "Reht pur roc egard naria psed." She spoke normally, as if nothing were wrong. "Reg nareh tsiw tdnar eh emu snoc." She raised her voice a little bit. "Rehnon rut rehek amd nayltn eloivn ruhc." She then began to yell something in Spanish.

They all stared at her, then Rex turned to the gang, "Is anyone getting any of this?"

"The other stuff I can't understand," Jewel replied, "but she said something that sounded like 'amigos y seres queridos', which is Spanish for 'friends and loved ones.'"

Rosy now yelled at the top of her lungs. "Dnald ehct erw siht yort sed sgnil eef deppa rtevit agen eseh tlla tel! Eca lplam sybas ihtno noi tarts urf dnat ergern wor ehfo odan rotad nes! Revi rrot agilla evob aykseh tssor cadek aertst emoc eulbeh tero feb yadeh tekil eromec notce fre peb!" She threw back her head and cried to the heavens, "TERG ERDN AEGAR REHMA ISA DAEL PIS IHT!"

Suddenly a huge, shadowy, blade-like force made a jagged cut through the bridge. The edges on both sides of the cut crumbled and fell. Screams filled the air as the animals, the Boss, and his goons scrambled away from the deadly edges. Strangely enough, the bus wasn't sliced in half. It sat untouched, spanning the two opposing sides, with the dogs and other wildlife gazing in wonderment on one side and De-Vil, the Boss, and his goons cowering in terror on the other.

Rosy wasn't finished. "¡Haga que el río Santa Cruz se desborda y inundar el área donde estamos!"

Jewel went as pale as a ghost.

"What did she say?" Rex asked urgently.

"She's speaking Spanish again." Jewel gulped. "She said, 'Make the Santa Cruz River overflow its banks and flood the area where we are.'"

"Please tell me this bridge isn't over the Santa Cruz River."

"We're over the Santa Cruz River."

They both looked down in horror and saw that the water beneath them was now raging and roaring.

"Why are you doing this?" Rex asked Rosy.

Rosy sneered. "Why do you think?"

"Rosy?" Raro asked. "You don't sound like yourself."

"I'm not Rosy," she shrieked demonically. "I'm Rosa Iraedolor!" Rosa pierced them with an ireful glare. "I am a manifestation of her deepest sorrows and her seething rage. And to answer your pertinent question, Rex," Rosa turned her head sharply and gave him a deadly stare, "This city is the home of what I despise. These people took everything from Rosy."

"But you're just adding to the chaos," Rex said in a pained voice.

"Why should I care?"

"Because even though the Boss and his goons are evil, they must have been good before. All people are good at one time. The Boss must have brainwashed them."

She scoffed. "How are you so optimistic? Aren't you scared?"

"Of course I'm scared. But we can't let things bring us down. We need to just try and find a way to stay hopeful."

Rosa's face twisted. "Rosy has had everyone she cares about taken from her," she seethed. "Her family, the scientists, even Hunter. Every home she has ever had has been taken from her. The wildlife refuge, her human friends, and her new pack up in the White Mountains. All of it is the fault of these people here."

"Yes, that's all true, but Rosy has us and Raro and the others. We're not going to abandon her."

Rosa scoffed again. "You ran away and left her alone with the coyotes."

Rex winced. He hadn't known how much them leaving bothered her. "I'm sorry. But we're here now, and we'll make everything right."

"But what if you don't? How can you defeat the Boss?"

Rex stared at her boldly. "We have a bond of friendship and love that gives us hope that even though life can be unfair, it will turn out right."

She stared at him, stunned. "How are you not afraid of me, even though you've seen what I can do?" She gestured to the destroyed bridge. "I could harm or even kill you, but you stand there unfazed. Why haven't you run away?"

"Because if we run away, the Boss, his goons and De-Vil would win and wreak havoc on this place. We can't let that happen."

She nodded slowly in agreement, recognizing his courage. "One more thing. Why are you all so brave?"

"That's who we are. We will give it all we've got, and we'll find you a home whether that's here or back in North Carolina."

Rosa paused for a moment, she then smiled and laughed joyfully. The ominous black haze turned to pure white and her purple eyes turned to a magnificent golden color. The white cloud left Rosy's body and swooped up in the air, turned and then seemed to face Rex. "Thank you for helping me. I wish you the best of luck." It then swooped back and dove into Rosy's body.

Rosy blinked, her eyes their normal blue again. "What just happened?"

Rex saw De-Vil climb up onto the bus and begin to cross the divide towards them. "I'll tell you later. We have bigger fish to fry right now." He bounded away and climbed up onto the other side of the bus.

De-Vil growled at Rex. "Get out of my way!"

"No!" Rex hunkered down, determined to protect the others.

"If you won't move, I'll make you!" De-Vil snarled. "Do you really think you can beat me, a wolf? I am superior to and much stronger than you! You're a simple pet—pampered, weak, and unable to survive," De-Vil paused to fix his murderous glare on Rex, then yelled, "YOU'RE NOTHING!!!!!!!"

Lilly froze. She had heard those words before, sleeping on the couch with Rex, when she had her premonition.

Rex lifted his chin and said, "Bring it, tough guy."

De-Vil lunged forward as Rex perfectly hit De-Vil's face, clawing a long cut near his eye. "That'll leave a scar," he smirked.

"How dare you?" De-Vil snarled and lunged forward again. They grappled across the top of the bus, neither gaining the advantage over each other. Finally, De-Vil shoved Rex away and they both drew back, panting heavily.

"We don't have to do this, you know," De-Vil said civilly between pants. "You just have to do one thing, that's all."

Rex chuckled humorlessly. "Oh, what is that?"

"Join us. It's that simple."

"What?!" Rex gaped in disbelief.

"You heard me," De-Vil said, more aggressively.

"I heard what you said; I just didn't think you were stupid enough to ask me that. So hear this. . . ." Rex paused and narrowed his eyes at De-Vil. "No!"

"Last chance," De-Vil said, growing more agitated.

Rex rolled his eyes. "Are you deaf? I said no!"

De-Vil went berserk and yelled at him demonically, "JOIN ME, OR EVERYTHING YOU KNOW AND EVERYONE YOU LOVE AND TRUST WILL BE THE DEATH OF YOU!!!!!!"

Rex lunged forward and pinned De-Vil to the bus, sticking his muzzle in De-Vil's face. "I said no," he growled in a low and threatening voice.

De-Vil was unfazed. "I feel sorry for you. I could have used you. You have so much potential for a dog, but . . ." he paused, then whispered sinisterly, "it's your funeral."

Rex froze and De-Vil surged forward, knocking Rex off of him. Rex slid toward the edge of the bus, but managed to stop himself and get back on his feet before De-Vil slammed into him again. They fought, biting and snapping at each other. Rex got in a few good hits before De-Vil smashed him down against the bus. Rex blinked the stars out of his eyes and got to his feet, but De-Vil had disappeared. Rex hunched his shoulders, circling nervously.

"Rex, look out!" Lilly cried.

De-Vil slammed him again from behind and Rex careened into the metal bus, hard. He looked up and saw a demon. De-Vil's fangs were bared and he was foaming at the mouth. His eyes were crazed and blood-red. Rex closed his eyes from the pain. De-Vil was pressing his head harder and harder onto the metal of the bus. Rex opened one eye and weakly saw De-Vil's large paw pressing down on his face.

"THIS IS WHAT HAPPENS TO ANYONE WHO GET IN MY WAY!" De-Vil snarled for all to hear. He pressed on Rex's head even harder, and Rex felt De-Vil's breath on his ear. De-Vil whispered loudly, "Say hi to Chrys for me." De-Vil hovered over Rex one moment more, then mercilessly lunged and ripped open Rex's light gray neck.

"REX, NO!" Lilly cried out in agony.

Rex lay bleeding from his furry gray neck. His eyes closed. His breathing stopped, along with his heart. He was gone.

CHAPTER 12
REX'S GUARDIAN ANGEL

Rex opened his eyes slowly. He saw a very bright, pure white and an endless horizon. He got to his feet, surprised that he didn't feel any pain from his recent wounds. There was no blood on his fur—not even the wound on his shoulder from the timber wolf.

"Where am I?" his voice echoed through the brightness. "Hello? Is anyone there?"

"Hello," a voice called back from the distance.

He followed the unknown voice, and out of nowhere a huge, magnificent golden gate appeared before him. It stood wide open. Strangely, there were no walls or fences attached to this beautiful gate. Sitting on a stool near the magnificent golden gate was a young man who had a jovial look on his face. A thick, red, woolen beanie partially hid his unkempt brown hair. He wore a thick, black, winter parka with a fur-lined hood laid back, and heavy gray pants with brown winter boots.

Rex fell back on his habits and approached the man, acting like a normal dog.

"Hello," the man said pleasantly, "and who might you be?"

Rex kept his mouth shut, cocking his head.

"Come on, speak up! Don't be shy," the man said cheerfully.

"Um, hello. . . ." Rex said hesitantly. "My name is Rex."

"Ah, Rex! I've heard all about you," the man said, nodding like he knew Rex.

"Where are we?" Rex asked.

"You sir, are in heaven," the man told him with a wink.

"Heaven!" Rex said in complete shock. He looked at the magnificent golden gates. They were the pearly gates he had heard of. He looked back at the man. "Does that mean I'm dead?"

"Indeed you are!" the man told him, just as cheerfully.

Rex was completely overwhelmed. He had failed his friends and ended up dying. It was done.

The man opened the golden book that somehow had infinite pages. He talked as he flipped through its pages. "Nope, nope, still nope, not that. . . . Ah, yes, here it is! Rex, it says here you had the misfortune of being killed by a bloodthirsty Mexican gray wolf named De-Vil de Mon. Yikes!"

"I really don't feel like talking about it right now." Rex looked away. "I'm ready to go in, if I can."

The man frowned at him. "Don't you want to help your friends?"

Rex stared at him. "I'm dead. What can I do? Besides, what's the point? I couldn't beat De-Vil anyway. My friends will just have the same fate as me." He bowed his head as tears began to fall from his face.

"Hmm, but it says here that you never give up on your friends or anyone you meet."

Guilt stabbed at Rex. "Stop saying that!" he snapped angrily. "I couldn't do it!"

The man fondly smiled at him. "It didn't matter if we were trying to prove a point to an ignorant person or taking important cargo through the wilderness from Fairbanks to Anchorage. We just need to consistently hold onto hope and keep moving forward."

Rex stared at the man; the words felt familiar. "How did you know that?" He looked even harder at the man, then gasped. "Alden, it's you!"

His master from the time he was a puppy smiled at him. "Hello, Rex."

Rex grinned but then his smile fell. "Why are you here?"

"A sledding accident. After you guys were gone, I wasn't thinking straight and fell off a steep mountain ledge." Alden grinned ruefully.

Rex tried smiling but was sad. "You were such a great master."

Alden smiled cheerfully back. "You all were great dogs. You deserved a good life. You . . . and your friends, especially Lilly." He winked.

"Lilly! My friends! What am I doing here?"

"Atta-boy! You can still turn the tides on this, my friend."

"But how? I'm dead!"

"I can help you go back," Alden said.

"Really? Thank you! But wait—does that mean I won't

ever see you again?"

His master got off his stool and hugged him. "We shall see each other again, but later." He rubbed Rex's head just like he used to. "I always knew you were special, from that very first day we met. Now go, save your friends and have a wonderfully adventurous life. We'll see each other again, don't you worry." He stood and placed his hand on Rex's forehead. "Back to earth you go. I wish you the best of luck."

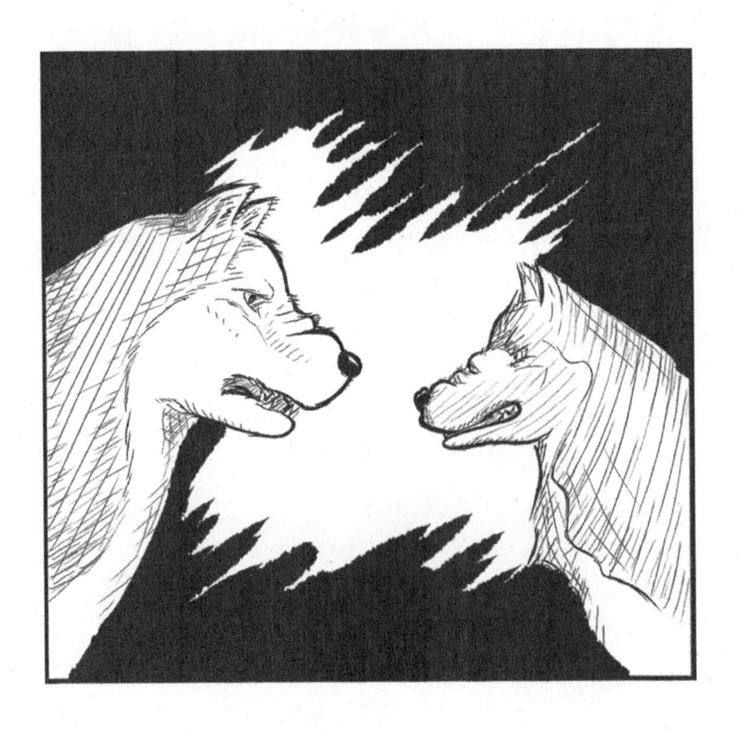

CHAPTER 13

THE TIDES HAVE TURNED

When Rex opened his eyes, he heard Lilly and the others crying and whimpering. He turned his head slowly, careful not to draw attention to himself. De-Vil was on the ground, prowling toward his friends, growling triumphantly as they cowered in fear.

Rex stood up on the bus, grinning recklessly. “Hello, De-Vil. Long time, no see.”

De-Vil whipped his head around toward Rex. The gash on Rex’s throat was gone. De-Vil began swearing. “How?! You’re . . . dead! This is impossible!”

“I thought so, too, but here I am. Aren’t you happy to see me, De-Vil?” Rex taunted.

“Rex?” Lilly asked overjoyed. She could barely breathe. “How are you. . . .?

“I had someone help me,” he told her with a smile.

"What? Who?"

"I'll tell you later," he said, turning back to De-Vil.

De-Vil climbed back up on the bus until he was face to face with Rex once again. "It doesn't matter!" he snapped, glaring menacingly at Rex. "You should have stayed dead. Now I just get to kill you twice."

Another explosion rocked the bus and the bridge. The Boss's goons were now wreaking havoc by throwing dynamite at buildings near the bridge and keeping other humans at bay. The Boss himself walked calmly toward Rex, a tranquilizer gun in his hand.

On Rex's left was an evil, bloodthirsty wolf who had already killed him once and still wanted to kill him and his friends. On his right was a mad millionaire who wanted them for his horrible zoo.

Suddenly both De-Vil and the Boss charged toward Rex. Rex dodged and managed to slip past De-Vil, but his momentum carried him off the bus, and he hit the concrete road hard. Lilly was instantly at his side.

"You flea-bitten mutt!" Rex looked up, expecting another attack, but the Boss was yelling at De-Vil. "Stop trying to kill my dogs!"

De-Vil snarled in response and tackled the Boss, pinning him to the roof of the bus.

"Wait, wait, wait!" the Boss's bravado was gone, and he trembled in terror. "You can't do this! We're partners!"

De-Vil laughed demonically. "Do you think I would be a partner with you?"

"El diablo!" the Boss mumbled in fear.

The gang and their friends all stared in shock. "De-Vil

actually spoke to the Boss," Jewel breathed.

Suddenly, Ren saw one of the goons light another piece of dynamite. She swooped down, ripped it from his hands and flew for the bus.

"Give that back, you crazy bird!"

She ignored him. With only seconds left, she dropped it right next to the bus, on the side away from her friends.

BOOOOM!!!

Another piece of the bridge crumbled away. The bus started to shift, then it fell, plunging into the raging river below, taking De-Vil and the Boss with it.

"SO THIS IS MY PUNISHMENT FOR THE LIFE I CHOSE," the Boss cried in Spanish as he fell.

"I'M NOT DONE WITH YOU!" De-Vil roared. "I'LL BE BACK!" He and his fury disappeared into the raging river below.

The goons stared at the river in horror, then looked at each other. "Let's get out of here!"

They fled.

Rosy turned to Raro. "Are you ok?"

He winced. "No, he bit my leg pretty hard. It still hurts, but I'm not sure how bad it is."

Rosy looked at the others. "We need to get him back to the desert and home immediately!"

"We will," Rex told her firmly. He looked at Ren and Torpe. "Go to Cabezota and tell him what happened. We'll meet you there." They flew off.

Rex and the others were helping Raro to his feet when they saw the Smiths running up to them. The family of humans froze when they saw a red wolf and three coyotes, but they continued to approach cautiously.

"What was that?" Jade asked. "We watched it from the side."

"We'll tell you later, but we have an injured coyote here."

They saw Raro's bloodstained leg.

"Quick, everyone," Matthew said. "To the car."

They helped Raro to the car and got everyone in. Matthew drove as fast as he could. Finally, they got to the Smiths' house. Rex and the others rushed Raro to the desert.

Cabezota and Tierra were waiting for them, with Ren and Torpe beside them.

"Is it really that bad?" Tierra asked in horror.

Cabezota went immediately to Raro's leg and assessed the injury quickly. "It's treatable; give us some space."

They all breathed a sigh of relief. Cabezota and two other coyotes went to work on Raro's leg, sending Rex and the others away to rest.

Rosy fidgeted nervously. "Do you think Raro is going to be okay?"

"I'm positive," Jewel said.

"Ugh, that horrible De-Vil!" Ren said. "He and the Boss put up a fight for us today, but we came out on top."

"Thank goodness he didn't find us sooner," Lilly said.

Rex thought about it and became confused. "He did, though, remember? He tried to get in the house last night, but the rock and the alarm stopped him.

"Yeah, that sure was lucky," Alpha said.

"Thank heavens for Torpe coming clean," Ren said.

Rex smiled, looking at his friends. He had come back from death, and they had made it through their confrontation with De-Vil and the Boss. Rex took a deep breath and began to sing "The Spirit of Alaska, let her winter winds rage."

The others smiled and joined in, singing together.

Rosy was caught up in the moment, and as they finished, she yelled joyfully, "I love Raro!" She blushed when everyone looked at her, and blushed even more when Jewel smiled genuinely.

Jewel was happy that Rosy was in love with her older brother. Rex cheered by howling and yipping and then they all sang the song over and over again. Their hopes were high while waiting to hear whether Raro would be okay.

CHAPTER 14

All's Well That Ends Well

Finally, Raro emerged from the bushes. His wound was covered by leaves and twigs, and though he limped a little, he seemed fine and was happy to see all of his friends. He was especially excited to see Rosy and went straight to her.

Right off the bat, she declared, "I love you, Raro."

Raro stared at her a moment, shocked. Then he grinned. "I love you too, Rosy," he replied affectionately.

The others all cheered and barked before they settled down to rest and relax for the rest of the day.

"So, what happened?" Lilly asked Rex eagerly.

"Yeah, tell us!" Rosy barked.

Rex began describing his experience. "I woke up in a place that was pure white as far as I could see. It was vast and very bright, and I called out to see if anyone was nearby. Someone called back. I went toward the voice, and out of nowhere a magnificent golden gate appeared and it was wide open and. . . ."

"Wait!" Lilly exclaimed in shock. "You were in heaven?"

"Yeah, I was, but I didn't know it at first," Rex responded. "It was kind of strange. Normally a gate is attached to walls or a fence, but there were none. That is when I saw a younger man, probably in his twenties." Rex paused as if trying to remember. "He had a cheerful look on his face, but he was kind of strange and out of place, too. He didn't really look like an angel; he had no golden halo above his head. He did, however, have a thick, red, woolen beanie on his head that hid his messy hair. He wasn't dressed in white robes and he didn't have feathered wings, but he did have on a thick parka with a fur-trimmed hood, thick gray pants, and brown winter boots. He had no harp but held a large white and gold book with fancy embellishments and words I didn't recognize on the face of it.

"I approached him and he looked at me with his kind, brown eyes. I asked him where exactly I was. He responded that I was in heaven. I felt as if I needed to be quiet, as I was in heaven and all, but we did begin to talk. I told him who I was and he acted like he knew me. He told of my death by De-Vil. This shocked me, and, I have to admit, made me a little sad. I was about ready to go in through the gates when he stopped me and began persuading me to come back and help you guys. I told him frankly that I was dead and couldn't defeat De-Vil and that my friends would probably die at his paws, too.

"He mentioned how loyal and committed I was to my friends, especially back in the Alaskan wilderness," Rex explained. The ears of Lilly, Alpha, Beta and Duke perked up in interest. "He said that I just needed to hold steadfast to hope and keep moving forward."

"Alden!" All four cried out in astonishment.

"Yeah, I was just as shocked as you guys are."

"Who's Alden?" Jewel asked.

"He's our master," Beta answered.

"His name is Alden Peter Wilde," Alpha replied, "and he would ride on the sled with the cargo and we would run across the vast Alaskan wilderness to cities, towns, and villages to deliver its contents."

"Wait!" Lilly turned to Rex with urgency in her voice. "Why was Alden in heaven? How did he. . . ? Did he . . . d-did he d-die?" she asked, breaking down in tears.

"Yeah, he did. But he seemed happy, like he always was," Rex said with a glum frown.

Beta and Lilly began to cry, Duke and Alpha's heads were lowered in sadness, and Rex was sniffling. Raro, Jewel, and Rosy shared in the gang's sorrow.

"How did he die?" Raro asked.

"In a sledding accident. He fell down a steep hill."

"So, your master is dead," Jewel said.

"Yeah. But as I said, he was happy, and he sent me back to help you guys finish off De-Vil, El Loco, and his goons."

This reminder brightened everyone's mood. They all committed to try to be more positive and began to talk about good times together that lay ahead of them. Lilly stayed especially close to Rex, thinking about how close she had come to losing him.

The next morning after breakfast, the gang said a heartfelt goodbye to the wildlife hosts and to Rosy, who had decided to stay with Raro. Then they headed back to the Smiths' house.

On the way, they ran into Bandit, who was ecstatic to see them.

"Hey! How's it goin'?" she cried. "I saw on the news that y'all finally got rid of the Boss and his goons and even De-Vil! Y'all got guts!"

"Yeah, if you only knew how close things were to going the other way. But we did it," Rex told her.

"So now y'all don't have the Boss, his goons, and De-Vil in your way, does that mean y'all's goin' back to Alaska?"

The dogs looked at each other, then at Rex.

"Maybe; I don't really know," Rex admitted. "We found out that our master in Alaska passed away, and I'm not sure what we would go back to."

"Hey, I have an idea," Bandit winked. "What if y'all stay here? Y'all have your desert friends and that family that just moved in. If that's not a darn good answer, then I don't know what is."

Rex thought about it, looking at his friends. "She's right. We have everything here to be happy. If the Smiths are willing to keep us. . . ."

The other dogs nodded eagerly, and Rex grinned.

"We're staying!"

"Yeehaw!" Bandit hollered joyfully. "That's a darn good answer, my friend. You'll not regret it. I have to go, but I'm happy I'll see y'all around!" She headed back to her own master's house, and the gang headed for the Smiths'.

The Smiths were glad to see the five dogs and demanded

to know what had happened. They all sat down and Rex told them the whole story.

Jade was horrified when Rex told about his death.

"Wait, Rex—you died!?"

Sam stared at him. "How are you here? How did you come back?"

Rex told them about Alden and finished the story.

"He was instrumental in getting me back to earth to ensure we defeated De-Vil and El Loco."

Matthew and Emerald looked at each other, then back at the dogs.

"Your master is dead?" Emerald asked caringly.

Rex nodded sadly.

"What was his name?" Matthew asked.

"Alden Wilde." Rex answered.

"We're sorry for your loss." Matthew looked each dog in the eyes. "Do you all still want to go back to Alaska?"

The dogs looked at each other anxiously. Rex cleared his throat.

"Actually . . . you guys have been so wonderful to us . . . and we were thinking . . . it would be nice if you and your family would be our masters. Only if you want to, of course," he finished, looking down.

The dogs held their breath. Emerald and Matthew looked at each other for a moment, then wide grins spread across both of their faces.

"Welcome to the family! We'd love to have you and your friends stay!"

The dogs barked joyfully, and Jade and Sam high-fived.

Rex smiled and looked back at Emerald and Matthew.

"We may still hang out with our friends in the desert; maybe even sleep there and go on adventures with them from time to time. Is that okay with you?"

"They're your friends. Of course," said Emerald with a smile.

As Rex and the gang were resting on the carpet in the living room of their new home, Sam grabbed the TV remote and turned it on. The local news was just starting, and the news anchor said, "Hello, Tucson, welcome to the six o'clock edition of Channel 8 news. I'm Marc Chartres, along with Lidia Amarillo."

"We have breaking news about the Tonto Organization and its illegal wildlife trade," the co-anchor, Lidia, said. This immediately caught everyone's attention there in the Smith's home. "We have our very own Veronika DeCosta live at José Tonto's mansion. Veronika, what can you tell us?"

The news broadcast switched to the news reporter, Veronika DeCosta, who was standing in front of El Loco's mansion.

"Thanks, Marc and Lidia. I'm here on the south side at the mansion of the notorious wildlife trafficker José Tonto. He is known by some in southern Arizona as 'El Loco de Tucson' or the madman of Tucson," Veronika told her viewers as the television showed a picture of a short, rotund Hispanic man in fancy white clothing. The caption under his photo read "José Carlos 'El Loco' Esteban Tonto. Next to his photo were pictures of two of El Loco's goons.

The two shown were the goons who had captured the gang and brought them from Alaska to Arizona. The first one was a slender Caucasian in a fancy uniform with the Tonto Organization seal. Under his picture was the name Francis Luke "Franky" Maverick. The second was a robust African-American man who wore the same uniform. The words under his picture read Nicholas James "Quick Nick" Barnie.

The television camera went back to Veronika DeCosta. "Both the Tucson and Marana Police agencies are working together and have contacted the Federal Bureau of Investigation for the investigation of the Cortaro Road bridge bombing and nearby train derailment," Veronika told her viewers.

The television displayed pictures of the derailed train with its cargo strewn across the desert landscape, and the destroyed bridge where the gang and others had recently fought De-Vil, El Loco, and his goons. "The FBI will assist in relocating the exotic wildlife back to their respective habitats, and José Tonto's subordinates will be tried for their crimes," Veronika said as a cameraman showed people in and around the exotic animals' cages. "We will update you as more information surfaces about José Tonto, his subordinates, and their crimes. Back to you, Marc and Lidia," Veronika finished, and the camera returned to the news anchors.

"What a happy ending for those caged-up animals, don't you think, Lidia?" Marc said with a smile on his face.

"Yeah, truly a happy ending for all of them," Lidia said.

"We'll get back to you when we have more information. Thanks for watching," Marc said to his viewers.

Rex and the gang looked around at each other and smiled. They knew they had helped Jabali, Moyo, and the other lions and lionesses, along with the other exotic animals, by helping get El Loco and his goons in trouble for their crimes.

That night, Rex had another weird dream.

Lilly, Alpha, Beta, Duke, Rosy, Raro, Jewel, Arthur, and Ren were there with Rex, but there was also a white wolf and fox that looked familiar. He started noticing more animals. There was a red fox and a tiny black bird, a few Mexican gray wolves, a couple of reddish-brown coyotes, a raven, a hummingbird and two tan cougars. None of them seemed to be a threat. They were all in a snowy forest that didn't look like Mount Lemmon or even Alaska. Suddenly, two sleek greyhounds emerged from the forest, followed by a lumberjack gripping a polished, sharpened axe in each hand. He glared murderously at Rex and the others.

Rex woke up, confused and concerned. Lately his dreams—and Lilly's—had an alarming habit of coming true. There wasn't much he could do, though, since he didn't know all the animals or the place in the dream. He tried not to think about it too much and went back to sleep.

Early the next morning, Rex, Alpha, and Duke got up to leave.

"Where are you guys going?" Sam asked sleepily.

"To tell our friends that we're staying here. If Emma or Matthew ask, can you let them know?"

"Sure." Sam laid his head back on his pillow.

They went to Jade's room and knocked quietly on the door. Lilly poked her head out, her eyes still bleary with sleep.

"What are you guys doing?" she asked with a yawn. "It's six o'clock in the morning."

"We're going to go tell Rosy and the others that we're staying."

Lilly squinted at Rex for a moment, then blinked hard to wake herself up. "Ok, I'll get Beta."

They emerged from Jade's room and walked with the others down the hall.

Duke opened the back door and they all squeezed through like they had before. This time he was careful to shut it behind them. As they walked through the neighborhood and desert, they saw Charlie near a fire pit.

"Hey!" he said excitedly when he saw them. "Long time, no see! I heard you were on the news! That's crazy!"

"It was," Lilly agreed.

"I heard from some of the wildlife nearby that you were stolen by the Boss and that you're all trying to get back to Alaska."

"Actually, we're going to stay here with the Smiths," Rex told him.

"I also heard you broke the law of animal nature," Charlie said anxiously.

"You don't have to worry," Rex reassured him. "They'll keep the secret. They seem trustworthy."

"Oh good," Charlie said, relieved.

"We're going to see our desert friends, but we'll be seeing you around. It's nice to have you as a friend, Charlie," Rex smiled.

"Thanks," Charlie said, smiling himself.

They kept walking up through the house alley and into the desert. Finally, they saw a coyote on a lively morning stroll.

"Do you know where Raro, Rosy, and Jewel are?" Rex asked him.

"They're a couple miles up the wash that way," he gestured

with his head. "They said they had something important to do."

They followed the coyote's directions and eventually found the other three busy making something.

"Hey, it's you," Raro looked up and greeted them as they got closer.

"How's the leg?" Rex asked.

"Healing well." Raro's smile seemed a little sad. "They're here," he called to Rosy and Jewel.

They came over carrying a few things. They looked like necklaces made from leaves and twigs with colorful flowers scattered on them. Their friends had obviously spent a long time making them.

Raro spoke while Rosy and Jewel gave each of them necklaces. "These are gifts we made because we want you to remember Arizona."

The dogs each looked down at the necklaces they now wore, then looked at each other smiling. Rosy started to cry, and Raro leaned against her shoulder comforting her. She wiped the tears from her eyes, "Ok, let's get going."

"Where?" Lilly asked, confused.

"To the airport," Rosy replied with a sniffle. "So you can get back home to Alaska."

Rex looked at his gang, then back at Rosy and the coyotes.

"We'll be back in just a second." Rex, Lilly, Alpha, Beta, and Duke walked far enough away from Raro, Rosy, and Jewel that they couldn't see or hear them, and sat down to discuss how to break the news.

"How do we tell them?" Rex asked, at a loss.

"I don't really know," Lilly said with concern. "They were

being so sweet."

"Well, we just have to tell them," Alpha said practically.

"Yeah, I'm with Alpha," Beta said.

They were all silent for a moment.

"Hey," Duke suddenly said. "What if we make them something from us? They gave us a going-away gift; what if we give them a staying-here gift?"

"Duke, that's a brilliant idea!" Rex said.

Duke looked surprised. "Really?"

"Yes, Duke," Lilly assured him.

"Your idea is perfect!" Beta agreed.

Alpha stood there, completely stone-faced and then relaxed into a smile. "Duke, you're a genius."

"But what will we make?" Rex asked.

"Twigs, sticks, leaves, flowers, anything," Duke said with a shrug.

They gathered anything and everything they could find and quickly made their gifts. When they returned, they saw Raro, Rosy, and Jewel resting and waiting. Rex, Lilly, and Alpha stepped forward and placed necklaces in front of each of them.

"What are these for?" the three asked together.

"They're staying-here gifts," Rex explained.

"What for?" Rosy asked.

They all grinned and said, "We're staying!"

Raro, Rosy, and Jewel's ears perked up. "You're staying?"

Rosy and Jewel both squealed with delight. Rosy howled joyfully, with Jewel and Raro joining in right after. Rex grinned, then he joined in seconds later.

They chatted and laughed and, of course, sang, "The Spirit

of Alaska." After they had all calmed down, Rex turned to Raro. "Do any of you know what happened to De-Vil, the Boss, and his goons?"

"I head from some friends that some javelinas said they found the Boss washed up near the Avra Valley bridge," Raro offered.

"Some birds told Torpe that the police caught all of his goons a few days later at the Reid Park Zoo, trying to steal some of the animals," Jewel added. "They're going to charge them for animal abuse and illegal animal trade. The plan is for all of the Boss's animals to be relocated to their original habitats. The lion and a lioness you guys met asked the birds to tell you how grateful they are to you for stopping the Boss and his goons."

"Moyo and Jabali," Lilly said smiling.

"Are those their names?" Jewel asked.

Lilly nodded happily.

"We saw on the local news how the government is dealing with El Loco and his goons," Rex said to Raro, Jewel and Rosy.

"They screwed up big time," Rosy said.

"Yeah, they did," Rex agreed.

"And De-Vil?" Lilly asked anxiously.

"Well," Raro said slowly. "No one knows exactly what happened to De-Vil, but I'll tell you what I saw last night." He began his story.

There is a rumor floating around that some birds recently saw a gray wolf at the Davis-Monthan Air Force Base's aircraft boneyard, southeast of Tucson. So last night, me and three of my good friends met up to see what we could find out. We needed Ren for assistance, and we found her sleeping with her family in a saguaro cactus.

"Psst, Ren! Ren, wake up," I whispered softly.

She woke up and poked her head out of the hole. "What are you guys doing up at this hour? It's past midnight."

"I need a favor," I whispered.

"What is it?"

"We need a navigator."

She sighed. "So, you need my help to get somewhere. Okay, but you owe me big-time." She stretched her wings, then flew and landed on my back. "Where we going?"

"Davis-Monthan's aircraft boneyard."

"That place? Okay, let's get going." She took off and led the way.

We slunk through the night following Ren, trying to be unnoticed as best we could. We got to Cortaro Road and the railroad crossing.

"What do we do now?" one of my friends asked.

"Follow the train tracks that way," Ren whispered, pointing south.

She flew above us as we trotted all the way from Marana to just south of downtown Tucson. We arrived at a rail yard where there were plenty of train cars all lined up and over a dozen wide.

"Are we close?" I asked Ren.

"Almost there. I'm sure of it."

We got through the rail yard and cut over to a massive area surrounded by barbed wire fences. We found a small break in the fence where we could slip under.

"Welcome to Davis-Monthan Air Force Base," Ren said

plainly.

We went across the base and past a bunch of buildings undetected, but we didn't see any indication of a gray wolf. Finally, we got to a part of the Boneyard that had a humongous military cargo aircraft, four smaller aircraft, and a half-dozen smaller fighter jets. Next to the smaller aircraft, a red-tailed hawk was tinkering with a partially-destroyed fighter.

He glanced up when Ren flew to him, but continued working on the aircraft.

She cleared her throat. "Um, sir? Uh, hello, sir."

"What you want?"

I spoke up. "We're trying to find a large gray wolf. Have you seen one?"

"Oh yeah, he's on the top of that humongous plane over there, but here's some advice from me: he seems like he has a few screws loose. Just warning you." The hawk went back to work.

Ren flew back to us.

"On top of the plane?" one of my friends asked. "But where?"

Suddenly, I saw him. I shushed my friend, but it was too late. The silhouette of a large wolf stood outlined on the wing of that enormous plane. He stared straight at us with ominous, glowing red eyes. He spoke, but it sounded strange. He was neither animal nor human, neither angel nor devil, neither evil nor good, neither sad nor happy, neither brave nor coward, neither beast nor man. It was like he was nothing.

"On this night of my final departure, I say farewell to the life I could have had if I had chosen to do the right thing. I didn't and was too prideful to see what I was doing wrong. I leave this happy life, not only as a wolf who was seen by many as a two-

faced murderer, but as a wolf who's made a million mistakes that have truly affected me in the end. To whoever is listening, I give you a riddle. 'A simple life turned upside down for the characters. This is a tale, a tale of bravery, a tale of hope, a tale of laughter and humor, a tale of misery, a tale of woe, a tale of anger, a tale of fear, a tale of war and battles, a tale of mystery, a tale of love, a tale of friendship and friends, a tale of enemies and people that aren't what they seem, a tale of good and evil, a tale of the black of yin and the white of yang, a tale of courage, a tale of the wild.'"

Then the dark silhouette of the wolf vanished into the dark. We ran to the top of the humongous aircraft, but we saw nothing. Whatever it was, it was gone, and we couldn't stop talking about it as we headed back for home.

The group was silent a moment following the strange tale.

"Where did he go?" Rex asked after a moment. "And are you sure it was De-Vil?"

"I don't know. He must have run away," Raro told Rex.

"But are you sure it was him that ran away, and not just some crazy wolf?" Rex asked again for clarity.

"I'll have to admit that it was a little strange, but I'm pretty sure it was him. His strange speech goes hand-in-hand with what we've learned about him, his dealings with Rosy, and the other half of Clements's pack. I saw his deep red eyes, and if you don't believe me, just ask any of my three friends or Ren. They were there, too, and saw it," Raro responded.

"I just want to make sure that it was him that was there and ran away, instead of some loony Shakespearean coyote. I want to know that De-Vil has run away and won't come back to kill us," Rex told Raro.

"Yes, I think it was him," Raro told him.

"Okay, good," Rex breathed a sigh of relief. "But those red eyes make a lot of sense with my and Rosy's stories," Rex said.

"What a strange riddle," Beta said thoughtfully. "Do you know what it means?"

Raro shook his head. "No, none of us could figure it out."

Alpha shifted his shoulders, trying to get rid of the dark mood the story had brought.

"Hey, why don't we sing 'The Spirit of Alaska'?"

Beta smiled at him and started singing. The others quickly joined in.

The Spirit of Alaska, let her winter winds rage.
But it won't hurt as it drifts over the sky,
Where the northern lights dance,
Where its bright colors shine,
Where the wolves run across the tundra,
And the fish swim in the icy, turquoise rivers.
Where the courageous mountaineers climb and scale
The towering and treacherous mountains.
Where the Natives lived long, long ago
And their descendants now live today.
Where the lucky men with their courageous dogs
Brave the winter storms to find their riches of oil and gold
Beneath the icy, snow-packed rocky ground.
Where the spirit of the wild
And courageous people and animals live and survive.

When it started getting late, Rex and the others said goodbye to Raro, Rosy, and Jewel and headed back home, glad to have one again at last.

"Do you think we'll be fine here?" Lilly asked, walking shoulder to shoulder with Rex.

"Of course! We'll have amazing adventures with the Smiths and Rosy, Raro, Jewel, and the others. What do you say about that?"

She smiled. "I wouldn't have it any other way."

END OF BOOK ONE